I0712801

# BE STILL MY HEART

K
♥
RED
K
♥

FOUR KINGS SECURITY

BE STILL MY HEART

CHARLIE COCHET

BOOK TWO

# FOUR KINGS SECURITY
# UNIVERSE

Welcome to the exciting Four Kings Security Universe! This ever-growing world filled with charismatic characters, action-packed adventures, lots of laughs, and, of course, heart-soaring romance includes several series with multiple books. New to this universe? You're in the right place. Love in Spades is the book that started it all. Looking for the universe reading order?

Check out: https://charliecochet.com/reading-order/.

Tell me I'm
enough for you.

Oh, darling,
you're more than enough.
You're everything.

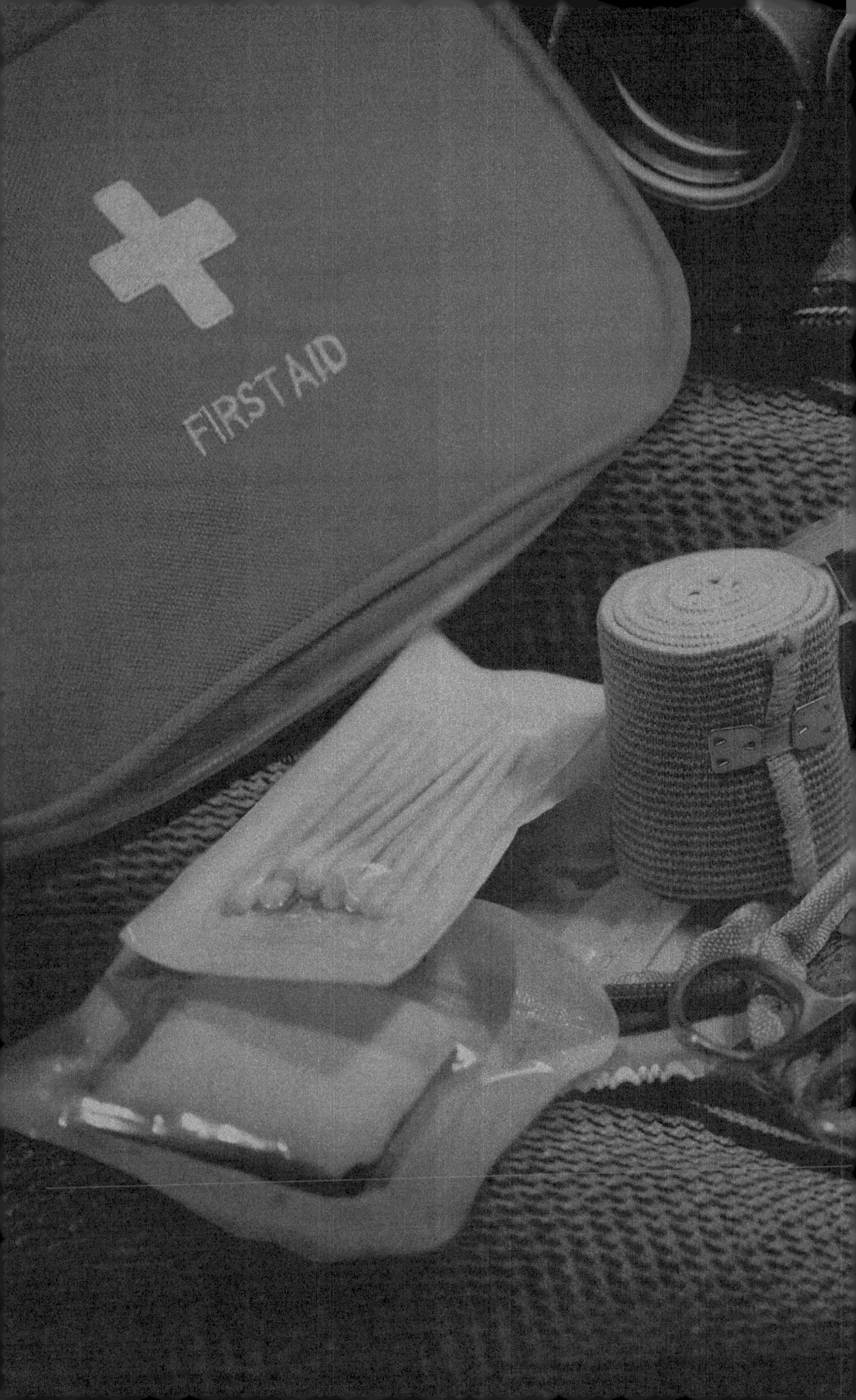
FIRST AID

# CHAPTER 1

"Are you trying to kill me?" Red shouted at Ace as his friend came careening around the bend, burning rubber, a Cheshire cat grin on his face. Whoever had decided it was a good idea to give Anston Sharpe a driver's license needed to rethink their life choices. The man was a menace behind the wheel, and years of defensive driving certainly didn't help his proclivity for challenging the laws of physics while in a moving vehicle.

"Where's your sense of adventure?" Ace laughed as his vehicle flew up a ramp and soared through the air.

"I left it back on that bridge you tried to drive me off of!" Red jerked his steering wheel and almost jumped out of his seat when Ace's car landed mere inches away. "You almost fell on me, you jackass!"

Ace's cackle was evil, and Red shook his head. He hit the accelerator, trying to outmaneuver Ace, who wasn't the only one experienced in defensive driving. At least Lucky wasn't here, or Red would be sharing the road with two overly competitive daredevils who reckoned themselves invincible. The cousins shared a knack for attracting trouble and approached high-risk situations like they were personal challenges. It drove their boss and best friend nuts. Red felt for King. They might all be equal owners of Four Kings Security, but King gave the orders, same as he always had. During their Special Forces years when they'd been part of the same ODA—Operational Detachment Alpha—they'd followed him to hell and back. They'd follow him there now.

"Did you see that?" Ace *whooped* loud, his car having taken out two other vehicles.

"Show off," Red muttered, skidding across the asphalt as he rounded one particularly harrowing bend, his teeth gritting and both hands on the wheel. He was so close. They were neck and neck. Red leaned forward, his grip fierce as he gained the few feet he needed to cut off Ace, the finish line coming up fast. *Come on.* He could do this.

The scenery whipped by in a blur, the noise around him nothing but muffled sounds. An object hurled toward him from out of nowhere, striking his car, and he cursed as his vehicle spiraled out of control toward the cliff's edge, Ace's laughter in his ears.

"You bastard! I can't believe you triple red-shelled me!"

Ace cackled as he sped past him. "Sorry, bro. It's every plumber for himself."

"I thought we were on the same team!" No way he was catching up now. As Ace was about to cross the finish line, the screen went black, and they both gasped.

"What the—damn it!" Ace jumped to his feet and whirled around to glare at King, who stood behind the couch, arms folded over his chest. "I was about to beat my personal best!"

"And I was about to beat your person. Period." King narrowed his eyes at Ace. "You have a very large, fully equipped game room at home. Why aren't you playing Mario Kart there?"

Red bit down on his bottom lip to keep from laughing as Ace mirrored King's stance. He lifted his chin and sniffed.

"Colton's getting ready for a two-week business trip in New York. He's flying out tomorrow, so he's working from home today. Being the loving, considerate boyfriend that I am, I didn't want to disturb him."

King arched a blond brow, turning to Red, who grinned wide.

"Someone thought it would be a great idea to upload his music library to the house's security system interface without figuring out volume control. Led Zeppelin's 'Immigrant Song' blasted through the house so loud it rattled Colton's bookshelves and everything fell off. Jack had to come out to fix it, and Colton told him to take Ace with him when he left."

The corner of King's lips twitched. "So what you're saying is his own boyfriend kicked him out of the house for being a pain in the ass."

Red shrugged. He was trying exceptionally hard not to laugh at Ace's unimpressed expression, but really, Ace had brought it on himself. Poor Colton. The sudden blast of drums, guitar, and Robert Plant's howling had scared him out of his office chair.

King turned back to Ace. "You know, when we stopped Colton from getting smuggled to another country, I assumed the threat to his life was over. Clearly I was mistaken. Do you always try to give your boyfriend a heart attack first thing in the morning?"

"You're hilarious. And for your information, he did not kick me out. I can go home anytime I want."

"Providing it's after five o'clock," Red pitched in cheerfully.

Ace gaped at him. "Whose side are you on?"

With no hesitation, Red pointed to King. "His."

"Wow, that quick, huh? Didn't even think about it. It's like I don't even know you anymore."

Red chuckled at Ace's mock disgust before they turned their attention back to King as he leaned his arms on the back of the couch, his expression stoic as usual.

"I love you both, you know that, right?"

They nodded.

"Good. Get the fuck out of my house."

"That's harsh, man. Red is injured."

Red opened his mouth to say he was fine—it'd been months since he was released from the hospital—but Ace held up a finger, cutting him off.

"You're kicking out poor, sweet, vulnerable Red?" Ace grabbed Red's chin and squeezed his cheeks. Red was not amused. "Look at this face. How can you kick him out?"

"I'm not. I'm kicking *you* out, and he's keeping you company. Unlike certain individuals whose life goal seems to be driving my blood pressure through the roof, Red actually listens."

"Aw, don't be so hard on Lucky. He tries. Sometimes. Not really. That *is* who you're talking about, right?"

Red snickered, and King let out an exasperated sigh. The four of them were family. Brothers. Ace and King were best friends, and few people outside their circle understood why. Anyone who didn't know them and witnessed the two interacting, assumed King couldn't tolerate Ace, but King's gruffness with Ace was all the proof of how much he loved the guy. King never lost it with someone he didn't care about. The man was an unmovable mountain, a fortress, his stone walls impenetrable. He'd held the rest of them up when they'd been on the verge of crumbling. King had a habit of carrying the world, and everyone in it, on his shoulders. Ace made sure King didn't get lost in the shadows of his own making. They were opposites in every way, and so they balanced each other out perfectly.

"Come on," Red told Ace, standing. He patted Ace's arm. "I'm hungry. Let's go get some breakfast at Bibi's."

At the mention of food, Ace was out the door before Red even rounded the couch.

"Keep him out of trouble, will you?"

Red congratulated himself on not laughing in King's face. Instead he blinked at him. "But I'm injured. The doctor recommended I take it easy for a while, remember?"

"Really?" King arched an eyebrow at him. "You're going to play the injured card?"

*Oh hell yes.* Red nodded, even went for the big guns. He jutted his bottom lip out a little.

"Fine. You know the drill. Call me if it looks like he's about to get arrested or cause more than ten thousand dollars' worth of property damage."

Red saluted him. "You got it." Technically he'd been given the all clear from his doctor weeks ago, but King had insisted he take some extra time off. A horn honked, and he shook his head in amusement as he grabbed his baseball cap off the couch before heading for the front door. He stopped by the polished wood side table to pick up his wallet and keys. After closing the ornate glass door behind him, he followed the pristine redbrick path to the impeccable driveway. Outside of a *Better Homes & Gardens* magazine, Red had never seen such a picture-perfect house, but then King never did anything by halves. His life and everything in it was as structured and organized as he could make it. Preparedness was as essential to Ward Kingston as oxygen.

Ace sat behind the wheel of his Chevy Camaro L1 convertible, wearing his favorite mirrored aviators, a big grin splitting his face. The top of the convertible was down, and alternative rock pounded through the car's state-of-the-art sound system. One thing Red could say for certain—there was never a dull moment around his brothers-in-arms.

Despite the early morning hour, the sun was glaringly bright. The weather was in the low nineties but felt like high nineties thanks to the humidity. Come August, the heat was going to be unbearable. Florida was a triple *h* threat: heat, humidity, and hurricanes. He couldn't complain, though. The rest of the year, the weather was spectacular, and he was never far from a beach, great food, or attractions.

Having been prepared for King to kick them out of the house— King could only take so much chaos before lunch—Red had dressed in a lightweight, soft gray henley T-shirt, khaki cargo shorts, and his comfy gray Vans. Once Red was in the passenger seat and buckled up, Ace pulled out onto Cypress Lake Court and headed for Colonial Drive, where he made a left. Since most of the roads around King's property were dead ends—thanks to King's neighborhood being pretty much in the middle of a forest—they had to loop around to get to State Road 206. Red loved the location of King's house, how quiet and peaceful it was.

When the Kings, Jack, and Joker had returned home for good, it was King who'd taken them into his huge family home. Their brother had been grieving himself, not to mention still recovering from his own injuries, but he'd kept them close, like he always did, protecting them, guiding them. Without King, Red doubted he would have survived. Not a day went by when he didn't think about their fallen brothers, or how close they'd come to losing King. How close *he'd* come to losing King, and himself. When enough time passed where it seemed like he might be leaving it all behind him, his head never failed to remind him of what he'd lost.

"Hey, bud. We're here."

Red blinked up at Ace, who stood on the other side of the closed driver's side door, his brows furrowed. Shit, how long had he been out of it?

"Sorry." Red got out and closed the door behind him.

"You okay?"

"Yeah."

Ace set the car's alarm but didn't move. "You want to talk about it?"

"It's nothing," Red promised. Years ago, Red had been in a very dark place, but he and his brothers had learned how important it was to communicate with one another. They trusted each other with their lives. Keeping everything bottled up wouldn't do them any good. Thanks to King, they understood the importance of talking things out, how asking for help didn't make them weak, didn't make *him* weak.

"Trouble sleeping?"

Red headed for the front door of Bibi's Café and opened one side for Ace, the little bell announcing their arrival. "No more than usual."

He was glad Ace accepted his word for it, but then Ace knew Red would say if he was having trouble. Like most of his brothers, sleep never came easy, but after being shot recently, his night terrors had returned. They weren't as frequent as they'd once been, which he was grateful for, but were still bad enough to have him waking up screaming and sobbing. Although he'd been eased off his medication years ago, he continued to check in with his psychologist once a month.

Pushing those thoughts aside, he smiled when Bibi came out from behind the counter, her blue eyes sparkling with mischief. "My brother kicked you out already? This must be a new record."

Ace kissed her cheek before shaking his head in shame. "You know, you could have left him with some sense of humor. You didn't have to go and steal it all for yourself."

Bibi laughed before turning to hug Red. He kissed her cheek. "Hey, hon." She pulled back and looked him over, her warm gaze becoming concerned. "How are you feeling?"

"Better. Thanks." He used to get so angry when people asked him how he was feeling, believing they were doing so out of pity or because they thought he was weak. It took some time to understand they asked because they loved him.

"Is that Ace?"

"No," Bibi called out behind her, cringing. "I was talking to myself."

"Lies!" Bibi's husband, Nash, burst through the swinging doors of the kitchen with flourish, all six-foot-three of muscular black man dancing a victory jig on his way over, his smile huge. "Yes! That's right, baby. Whoop!"

"Damn it." Bibi crossed her arms over her chest, her narrowed eyes on Red. "Thanks a lot."

"What did I do?"

Ace laughed at her pout. "Oh my God, you lost another bet? Seriously, Bibi, you need to stop betting against your man. You especially need to stop betting on the Kings. What was it this time?"

Nash waggled his eyebrows. "Bibi said King wouldn't kick you out until after lunch. I told her he wouldn't make it to breakfast."

Bibi planted her hands on her hips with a huff. "I figured Red would provide enough of a buffer."

"Yeah, but you didn't take into account that by Red staying with King while he recovered, Ace would be there more than usual and slowly the pressure would build until *kaboom*! Quite frankly, I'm surprised your brother lasted this long. I figured he'd be done after a week." Nash did another little victory dance.

Bibi and Nash were part of their little family. They were also proof that true love and happy ever after did exist. It hadn't been an easy road for them by any means. Bibiana Kingston and Nash Sherwood met in high school, and when they fell in love, the two faced a world of prejudice and hate, because not only was Nash black, but a Cuban immigrant.

Their families might have been accepting, but society had not been. Thankfully, Bibi was not a woman to be trifled with. She also had her little brother, her man, and his siblings to make sure no one messed with them. As of several years back, they also had all the Kings.

Bibi and Nash showed the world what it could do with its ignorance, and after successful law careers, both retired in their mid-forties and opened a café near the beach. The two had been married twenty-seven years and looked at each other like they'd just fallen in love. Except now. Now Bibi was glaring at her husband like she was plotting his demise.

"What did you win?" Red asked, amused.

"I get to pick our next vacation. *Someone* wanted to do hiking and a bunch of other exhausting 'not my idea of a relaxing vacation' stuff, and I wanted to do something chill. Bora-Bora, we are going to be on you!"

"Enjoy your victory, because next time, I will crush you."

Nash let out a hearty laugh. "Baby, I do love your optimism. I shall now direct your attention to the board." He swept an arm dramatically to the blackboard behind the counter that kept tabs on their monthly bets. Red winced.

"I can still catch up," Bibi muttered.

Ace shook his head. "Nooo, you cannot."

With what sounded like a growl, Bib jabbed a finger toward the nearest chair. "Park it, pretty boy."

"Yes, ma'am." Ace quickly took a seat and grinned up at Nash. "Did you hear that? Your wife thinks I'm pretty."

Nash pursed his lips in thought, then shook his head. "Nope. Lucky's prettier."

Red laughed at Ace's scandalized expression and took a seat opposite Ace. It was always a battle of wits between these two, and a highly entertaining battle at that, especially since Nash usually ended up the winner. Red had to give it to Nash. Anyone who could beat Ace at his own game had major skills.

"*What*? Are you kidding me? I am way prettier." Ace motioned to his face. "This here is irresistible."

"And I'm sure when Colton says it, he means every word," Nash said, laughing when Ace flipped him off.

They put in their order, and with a kiss to his wife's cheek, Nash disappeared into the kitchen, whistling happily. Bibi brought them their usual drinks—a latte for Ace and a protein smoothie for Red.

Ace smiled brightly at her. "You are *terrible* at placing bets. You should really stay away from Vegas."

"Shut it, mister." She went off to check on the other customers in the café, leaving Ace to focus his attention on Red. His sudden innocent expression was fooling no one, least of all Red.

"What?" Red asked.

"Have you spoken to Laz?"

"Ace," Red warned. "Why can't you just drop it?"

"Because there's clearly something between you two, and you're being an ass."

"*I'm* being an ass? How am I being an ass? He left without a word and hasn't called me since, hasn't even texted." He'd spent all that time wondering if he'd done something to upset Laz, and like Ace, Red had thought there was something special between him and Laz, but apparently it had been one-sided. What else would explain Laz taking off the way he had? Red thought of the developments over the last few months.

Paxton Connolly had finally retired as Chairman and CEO of Connolly Maritime after signing a contract with Four Kings Security to provide security for the company. They'd saved his son's life. Colton falling in love with Ace—who had been tasked with his personal round-the-clock protection—had been unexpected to both Paxton and to the Kings. And the job had resulted in a relationship for Ace and two bullets to Red's gut—along with Red meeting Lazarus Galanos, a close friend of Colton's. The moment Red laid eyes on the beautiful fashion photographer, something inside him shifted. He'd never had such a strong reaction to someone he'd just met. His protective instincts had gone into overdrive, especially after Laz had been injured during a fight with his now ex-boyfriend. Laz had clung to Red who'd held on tight. No one had ever looked at him the way Laz did—like all he needed was Red.

Laz had not only accompanied Red in the ambulance, holding his hand the whole ride over, but after surgery, Laz's beautiful face and stunning blue eyes were the first things Red saw when he opened his eyes. Laz remained at Red's bedside while he was in recovery, holding his hand, reading to him, and offering comfort. As soon as the Kings had been able, they'd rushed to the hospital, and Laz disappeared without a word. Red hadn't heard from him since.

"Here we go," Bibi said, placing Red's feta, spinach, and egg sandwich in front of him. His mouth watered. He didn't usually indulge in the croissant sandwiches, but after being shot, he was entitled to spoil himself a little. Also they were so damned good, but then so was everything on Bibi's menu. She placed a bowl of something in front of Ace, and Red almost choked on his smoothie. "Be right back with another latte for you."

Ace picked up his spoon, then started searching through his food.

"What are you looking for?" Red asked.

"Bacon."

"In oatmeal?" Was he really surprised? This was Ace, after all.

"No. In what's supposed to be Bibi's Breakfast Bacon Egg-stravaganza."

Bibi returned, and Ace peered up at her. "What's this?"

She squinted at him. "Oatmeal."

"Thank you for clarifying, but that's not what I ordered."

"It's what his majesty ordered for you."

Ace's eyes went wide, and Red stifled a laugh. "He didn't."

Bibi grinned wickedly. "Oh, but he did. Would you like the granola topping? Or the berries?"

"I'm going to kill him." Ace pulled his cell phone out of his pocket, and Red took a big bite out of his breakfast sandwich while Ace growled into the phone. "What the hell, King?"

Red didn't need to hear King's side of the conversation to know he was being all calm and collected, and secretly enjoying every moment of torture he was inflicting on Ace.

"Haven't I been punished enough?"

Bibi laughed all the way to the kitchen.

"*Fine*." Ace hung up, then glared at his oatmeal like he was telepathically trying to set it on fire. "Stupid King. How long is he going to make me pay?"

"This is King we're talking about," Red reminded him, smiling when Ace let his head fall back with a loud groan.

The four Kings built a company based on trust. Without trust, they had nothing, so becoming involved with a client was a line they never crossed. When Ace became romantically involved with Colton, he hadn't simply crossed the line—he'd annihilated it. He should have pulled himself off the case, but he didn't. Had Colton not smoothed things over with his father when Paxton discovered what was going on between his son and the man he'd hired to protect him, the Kings, and everything they'd built over ten years, would have been in ruins.

As co-owner of the company, Ace's contract wouldn't be terminated, as it would have been for someone else, but it didn't mean he was excused from facing the consequences of his actions. The four of them spent hours going over Colton's case, with Ace accounting for every minute spent in Colton's company. Learning about the many times Ace and Colton had engaged in sex was not Red's idea of a good time, but it had been necessary to determine the appropriate disciplinary measures.

Ace was suspended for two weeks without pay, and in addition to that, every case he was assigned to, until further notice, came with personal supervision from King, which translated to babysitting, something Ace hated far more than anything. More than the suspension without pay. More than having to be at the beck and call of the pop divas he was continuously assigned to protect. More than having King call Bibi to change his meal order, driving him batshit crazy. No one wanted to disappoint King, especially Ace.

Nash appeared at their table and placed a plate piled high with bacon in front of Ace.

Ace blinked up at Nash. "Oh my God, leave your wife for me."

"Yeah, I love you too, bro, but this right here requires a favor in return."

Ace peered at him, and when Nash waggled his eyebrows, Ace gasped and shook his head before leaning in to whisper conspiratorially, "Are you insane? Do you know what your wife will do to me if she finds out I've been letting you take Lucky's motorcycle out for joyrides? She will murder me dead, and if by some miracle I survive, she'll tell King, who'll force me to eat oatmeal for the rest of my life!" He pushed away the plate of bacon. "Take your delicious, iniquitous bacon with you."

Nash arched an eyebrow. "Iniquitous, huh?" He moved his questioning gaze to Red.

"He installed a 'word of the day' app on his phone to impress Colton."

"Ah." Nash let out a sigh. "Well, that's a shame. Looks like I'll have to eat this crisp, crunchy, mouthwatering bacon all on my own." He bit into a strip and moaned. "Mm, this is damned good. I think I outdid myself." He held the plate out to Red, who took one, knowing it would be cooked to perfection.

"Oh God, Nash," Red said with a moan. "This is incredible. There's a hint of something sweet."

"Canadian maple syrup."

"I hate you both," Ace said with a growl.

"There's still plenty left." Nash waved the plate of bacon under Ace's nose. "King doesn't have to know. I can keep Bibi busy long enough for you to enjoy every crunchy, salty-sweet, satisfying strip."

Ace held a hand out for the plate. "I hate you so much right now. Evil bastard."

"It's only fair when you got this much game going on." Nash grinned wickedly as he handed Ace the plate. "Bibi's got her book club next week. I'll call you with a date and time."

Red shook his head in shame at his friends. "I love how you two are still under the illusion that she won't find out. She was born a Kingston. If she ever decided to go into private security, she'd put us all out of business."

"Hey, don't you be throwing those bad juju vibes my way," Nash said, giving him a pointed look. "She has a sixth sense for shenanigans. Do you realize how hard it is to get away with anything around her?"

Ace was unimpressed. "Yes, we do. Her brother's our boss, remember?"

Nash winced. "Damn. You need to get that man laid. Release some of the tension."

"Try telling *him* that," Ace said with a laugh. "No, please do, but make sure I'm around to hear it. If the vein on the side of his neck starts to pulse, that's your signal to haul ass."

Nash laughed before patting Ace on the shoulder, then heading off toward the kitchen.

"How long has it been now?"

Ace's question threw Red off guard, and it took his brain a moment to catch up. He should have known Ace wouldn't let the matter of Laz drop. "Almost three months." He let out a heavy sigh. "It's better this way."

Ace peered at him. "That makes no sense. Explain."

"Well, for one, I'm ten years older than him. He travels more than I do, and all over the world. His lifestyle couldn't be any more different from mine. His ex-boyfriend was a gorgeous model—"

"Who cheated on him, treated him like shit, and scarred him for life." Ace leaned in, his eyes never leaving Red's. "The fact that you're the complete opposite of that asshole Bryan is a good thing. Stop putting yourself down, Red. Anyone would be lucky to have you. You're the sweetest guy I know, loyal to a fault, and you make Laz feel safe. He needs that."

Red couldn't bring himself to respond. Relationships were never easy, especially when his sexuality came into play. Was it really that difficult to understand? He was attracted to people, to their personalities, their hearts, their sense of humor, their smile—not their gender or what was between their legs. That never mattered to Red. Unfortunately, it mattered to others, even to members of his own community.

Just because he was attracted to all kinds of people, didn't mean he was attracted to everyone he met. It had been one of the many reasons his last relationship imploded. His girlfriend, Naaz, became jealous of everyone Red so much as smiled at, and despite being adamant she didn't care about his sexuality, she'd continuously tell him how hard it was for her to not only have to compete with other women, but with the whole world. It made no sense to him. She didn't have to compete with anyone. He was with her, and only her, wanted her, *loved* her, but in the end, none of that had been enough. He'd tried to salvage their relationship, he really had, but then she'd presented an ultimatum. Her, or the one man she knew Red could never give up, the one man she was most jealous of.

King.

Naaz had been convinced something was going on between him and King, and the fact he sometimes called for King in his sleep didn't help. When he'd explained why, that it was nothing sexual, she said she believed him, but she didn't, because after he had a particularly bad nightmare, she'd made up her mind. It was her or King.

For years Red fought against the feeling something was wrong with him, and when he'd finally accepted himself, he ended up fighting a different battle. Now it was easier to not get involved. Less chance of getting his heart broken, of being made to choose.

Bibi appeared beside their table, snapping him out of his thoughts. She placed a brown takeout bag in front of Ace. "Here you go."

Red arched an eyebrow at Ace. "Didn't you just eat?"

"It's for Mason. He's stuck at the beach covering an event." Ace stood and kissed Bibi's cheek. "Thanks. See you later."

"Say hi to Mason for me," Bibi replied before bringing Red in for a hug. "You take it easy. Let us know if you need anything."

"I will. Thanks, Bibi." Red kissed her cheek, then headed for the door after Ace, who handed him Mason's food to hold. They got into the car, and Red lowered his sunglasses. "Your new boyfriend doesn't mind you taking your old boyfriend breakfast?"

"Nope. Colton knows about Mason. We don't keep anything from each other."

"Colton doesn't mind that you and Mason are still friends?"

"Colton trusts me. I also know that if I suddenly turned into a cheating asshole, he'd rip my balls off and feed them to his neighbor's golden retriever."

Red cringed. "Yeah, your boyfriend's a little scary sometimes."

"Isn't he?" Ace's smile stretched from ear to ear. "God, I love him. He's so fucking adorable, but piss him off, and *bam* you've been eviscerated. We were meant to be."

"I worry about you sometimes."

"I appreciate the love."

"That wasn't a compliment."

"Really? Because all I heard was how much you love me."

"You're exhausting."

Ace laughed. "Now you sound like King."

Despite the circumstances of how Ace and Colton got together, Red was happy for Ace. He wasn't kidding when he said the two were meant for each other. Ace might drive his boyfriend nuts, but Colton was one of the few people who could handle him, and Ace was so in love with the man, he'd do anything to make him happy. They also had Colton to thank for Ace's newfound ability to question his actions *before* carrying through with them. Not always, but some of the time was better than never.

"What part of the beach?" Red asked.

"Pope Road. Next to that new hotel they're building. Fewer beachgoers."

They were only on A1A Beach Boulevard for about two minutes before they were making a right onto Pope Road. Ace drove to the end of the sandy path, where Mason's patrol car was parked. A medium-sized group of people were scattered on the beach near the water's edge, some sitting on colorful folding beach chairs, others standing beneath large black umbrellas. Several stands were stuck into the sand, some with screens attached, others with huge lights. A lone, half-naked man knelt on the shore as waves crashed against his toned body from behind. It wasn't the sensual figure that caused Red's pulse to speed up, though, but the slender man kneeling in the sand with the camera. Heat flared through Red, anger quickly following. He unbuckled his belt, then turned in his seat to growl at Ace.

"Explain."

"Explain what? I told you. I'm bringing Mason breakfast."

Red thrust a finger toward the beach. "Explain *that*."

Ace peered ahead. "Well, Russell, it would appear some sort of fashion shoot is taking place."

"Unless you want to eat nothing but oatmeal for the rest of your life, you'll tell me what you did."

"Me?" Ace asked with a dramatic gasp. "You think I arranged this?"

"Ace," Red warned.

"Okay, I possibly, maybe, might have asked Colton if he knew of any local fashion shoots coming up, and Colton may or may not have mentioned this particular one, and I may or may not have asked Mason to get himself assigned to it." Ace cleared his throat and met Red's gaze. "I meddled. I'm a meddling meddler. It's Laz."

"No shit."

"I had Colton ask him for his schedule, told Mason he needed to be here so he could keep me informed; then I tricked you. I should apologize."

Red narrowed his eyes.

"I'm not going to. I'm not sorry. Go talk to him."

"I'd rather strangle you," Red said with a growl.

Ace held up a finger. "You could, and I'd deserve it, but just hear me out. How about instead of strangling me, you go say hi to the cute guy who wouldn't leave your side in your moment of need."

"Really? You're going to guilt-trip me?"

"Absolutely. Is it working?"

With a frustrated growl, Red shoved the car door open and got out. He leaned in to glare at Ace. "This isn't over."

"Whatever you say. Go get 'em, tiger."

Red grunted and turned to leave, but Ace called out to him.

"Wait."

*God, what now?* He spun on his heels, his jaw clenched tight at Ace's stupid smile and the roll of mints he held up.

Ace shrugged. "You never know."

"You're an ass." Red marched off and got halfway to Mason's car before he turned and marched back to Ace, who was still sitting in his car and grinning like an idiot. He snatched the roll of mints, popped one into his mouth, then tossed the roll back at Ace and left before the urge to push Ace off the pier became too great to ignore.

# CHAPTER 2

He was cursed. He had to be.

Laz pinched the bridge of his nose, closed his eyes, and summoned patience. Clearly the universe was against him. The day had started out so promising. The weather had been gorgeous, the brilliant blue sky filled with perfect white fluffy clouds, the heat bearable, and the beach scarcely populated. The art director, Esteban, had been on time and so had the stylist, Emily, the hairstylist and Laz's friend, Fitz, and Vic, the makeup artist. The models had been ready with minimal hassle and almost on time, which was an improvement from the usual. Then Esteban smiled at one of the models, and everything went to hell.

It wasn't a friendly smile. No, it was an "I can't wait to get you out of that wet Speedo" smile, one that made it clear the two were intimately acquainted. It wouldn't have been a problem had two other models not witnessed said smile. Two models who'd been on the receiving end of that very look earlier that morning. Damn it, why couldn't they keep it in their pants? Or Speedos.

After spending half an hour defusing the situation, the weather turned against him as well, with a breeze strong enough to whip against his equipment. Esteban was hiding behind Emily, Fitz and Vic kept trying to one-up each other, and the models were competing for the title of world's biggest diva. Perfect.

"Let's take a break," Laz announced, finally looking up and spotting several of the models smiling coyly at someone somewhere behind him. He turned and his heart lurched to a stop, or so it felt. Jesus, the man was something. Not the kind of gorgeous some would use to describe the models he was currently working with. But a different kind of beauty, one that encompassed the man both inside and out.

Russell "Red" McKinley was handsome, no doubt about it, but it was everything else that made him stunning. Yes, Red had an incredible body, his muscles bunching and straining beneath the gray T-shirt as he walked, his broad shoulders and wide chest tapering down to a trim waist. He was sexy as sin, but also kind of adorable. Something about his soulful, hooded hazel eyes mesmerized Laz, but it was Red's smile that always stole his breath away. Laz loved how it reached his eyes, forming little creases at the corners.

Red stopped in front of him, his boyish grin kind of shy as he removed his baseball cap and ran a hand through his hair. "Hey."

"Hi." Laz couldn't help his wide smile, or the way his heart skipped a beat. Being so close to Red made him feel light-headed. The breeze ruffled Red's already tousled auburn hair, and the sun made his freckles more prominent. Laz wanted to kiss each one. "What are you doing here?"

Red motioned behind him, where Ace was talking to Officer Cooper. "Mason's a friend. Ace was bringing him breakfast."

"That's nice of him. Officer Cooper's been really patient with us."

"Yeah, Mason's a great guy." Red placed his cap back on his head before shoving his hands into his pockets. Was he nervous? Laz certainly was. "It's good to see you."

"It's good to see you too. How have you been?"

"Good. Supposed to take it easy, nothing too strenuous, but other than that, I'm feeling right as rain." He smiled at Laz, and Laz could have melted then and there. Red's face flushed pink, and Laz wondered if it was a result of the sun's heat against his fair skin or something else. He secretly hoped it was the latter.

"I'm glad. I've been worried," Laz admitted.

Red's smile widened. "Yeah?"

"I'm sorry I didn't call. I didn't want to be a nuisance." Things between them had been going so well, the last thing he'd wanted was to overstay his welcome. When the rest of the Kings, Jack, and Joker arrived at the hospital to see Red, Laz felt like he was intruding. He'd also felt a little intimidated being in a room full of men who'd sacrificed so much, who despite no longer being in the military still risked their lives to protect others. What could *he* possibly offer a man like Red? Laz had slipped out of the room and hadn't called since, too embarrassed by his cowardly retreat.

"I would never think of you as a nuisance. I'm sorry I worried you, but at the same time, I'm kinda glad to hear it."

Laz's heart did a flip. "You are?"

"Yes."

"I'm sorry."

"For what?"

"I should have called. After everything, I just took off. You must have thought I was an asshole, disappearing like that." Laz looked away, his face burning from embarrassment.

"Hey." Red stepped closer and placed his fingers gently beneath Laz's chin, turning his head so their eyes could meet.

This time the heat in Laz's face had nothing to do with embarrassment and everything to do with Red's proximity. His stomach was full of butterflies, and he struggled not to drop his gaze to Red's lips. What would his lips taste like? How would it feel to have those big, strong hands caressing his body? He knew from experience how good those arms felt around him. How would the rest of him feel? *Okay, get it together. The guy's being all sweet and understanding, and you're thinking about jumping his bones.*

"You were there when I needed you, and I won't forget that. Ace said you were really upset when you saw me. I'm sorry I scared you."

"Scared? I was terrified." Laz swallowed hard, thinking back to that horrible night, and the fear he felt knowing he might never get to see that smile again. "When I saw you lying there covered in blood, I thought you…. There was so much blood." He closed his eyes, allowing himself to be pulled into Red's embrace.

Laz wrapped his arms around Red's waist and let his head rest against Red's chest. No one had ever made him feel so at ease. How was that possible? He didn't know all that much about Red, only what he'd experienced while at Colton's, and what he'd learned from online articles about the four Kings. His browser history made him look like a stalker. The thing was, as much as he liked Red, all of it was too perfect. Laz knew better than to fall for illusions. There was no such thing as perfect, and anyone who appeared too good to be true was hiding something.

"It's okay. Everything's okay now."

Laz nodded. His stomach rumbled, and he let out a self-conscious laugh as he pulled away. "Sorry. I haven't had anything to eat since four this morning."

Red's brows drew together in concern. "Are you due for a break soon?"

"I can't. We've fallen behind, and—"

"You promised me you'd take care of yourself, Laz."

"And I have been," Laz promised. Coming from anyone else, he might have been annoyed at being fussed at, but Red had been the first to call him out on his stupidity. With sweet words, he made Laz realize what he'd been doing to himself because of Bryan.

Laz had been underweight and unhealthy, believing Bryan when he said Laz needed to lose weight or no one would want to hire him, how he looked bloated and was always stuffing his face, despite the fact Laz had already been skipping meals. It was a misconception that models didn't eat, when in truth, many of the models he worked with enjoyed food. They simply made sure to eat healthy with the occasional cheat day. Bryan and his friends were not those models, and they sneered at anyone who didn't "sacrifice" what they did for their beauty. Somewhere along the way, Laz had allowed himself to feel ashamed of eating. His poor nutrition habits and severe work schedule had started to take a toll on his body and health without him even realizing. Until the day of his party at Colton's house, where he'd met Red.

They'd only just been introduced when Red challenged Bryan, who'd been having a go at Laz for daring to eat something. Red called Laz gorgeous but expressed his concern at how underweight Laz was for his height and build. After that, Red had taken it upon himself to look after Laz and make sure he was eating properly and not skipping meals. He never came off preachy or condescending, his concern genuine and sweet. Thanks to Red, Laz was now at a healthy weight, and felt so much better than he had in a long time.

Red tapped away at his phone, then handed it to Laz. "Tell me what you'd like, and I'll go get it for you."

"You don't have to do that."

"Bibi's is two minutes away. It's not a problem."

"You really don't need to." The butterflies in his stomach fluttered wildly when Red smiled playfully and winked at him.

"I know. But I want to."

"Okay." Laz scanned the menu, his mouth watering with each description he read. He picked a breakfast sandwich since it would be easier to eat on the beach, and an iced coffee because he could really do with the caffeine. The iced part was a bonus.

"Do you want to ask around, see if anyone wants anything?"

"Thanks, but Esteban's assistant takes care of everyone else. She has enough on her plate, so I didn't want to take up any more of her time with a food run just for me."

"You don't have an assistant to take care of you?" Red asked, his expression concerned.

"Can't afford one. Not yet. But I should be able to hire someone part-time soon."

Red nodded his understanding. "Be right back, then." He was off before Laz could reach for his wallet. Laz watched him go, his eyes following Red's muscular form. Red's T-shirt was rucked up and caught in the waistband of his shorts, leaving Laz with a spectacular view of his ass.

"Good God. Please tell me you're letting that man do filthy things to you."

"We're just friends," Laz murmured, feeling his face heat. Quickly pushing Red from his thoughts, he turned to narrow his eyes at Fitz. "What's going on with you? Esteban said windswept. Why does Lonny look like he can stab someone with his bangs?"

"Funny," Fitz muttered, his frown deep. Something was obviously bothering his friend, and it wasn't like him not to confide in Laz.

"I'm serious. He's like Cameron Diaz in *There's Something About Mary*. Is that what you were going for? That 'I've got dry jizz in my hair look'? Because I hate to break it to you, that trend has come and gone. Pun totally intended."

Fitz's lips twitched. "Are you done?"

"Absolutely not. I want to know what the deal is with you and Vic. Between Lonny's hair and Han one smoky-eyed expression away from looking like the Joker, I'm getting concerned."

Fitz burst into laughter before his eyes welled up and he broke into a sob.

"Oh my God, Fitz, what happened?" Laz quickly but discreetly led Fitz away from the others. The last thing he wanted was for someone to overhear their conversation and gossip about whatever was causing poor Fitz so much pain. Laz always set up an umbrella and folding chair far enough away from the shoot to allow for some privacy. The truth was, he sometimes needed a break.

Fitz wiped at his cheeks, then let out an unsteady breath. "Jiles moved out two days ago. I caught him cheating on me. With Vic."

Laz gasped. "What?"

"Oh, baby, it gets better," Fitz said with a bitter laugh. "He's married."

Laz blinked at him. "Vic is married?" How had he not known that? Vic had a different guy on his arm every week. Maybe he and his husband were in an open relationship. A *very* open relationship.

Fitz shook his head, his bottom lip trembling. "No. Jiles."

"Wait. Jiles? As in your boyfriend of ten years who said he wanted to marry you? That Jiles? He's *married*?"

Fitz nodded.

"Oh my God." Laz couldn't believe it. "That son of a bitch! How long has he been married?"

"Three years, but he's been with his husband for twenty. *Twenty years*, Laz. I'm such a fucking idiot. I gave that lying, cheating son of a bitch ten years of my life!" Fitz burst into tears again, and Laz brought him in for a hug, holding him tight, his heart aching for his sweet friend.

Fitz was a couple of years older than Laz and a highly sought-after hairstylist. He could have his pick of shoots, but he always accepted jobs where Laz was the photographer. They'd met years ago on a shoot for a fashion magazine down in Miami, where Laz had been an intern. It had been Laz's first day, and he'd been so nervous. Fitz had come to his rescue when Laz screwed up a coffee run, forgetting the photographer's Chai latte. Laz had been about to admit he'd gotten the order wrong when Fitz stepped in and told the photographer he'd taken the latte, thinking it was his. The photographer had ranted and fumed, but he couldn't fire Fitz like he could Laz. No intern had lasted longer than a month with the man. Thanks to Fitz's guidance, several months later, Laz walked away with a glowing reference.

"You're not an idiot," Laz said softly. "The man was living with you, for Christ's sake. How the hell did he pull it off?"

"He and his husband have a house together in Atlanta. Now it's so obvious, but at the time, all the traveling made sense," Fitz said with a sniff. "I mean, that's where the company's corporate office is, so of course he'd be traveling there a lot. When he said he was too tired to drive back and would be staying the weekend or that he had a weekend golf game with important clients, I didn't think anything of it."

"Because you loved him."

"I trusted him." Fitz pulled back and wiped at his reddened eyes. "The worst part was that I found out from Vic. Like it wasn't bad enough I walked in on them having sex in *our* bed. I was kicking Vic out of the house when he said I shouldn't be so surprised about how things turned out, how it was what I got for getting involved with a married man. I couldn't breathe. I told myself Vic was just being a spiteful bitch, but if Jiles was cheating on me, how farfetched would it be that he really was married? You know what Jiles did when I confronted him?"

"What?" Laz asked, wiping a freshly fallen tear from Fitz's cheek.

"He laughed at me. Then he told me I was naïve. How gay men weren't made to be monogamous."

"That's bullshit," Laz spat out. Fitz arched an eyebrow at him, and Laz sighed. "Okay, so we were both cheated on, but that doesn't mean all men are lying, cheating assholes. I'm so sorry, Fitz."

"Yeah, well, it is what it is. Enough about me and my sad, pathetic love life. Tell me about your new man."

"He's not my man." The thought of Red being his made him shiver in the most delicious way. "We're friends." Sort of. Were they friends? He hoped so.

"Why? Is the sun in your eyes? Have you not seen the man's muscles? I bet you could eat off his abs, or you know, just dine on other parts of him."

"Get your head out of the gutter. Yes, he's gorgeous, but he's also ex-Special Forces, incredibly sweet, attentive, caring, protective, and he saved my life."

Fitz's eyes went wide. "Wait, *he's* the guy you were telling me about? The hottie from Colton's party who saved you from drowning when you hit your head and fell in the pool?"

Laz nodded.

"I'm sorry I wasn't there, by the way." Fitz squeezed his arm. "It's probably a good thing I wasn't. I would have grabbed a Taser off one of those security guys and tased Bryan in the balls. Also, I'm waiting for the part where you tell me your Superman is really a soul-sucking vampire or something, because that's the only reason I can think of for you not climbing him like a tree. Personally, even if he was a soul-sucking vampire, I'd take my chances."

Laz chuckled. "I bet." His smile fell away, and he sighed. "That's the thing, Fitz. He's amazing."

"And… that's a bad thing? I'm really confused here, babe."

"He's too good."

"Ah. You think he's going to turn out to be like Bryan."

"Maybe not exactly like Bryan, but there's got to be something, right? The guy can't be hot, a super soldier, and a great guy."

Fitz shrugged. "Maybe he puts ketchup on his mashed potatoes or something."

"Gross. No. Red's a great cook."

"Oh my God, he cooks too? Why aren't you chaining him to your radiator?"

"First, this is Florida. Where am I going to find a radiator? Second, because that would be illegal."

"Whatever. My point is, he sounds amazing. You don't actually think he's perfect, do you?"

"No, of course not. What I mean is, guys who seem too good to be true, usually are. When you first hook up, they say and do all the right things. Then when you're in deep, it all falls apart, and you end up wondering how you could be so blind. I can't… I can't go through that again. I'm only just making sense of all the shit Bryan put me through." Laz swallowed hard, his skin crawling and the back of his eyes stinging when he thought about his fucked-up relationship with that asshole. "I was in an abusive relationship and didn't even know it. If I hadn't gotten out when I did, I don't know where I would have ended up."

"No one says you have to jump into a relationship with him." Fitz elbowed him playfully, his expression lecherous. "Doesn't mean you can't jump into bed with him. I'll be very disappointed if you don't let that sexy soldier wreck you. He is gay, right?"

"Pan."

Fitz's eyebrows shot up. "How did that conversation go?"

"Actually I, um, watched an online interview *LGBTQ Nation* did with the four Kings a couple of years ago. They don't hide who they are, especially after having to serve under Don't Ask, Don't Tell. It was really inspiring. Anyway, I may have done a little research on Red. Okay, a lot of research."

"Stalk much?"

"Shut up," Laz grumbled before covering his face with his hands and groaning. "Oh God. When did I turn into a teenage girl?"

With a laugh, Fitz wrapped an arm around him, giving him a squeeze. "Hey, you do what's best for you."

"What if Red *is* what's best for me? Am I going to let Bryan ruin that for me? I know it's easier said than done, and God knows Red doesn't need my baggage, but I'm sure he has his own. Who doesn't? Screw Bryan. I deserve to be happy, and so do you."

"That's the spirit. Now pout those pretty lips."

"What?"

"Your man's heading this way."

Laz's pulse sped up, and heat flared through him as Red approached. Red smiled at Laz when he reached them. "Hi, sorry to interrupt." He handed Laz a brown bag and an iced latte. "Here you go."

"Thank you. I really appreciate it. And you weren't interrupting."

"Well, hello," Fitz hummed, raking his gaze over Red. He wasn't even trying to be subtle.

"Fitz, this is Red. Red, this is my friend Fitz. He's a very talented hairstylist and was just leaving."

"Enchanté," Fitz purred, holding his hand out to Red, who shook it with a bemused smile.

"Um, likewise."

"Tell me, Red. Any marriages Laz should know about?"

"No. What? No. I've never been married." Red was puzzled and rightfully so. Could this conversation get any more awkward?

"Wonderful. Laz is free this week, by the way. You know, in case you wanted to ask him out to dinner or something."

Apparently, it could get more awkward.

Laz glared at Fitz. *I am going to kill you!* As if sensing his murderous thoughts, Fitz chirped a quick "Bye" and hurried off.

"I am *so* sorry about that," Laz said. "He has no filter."

Red chuckled. "That's okay. I know a thing or three about meddlesome friends." He shrugged. "They mean well." Red motioned to the folding chair. "Why don't you go ahead and eat."

"You sure? I feel kind of weird being the only one eating."

"It's fine. I already ate. Besides, you shouldn't feel guilty about eating when you're hungry."

It was a bad habit. One he'd picked up thanks to Bryan. It was amazing how much better he felt about everything since he'd left. Only now could he see how toxic their relationship had been. How much of himself he'd given up and allowed to be manipulated. Laz sat on the folding chair, surprised when Red took a seat in the sand beside him, his knees drawn up and his arms resting on them as he gazed out at the ocean.

"You're going to get sand all over."

Red shrugged and smiled up at him. "I live and work in Florida. Occupational hazard. You were kneeling in the sand when we arrived."

"Oh, yeah, I have enough sand in my shoes to build at least two sand castles," Laz replied, loving the sound of Red's rich laugh. It was nice sitting here together. They made small talk as Laz ate his sandwich. At first, he was a little self-conscious about eating in front of Red with Red not eating, but as Red leisurely made conversation, Laz found himself forgetting about his insecurities. He made a mental note to stop by Bibi's more often. He had no idea King's sister and her husband owned a café so close to St. Augustine Beach. He also discovered Mason and Ace dated for a year before Ace broke things off, yet the two remained good friends. Apparently, Colton knew all about Mason, but then Laz wasn't surprised. Ace and Colton had built their relationship on trust. They didn't keep anything from each other. It must be nice, knowing the person you loved could be counted on so completely.

Once he'd eaten and finished his coffee, he headed back to the shoot with Red beside him. Laz was about to grab his camera when he heard the resounding *smack*.

Lonny covered his reddening cheek before he launched himself at Han. "You skank!"

Laz groaned. Just what he didn't need. "Great. This is going to leave a mark." He made to head for the catfight when Ace strolled by.

"I'll take care of it," Ace said, heading for the group of bickering male models who'd gathered around the pair clawing at each other.

"I don't think that's a good idea," Laz called out, trying to warn Ace before turning worriedly to Red. "You have to do something. They're going to eat him alive."

Red groaned. "Too late."

"What—" Laz turned and gasped. "Oh my God." Lonny was wrapped around Ace, arms around his neck, screeching at him, while two more models attempted to climb him just before Han smacked him.

"That's not what I meant! Ow! My spleen! Hey, Zoolander, go Blue Steel yourself somewhere else. Oh my God, where are they all coming from?"

Incredible. Laz had never seen anything like it. "Wow, that escalated quickly."

"When Ace is involved, it usually does," Red mumbled, removing his phone from his pocket.

"What the hell is goin' on?" Mason stopped beside them, hands on his utility belt as he shook his head at the spectacle before them. "How does one man cause so much havoc just by opening his mouth? 'Course I shouldn't be surprised, considering the man got himself cussed at by a nun."

Laz's jaw dropped. "A nun cursed at him?"

"Yep. She used cuss words I've never heard before, and considering my acquaintance with the Kings, that's saying something. I don't know what he said to her, but she condemned his soul to hell right then and there. I reckon she would've made a deal with the devil himself to have him dragged away. Boy's got talent for making folks lose their damn minds."

Laz wouldn't have believed it if he hadn't seen it. Granted, he hadn't known Ace very long, and from what he'd gathered, Ace could be a little over-the-top sometimes, but Laz had only ever experienced the playful, caring side of Ace. When Laz had been hurt, Ace had been good to him, looked out for him. What's more, Colton was madly in love with Ace, and Colton wasn't the type of man to play fast and loose with his heart. Though now that Laz thought about it, he did often hear Colton threatening Ace with bodily harm.

"I better step in before he makes things worse," Mason grumbled.

"Worse? How can he possibly make things worse?" Every model at the shoot was currently dogpiling Ace, and yet the man was still standing. It was clear he was trying hard not to hurt any of them. Like the rest of the Kings, Ace was a former Green Beret, and although he was a couple of inches shorter than Red, and not as muscular, he was still bigger and stronger than everyone at the shoot, with the exception of Officer Cooper, who reminded Laz of one of those romance novel cowboys, all rippling muscles and swagger, with a sexy Texas drawl.

Ace could easily throw any of those young men off him, but for some reason he kept trying to talk himself out of it, which only brought about more high-pitched shrieks.

"It's Ace. He can *always* make things worse." Mason took a step forward, but Red grabbed his arm.

"No need," Red said, smiling widely. He waved his phone at them. "I just sent King a video. He's two minutes away."

Mason groaned. Loudly. "Goddamn it, Red. Why would you go and do a fool thing like that? King's gonna be spitting nails, and I just know I'll catch hell from him."

Red chuckled and patted Mason's arm. "Don't worry. Only one King's going to blame is the smartass who pissed off a bunch of models."

"Are you sure calling King was a good idea?" Laz asked Red. "He's kind of… intense." King had always been nice to him, but the guy had a larger-than-life presence. When he walked into a room, he captured everyone's attention, and although he was a good-looking man, it wasn't what had everyone fascinated. He exuded strength and confidence, along with something else Laz couldn't quite put his finger on, something that made Laz feel as if he'd known King for years, although they'd only just met. It was odd.

"You think King's intense?" Red frowned thoughtfully.

"Yes. To the rest of us mere mortals," Mason drawled, "the almighty Ward Kingston is fuckin' terrifying."

As if summoned, King approached, dressed in a stylish white button-down shirt tucked into the waistband of his blue-gray slacks, the sleeves perfectly rolled up to reveal his muscular arms, and the top button undone. He paused beside them long enough to let out a heavy sigh, as if he were mentally preparing himself to deal with Ace and the mess he'd gotten himself into. Laz stood enthralled as King strolled up to Ace and the mountain of models he was currently under. He didn't yell, didn't bark orders or pull anyone off Ace.

"Holy shit," Mason whispered hoarsely. "Is that… a smile? Is King smiling?"

Sure enough, he was, and when he spoke, his voice was soft, friendly, but firm.

"Excuse me."

Everyone's head whipped up, their attention locked on King. The models, their eyes huge, slid off Ace and stood to face the ruggedly handsome man.

"Hi, I'm Ward Kingston, but you can call me King." He put a hand to his chest, and their eyes followed the movement. "Wow, it's hot out here, huh? Why don't we go and chat under one of those big umbrellas over there? I'm sure it's a little cooler." He turned, and Laz's jaw all but hit the sand when everyone followed King like he was a mama duck and they were his ducklings.

"What's happening right now?" Mason asked, scratching his head.

King stopped beneath the umbrella next to them, and the models crowded around him. He asked them how they were, if they were staying hydrated, were they local, how long they'd been modeling. His smile never left his face, his sparkling blue eyes moving to each model as he spoke to them. They leaned in to him, smiling wide, giggling and laughing, hanging on his every word. He had them eating out of his hand.

"I think I may be suffering from heatstroke," Mason murmured.

Laz stifled a laugh at Mason's startled expression.

"I'm so sorry about my friend," King said sincerely. "He's a little excitable, but he really does mean well."

"Oh, of course," Lonny said, hands wrapped around King's arm. "I shouldn't have been so quick to go off. Low blood sugar, you know?"

"I understand completely," King said, patting his hand. "I hope you're all taking good care of yourselves." They all nodded, and when King's smile brightened, Laz heard the dreamy sighs.

Ace limped over to them, grumbling under his breath. He glared at Red. "I can't believe you called King."

Red shrugged, amusement written all over his face. "I can't do any heavy lifting, remember? Someone had to step in."

Ace thrust a hand at Mason. "How about the giant Texan in uniform and shiny badge that's trained for this sort of situation?"

Mason rubbed his stubbled jaw, his grin cocky. "Well, I don't know about being trained for *this* particular situation. Don't remember the academy covering any incidents involving loudmouthed smartasses swarmed by pissed-off models."

"Screw you too," Ace spat out at Mason, his arms folded over his chest and his pout fierce.

Mason and Red burst into laughter, and Laz couldn't help but join in. He couldn't remember the last time he'd had this much fun. He liked being around Red and his friends.

Maybe today was going to be a good day after all.

# CHAPTER 3

"Thanks for not arresting any of my men," King told Mason, following up the remark with a pointed look before Han stepped up to ask King something. He turned to give the young man his full attention, and Mason took the opportunity to whisper hoarsely at Red.

"It was one time. One time!"

Red chuckled. Poor guy. If Mason was waiting for King to forget, he'd be waiting a very, *very* long time. King might forgive, but he never forgot, though Red suspected King enjoyed getting a rise out of the rough-and-tough cowboy.

The familiar rumble of Lucky's motorcycle had them searching him out. He parked his bike next to Mason's patrol car, and as he removed his helmet to secure it to his bike, Mason's frown deepened.

"I can't believe he's still ridin' that damn thing. This is Florida. It's like goddamn bumper cars out there."

"You forget Lucky rides his motorcycle in Miami," Ace reminded Mason. "Where do you think our security officers go to learn defensive driving techniques?"

"You send your security officers to train in Miami?" Mason looked horrified, making Red laugh. Despite having lived in Florida for years now, Mason continued to be baffled by its residents. He was convinced something was in the water. That, or the humidity was affecting people's oxygen intake. Ace loved to poke and prod Mason just to hear him rant. It was highly entertaining.

"I'm sorry, but have you tried making a left turn in Miami during rush hour?"

"Nope. Too busy trying to figure out which of the ten cars driving with their hazard lights on during a thunderstorm actually has an emergency. I'll give you a hint, none, because they're not using the damn thing like they're supposed to."

"Well, we do live in the state of shoplifting turkeys," Ace said with a grin.

"Someone shoplifted turkeys?" Laz asked, confused. He was so damned cute.

"No, someone dressed like a turkey was arrested for shoplifting."

Laz opened his mouth to reply, then closed it. He shook his head. "I got nothing." The wind blew his hair into his face, the soft dark curls calling to Red, and he couldn't help reaching out to tuck a lock of hair behind Laz's ear, earning him a sweet smile. "Thanks."

Red returned his smile and shoved his hands into his pockets, the urge to touch Laz overwhelming. Laz was a good half foot or so shorter than Red, which meant he had to look up to meet Red's gaze, and for some reason Red found that endearing. He wasn't sure why. At six-foot-three, most people had to look up when talking to him. Maybe because he liked how Laz felt tucked against his body. How well they fit together. One thing he did know was that the more time he spent around Laz, the more he wanted to bring him into his arms and kiss him.

"Well, hello, Officer Cooper." Lucky swaggered over, blatantly checking Mason out like he always did, and like every other time, Mason ignored him. "You are looking particularly fine today."

"Lucky," Mason grumbled by way of greeting, folding his beefy arms over his chest, his bulging biceps straining against the shirt sleeves of his uniform, drawing Lucky's hungry gaze. Red stifled a laugh and exchanged glances with Ace, who waggled his eyebrows. Mason had no idea how much he flexed when Lucky was around. For all his bitching about Lucky's "manwhore" ways, he preened an awful lot around the guy. "When are you gonna get rid of that death machine?"

"Why? Are you worried about me?"

Mason let out a snort. "Yeah, I ain't touchin' that."

"You should. Who knows. You might like it." Lucky winked at him, and Mason rolled his eyes.

"How did you know we were here?" Red asked Lucky. It's like his friend had an internal radar. Wherever a group of young beautiful people were gathered, Lucky was bound to be there.

Lucky held up his phone, his grin wide. "You uploaded the video to the cloud by mistake. I would have been here sooner, but I had to pull over because I couldn't see from the tears, I was laughing so hard."

*Oh shit.* Red cringed. "Oops."

"Oops?" Ace punched Red in the arm. "Thanks a lot, asshole. You know what's going to happen now, right?"

"I'm sorry." He was. He really was. He wouldn't wish what was about to happen on anyone, not even Ace. Okay, maybe sometimes he did wish it on Ace because… well, it was Ace, so he probably did something to deserve it, but this was on Red.

Ace's phone rang, and when he answered, he didn't bother with a greeting. "Fuck you. The both of you."

Wow, that was quicker than expected.

Ace put his phone on speaker, Jack and Joker's loud peals of laughter filling the air. Jabbing a finger at his phone, Ace hung up and glared at Red. "This is your doing. I hope you're happy."

He wasn't. Not really. Okay, maybe a little.

"I can't wait to see what Jack does with the video," Lucky said, rubbing his hands together in glee. "Ooh, this means another training video."

Ace spun to thrust a finger in King's face. "Stop putting me in training videos!"

"What's he talking about?" Laz whispered at Red.

Red leaned in to reply quietly so Ace wouldn't hear him and give him another reason to yell. "Anytime someone catches Ace doing something like today and records it, King puts it in a training video on how to *not* do that thing."

"I'll stop putting you in training videos when you stop expertly demonstrating all the wrong ways to defuse a situation," King growled, swatting Ace's finger away from his face. "Do that again and you'll be featured in a new video on broken fingers and how not to get them broken."

Ace opened his mouth to reply, but King narrowed his eyes, his jaw muscles working and his expression daring Ace to mouth off.

"So," Ace said, pivoting toward Mason, "tell 'em your good news."

"Oh, um, I'm joining the Major Crimes Unit. I made detective."

"That's fantastic! Congratulations." Red shook Mason's hand and patted his shoulder. Mason would make a great detective. He was honest, dedicated, and fearless. "Local?" It would be great if they could continue to work with him. Working security was always easier when you had an in with the local police. Thanks to Mason's friendship, they had an inside man, so to speak.

"Yep. St. John's County Sheriff's Office."

"Congratulations." King held his hand out to Mason, who looked stunned before quickly taking it.

Mason smiled wide. "Thanks, King." He received a hearty pat on the back from Lucky.

"Congratulations, bro. I knew you could do it."

"Wait, you knew about it?" Mason narrowed his eyes at Ace. "Really? What happened to 'don't worry, Coop, I won't say a word 'til it's official'?

"In my defense, you should know better by now."

"That's not—" Mason gave up, most likely realizing he wasn't going to win. "Never mind. I haven't had nearly enough caffeine to deal with you."

"Hey, you're the one who dated him," Lucky offered cheerfully.

Mason scoffed at that. "In *my* defense, I was deceived into believing he was a rational adult."

"Yeah, that would have been the painkillers," Ace explained to Laz. "I was recovering from a nasty fall I received while working a case, so I was a little out of it when we met. He mistook that for boring."

"Behaving like an adult does not translate to boring," Mason grumbled.

Leaving his friends to tease poor Mason, Red gently pulled Laz to one side. He ignored the butterflies in his stomach or the insecurities threatening to get the better of him. "I thought maybe we could grab a coffee or something when you're done here, if you're not busy?" Laz's smile was stunning, and Red's breath hitched. He was so beautiful. Red fought down the urge to brush his fingers down Laz's jaw, to feel the faint stubble, and run his thumb over Laz's bottom lip. It was pink and plump, and Red wanted so desperately to nibble at it. He quickly pulled himself together.

"I'd like that. Actually, I'm about to wrap up here, if you don't mind hanging around for about a half hour? The wind's not cooperating, which means water and sand getting everywhere."

Red couldn't contain his smile. "I can wait. Did you get the photos you needed?"

"I always take a few extra shots, so it'll be fine, plus I have shots I took last week at a different location. I'm just going to let everyone know we're done for the day and they can go. Then I'll pack up my equipment, and I'm done."

Laz was about to leave when Red heard it. Or rather *didn't* hear it.

The Kings had gone silent.

"What's wrong?" Mason asked, looking from Ace to Lucky and back.

Red's heart pounded in his ears, the hairs on the back of his neck standing on end before he steadied his breathing, his senses on high alert. The air around him changed, and instinct took over. He grabbed Laz and pulled him against his body, a hole appearing in one of the large screens in the sand where Laz had just been. King sprang into action, and the rest of them followed, moving before the words were out of King's mouth.

"Shooter! Everybody, move! Take cover!"

Red kept Laz close to him as he took off toward the parked cars, King shouting behind them. "Get behind the cars! Move, move, move! Mason!"

"I'm on it," Mason replied, calling for backup on his radio as he helped the Kings get everyone to safety behind the cars.

"Lucky, Ace!" King motioned toward the hotel under construction to their left, and the cousins took off, using the cars to shield themselves as they headed for the side entrance.

Red headed for Ace's car, Laz in tow, when a bullet whizzed past him. *Shit.* They weren't going to make it. He had to get Laz off the beach. They were sitting ducks out here. The closest thing to cover they had was several feet away.

"The pier," Red told Laz, pulling him to his left side and keeping himself between Laz and the hotel on the right. With the tide out, they could take cover beneath the pier. They made a run for the concrete walkway that stretched beneath the end of the pier, its wall providing some protection. It wasn't high enough for them to take cover behind, but the shooter missed twice, so they had a chance. Chunks of concrete burst from the wall beside his head, confirming his fears concerning who the target was. He was grateful it wasn't a weekend, or the beach would have been filled with panicking beachgoers. But even with it being a weekday morning, there were families and kids in the water park, on the dock, the gazebo, and scattered around the beach. If he or Laz were drawing fire, he had to do everything in his power to avoid those places yet keep Laz safe.

Sirens filled the air in the distance, and Red hoped it would be enough to spook the shooter, though he'd much prefer it if Ace and Lucky got to the bastard first. They sped toward the pier, sand kicking up behind them, the resounding echo of gunfire splintering the air. Red jerked Laz with him behind one of the pier's large wooden support beams, then pushed Laz up against it. He shielded Laz with his body, using his larger frame to envelop Laz's smaller one, his arms cradling Laz's head.

"Oh my God. Oh my God. I don't want to die." Laz dug his fingers into Red's sides as he clung to him, his entire body shaking uncontrollably. Everyone handled danger differently, and unsurprisingly, Laz was inexperienced when it came to life-and-death situations. Most folks were. It was easy to think a person would react a certain way when faced with danger. Movies and TV made it look easy. That common sense or rationality would prevail, but the truth was that unless someone was trained to make split-second decisions, the human brain reacted on instinct, and for most people it meant self-preservation, whether it was fighting back or running from the danger, the latter tending to be the most common. In some cases, the person simply froze up from the terror of not knowing what to do.

"You're not going to die," Red assured Laz, soothing him. "I'm right here. I won't let anything happen to you."

"Why is someone shooting at us?"

"Breathe," Red instructed calmly, pulling back enough to put his hands to Laz's shoulders. "Look at me."

Laz's eyes were shut tight, and he shook his head, his lips pressed together. He was pale, trembling, and his brow beaded with sweat. If Red didn't keep Laz calm, he was going to shut down, and he couldn't let that happen.

"Laz, look at me." Red cupped Laz's face, smiling when Laz finally opened his brilliant blue eyes. "There you are. Just do what I do, okay?" Red demonstrated how he wanted Laz to breathe, and thankfully, Laz followed along. "That's it. Breathe just like that. You're doing great. You're not alone. I'm here with you, and I'm trained for this, remember?"

Laz nodded fervently. "Why is this happening?"

"I don't know, but I promise you we're going to find out." Red swept Laz's hair away from his brow. He kept his hands on Laz in the hopes it offered some comfort. "We're just going to stay here until it's safe to go back out there." As much as he wanted to be out there backing up his brothers, Laz was the intended target, and Red would do everything in his power to keep him safe.

"Fitz!" Laz tried to wriggle out from Red's hold, but Red didn't budge. "Red, please. He's my friend. What if he's hurt? What if he's—"

"He's fine. King and Mason got everyone to safety. As soon as I get the all clear, we'll go find him."

"I can't—I need to make sure he's okay. Please."

"Laz, you can't go out there."

"Why?"

"Because *you're* the target."

Laz froze. He stared up at Red, his eyes wide. "What?" The word came out as a whisper. "What are you talking about?"

"I'm sorry, but they weren't shooting at us. They were shooting at *you*." It had become clear from the first shot. Whether the shooter was a crappy marksman, or they were purposely missing, the fact remained that Laz was the target.

Something felt off, and Red stilled. "Shit." The shooter was on the move. "We can't stay here."

"What? How do you know?"

"A feeling." Red dropped into a crouch, bringing Laz with him as a gunshot exploded through the air, the bullet piercing the beam, splintering the wood.

"I thought we were safe here!"

"I thought so too. We need to go." Red quickly scanned the area before moving his eyes back to Laz. "Okay, here's what we're going to do. When I give the signal, we're going to run as fast as we can to the end of the pier and climb out onto the street. We'll use the cars in the parking lot for cover, if you can safely get behind where the engine is, you do that. There's a small fire station to the left at the end of the lot. Stick close to me, go around the station. There's a back entrance, and the garage is usually open. Fire and Rescue have probably been called out, but someone would have stayed behind. Ready?"

Laz nodded. "I trust you."

"Good." Red took a deep breath and said a little prayer. "Now!" He bolted from behind the pillar, Laz to his side. He made sure to cover Laz as they sped for the end of the pier. When they reached the concrete wall, Red climbed up first, knowing he was quicker. He was up and over in seconds, then reached down to grab Laz and haul him up, making sure to keep himself between Laz and the hotel as they took off into the parking lot. They had to stay clear of the water park. Using the cars for cover, they quickly but carefully made their way through the lot. A bullet pinged a lamppost to his right, and they ducked behind an SUV.

"Just two more rows to go," Red said, checking on Laz. "You doing okay?"

Laz nodded.

"We're going to briefly be out in the open when we hit the sidewalk, but if we head straight to the front of the garage, we'll be completely exposed. Going around is our best bet." Red took off his baseball cap and put it on Laz.

"What are you doing?"

"When we run out, it'll take the shooter a moment to realize the guy in the baseball cap is you and not me. Every second counts. Ready?"

"No, but what choice do I have?" Laz blew out an unsteady breath, then nodded.

"Now!" Red grabbed Laz's wrist, and they bolted out from behind the truck, weaving their way through the remaining two rows and out onto the sidewalk, around the side of the station. As he'd suspected, the first bullet hit a car to Red's right before the second shot was fired at Laz, hitting the flagpole outside the station. Red threw open the station's back door, and ushered Laz through. A paramedic and firefighter sat at a small table inside, both jumping to their feet when Red and Laz sped inside.

"We need help," Red told them, knowing they would have been apprised of the situation the moment the first emergency call went through. From the looks of the place, their guys were already onsite. "My friend's the shooter's target. We need to keep him safe."

"Shit. I'll tell the captain," the firefighter said, darting off. The paramedic was about to follow when he abruptly changed direction and hurried over to them.

"Your friend is hurt."

Laz put his fingers to the side of his head, and his eyes went huge. "Oh God, Red, I'm bleeding."

"Let me see." Red removed the baseball cap, the rim stained with blood. He turned Laz's face and cursed under his breath. "I need a medical kit."

"You know what you're doing?" the paramedic asked as he walked backward toward the doorway that most likely led to the lockers and equipment.

"Yeah, I was a Special Forces medical sergeant."

The guy nodded before taking off to fetch the medical kit. At the end of the room was a long comfortable-looking couch. Red hauled Laz over and sat him down.

"I've been shot," Laz said quietly.

"It's okay. You're okay. Focus on me."

Laz's eyes fluttered, and he swayed. He was on the verge of passing out.

"Laz, stay with me. Breathe, just like I taught you." Red thanked the paramedic, and quickly went to work checking Laz's wound. "It's just a scratch. You won't even need stitches."

"Then why is it bleeding so much?"

"Head wounds bleed a lot, no matter how small. Your brain needs huge amounts of oxygen, which means lots of blood vessels, and your scalp has all these tiny arteries and veins close to the skin, so even a small laceration can result in a large amount of bleeding. I'm going to clean you up, okay?"

Laz nodded.

"Is there something I can help with?" The paramedic stood to one side of the window, and peered out through the blinds.

"What's your name?" Red asked as he pulled on a pair of gloves from the medical kit.

"Jerome."

"Jerome, I'm Red from Four Kings Security. This is Laz. Can you keep a lookout for me? It's unlikely whoever's after Laz here will show up, but I don't want to take any chances. Unless it's one of my guys, your guys, or law enforcement, no one else is cleared to come in. Make sure everyone stays away from the windows."

"You got it," Jerome replied. "I've heard of you guys. Thank you for your service."

Red smiled at Jerome, nodding a "thanks" before getting to work cleaning Laz's wound.

"Seems like you're always looking out for me," Laz said softly, his blue eyes glassy. He'd been through a real ordeal, and it was only going to get more complicated, but that was a conversation for later.

"I don't mind. I'd rather you not be bleeding when you end up in my arms, but if you are, I'll take care of you."

Laz chuckled. "Thanks. Man, I'm beat."

"You're crashing. It happens after an adrenaline rush like the one you just experienced." Red clicked on the small flashlight. "Look straight ahead." Laz did as asked, and Red checked his pupils. "Follow the light with your eyes. Good. That's good." He clicked off the flashlight and went back to tenderly wiping the blood out of Laz's hair. "Do you feel dizzy?"

"A little. My head hurts."

"I'll give you some Tylenol."

Jerome handed him a bottle of water.

"Thanks."

"No problem."

Red handed the water bottle to Laz, then popped the cap off a small bottle of Tylenol. He tapped a couple of pills out onto Laz's palm. "Take those." He finished patching Laz up and had just tossed his gloves in the bin when his phone rang. Relief flooded through him. "Hey."

"Are you both okay?" King asked worriedly.

"Yeah, Laz has a minor flesh wound, but he's fine. Is everyone safe?"

"They're shaken up, but safe. Where are you?"

"The fire station."

"Good. Mason's heading over to pick you guys up and take you to the precinct. I'm sending Lucky with him in case you need backup. Ace and I will meet you there. Roadblocks have been set up, SWAT is all over the hotel, and the police are canvasing the area, but my guess is the shooter's long gone by now. Everyone on Laz's photoshoot is currently being questioned."

"You think it could have been one of them?"

"I doubt it, but the police need to look into everyone. Laz was clearly the target. See you in a few minutes."

"Okay. Thanks." Red hung up and put away his phone. "That was King. No one was hurt. It's likely the shooter's gone, but just in case, Mason's coming to pick us up. He'll drive us to the precinct."

Laz blinked at him. "The precinct? You mean the police precinct?"

"Yeah. They're going to need to take your statement and ask you some questions."

"I… I can't believe this is happening." Laz's eyes went huge, and he looked like he was on the verge of panicking. "Please come with me. I need… I need you to stay with me."

"Of course." Red brushed his fingers down Laz's cheek. "I'm not going anywhere. I promise."

Laz nodded. He was still pale and a little shaky, so Red held on to him. Thankfully, Mason arrived within minutes, Lucky behind him as they came in through the back door.

"You two okay?" Lucky asked, checking Laz over. He took hold of Laz's chin and turned his face. "What happened?"

"Bullet grazed him."

"I'm okay," Laz promised.

Mason motioned toward the door. "We should go."

"Right." Red turned to Jerome. "Thank you so much for your help."

"Sure thing."

Lucky held his hand out to Jerome, his smile wide. "Thank you for taking such good care of my friends."

Jerome smiled, his gaze dropping to Lucky's mouth. "You're welcome, Mr.…?"

"You can call me Lucky."

Jerome's laugh was husky. "That your name or a pick-up line?"

Lucky opened his mouth to reply, when Mason grabbed Lucky's arm, jerking him to his side. "Thanks for your help, Jerome, but we gotta go."

Jerome nodded, bemused by Mason's gruff reaction.

Mason dragged Lucky with him as they made their way to the car.

"Why are you manhandling me?"

"Because we're in the middle of a very serious situation and you're thinking about your dick," Mason growled.

"¿Qué?"

"Just get in the goddamn car, Edward."

Lucky stared at him. "The fuck did you just call me?"

"I called you by your name."

"No, because then you would have said Eduardo," Lucky spat out, poking Mason's shoulder. "Do I look like a fucking Edward to you?"

"Fine. Get in the car, *Eduardo*."

"You have anger issues, my man."

"No, I have *you* issues." Mason jerked open the passenger door and shoved Lucky into the seat before turning to Red. "What?"

Red threw his hands up in surrender. "Nothing."

"Let's go." Mason stomped over to the driver's side, threw the door open, and then slid in behind the wheel.

*What the hell was that about?*

"Maybe he's stressed out," Laz said quietly.

"Yeah, well, Lucky'll do that to you." Red opened the back door for Laz, and as soon as Laz was in, Red slid in next to him, then closed the door. He placed a hand on Laz's forearm, giving it a gentle squeeze. "We're going to get through this. I promise."

"Thank you."

Red made to move his hand away, but Laz covered it with his own.

The ride to the police station was awkward. At least in the front half of the car. Lucky was uncharacteristically quiet. Mason wasn't usually a big talker, but the man's jaw was clenched so tight Red was afraid he was going to break something. They stopped at a red light, and Mason let out a heavy sigh, his voice low when he spoke.

"I'm sorry I called you Edward. It wasn't a slight against your heritage or nothin'. I'm just kinda self-conscious about how I sound when I speak Spanish, so I took the easy way out."

"It's fine," Lucky grumbled, leaning against the door, his gaze out the window.

"No, it's not. I clearly upset you, and I apologize."

"I accept your apology, but it's not completely your fault. It's a touchy subject for me."

"You, uh, wanna talk about it?"

Lucky shook his head. "Otro día."

"Okay, erm…." Mason cleared his throat. "Está bien."

Lucky's lip curled up in a smile on one side, but he didn't respond.

"Red?" Laz said quietly, drawing Red's attention.

"Yeah? You okay?"

Laz nodded. "I need to call Fitz. He's probably freaking out."

"Oh, eso ya pasó," Lucky said, meeting Laz's gaze through the rearview mirror. "Big-time. He freaked out big-time."

"What?" Laz sucked in a sharp breath.

Unbelievable. "Jesus, Lucky. Come on. What the hell's wrong with you?"

"No, but it's fine," Lucky said quickly. "Fitz is okay."

"How can he be okay?" Laz asked worriedly. "You just said he freaked out big-time!"

"Sí, pero now he is fine because Jack is with him."

Laz peered at him. "What does that mean?"

"We needed help, so King called Jack and Joker. Your friend was freaking out very bad when they arrived. I was trying to calm him, but it was only when he saw Jack that he stopped freaking out. Jack saw this, and he came over to make sure Fitz was okay." Lucky smiled knowingly. "The way your friend looked at Jack? I think maybe he was a little more than okay."

"Oh." Laz's lips spread in a tentative smile.

"Don't worry," Mason assured Laz. "Jack is a standup guy, and he's damn good at his job. Your friend is in good hands."

Lucky narrowed his eyes at Mason, who glanced over at Lucky, then cleared his throat, shifting uncomfortably in his seat.

"Anyway," Lucky grumbled. "We told Fitz you were okay and that you would call him when you were able."

"Thank you, Lucky."

The car plunged back into awkward silence. Whatever the hell was going on between these two was bound to be explosive. Red just hoped the rest of them didn't get caught up in the blast when it happened.

# CHAPTER 4

"Here you go."

"Thank you." Laz took the hot cup of coffee with creamer from Red with a small smile. He just couldn't seem to get warm, which was crazy, considering it was ninety-something degrees outside. What the hell was going on? It was like he was in a strange dream, surrounded by a fog of colors, shapes, and sounds he couldn't quite make sense of. He'd given his statement, but it was as if someone else was talking through him.

This couldn't possibly be happening to him. He was a nobody. A regular guy who geeked out over new Photoshop filters, binge-watched cheesy TV shows, and had an unhealthy obsession with Pinterest. Bugs grossed him out, he hated green peppers, and he owned a flamingo pool float he wasn't afraid to use. Who the hell would want to kill *him*?

"I don't understand. Why is this happening?" Laz took a sip of coffee, his gaze focused on the milky liquid. He never liked creamer. It tasted weird to him. Right now, he couldn't taste anything. God, he was so tired.

"That's what we'd like to know," Ace said gently from where he sat beside King, arms folded over his chest.

Thankfully, the Kings had been allowed to accompany him. Laz had no idea what he would have done if he'd had to do this alone. He'd never even been inside a police station before. When they'd reached the precinct, he'd expected it to be like the movies. A bustling bullpen of officers and detectives hauling in angry suspects, phones ringing off the hook, case files piled high on desks. In reality, the precinct was pretty quiet, with less than a handful of officers and other personnel around. The station was small and looked like it could have been someone's home if that someone had a cell built into their living room. According to Mason, there were only about twenty or so officers, but when they needed help, officers from other precincts came in to assist.

Like in the movies and TV shows Laz watched, he'd expected to be taken into an interrogation room for questioning. Mason had been kind and not looked at him like he was an idiot. He'd escorted Laz and the Kings into a medium-sized conference room. After they all filled out detailed reports of what they'd witnessed, Mason collected the reports, went over everything with them, asked them questions, then informed them he'd be right back before leaving the room. The Kings all talked among themselves, and Laz zoned out.

The door opened, and Mason returned with a padfolio. He took a seat across from Laz. "Looks like your case will be my first investigation as part of major crimes."

Laz blinked at him. "You've been assigned to my case?" Oh God, he had a case. A case that would be handled by a unit dedicated to major crimes. Crimes like homicide. Attempted murder. *His* attempted murder. *Breathe. It's going to be okay. Just breathe.*

"It made sense to put me on this investigation since I have strong ties with the Kings, and through them, know you. Any avenue that can get this shooter off the streets as quickly as possible is worth pursuing. My official start date was scheduled for the end of the month, but the chief's agreed to let me go early to work this." His blue eyes were intense when he met Laz's gaze. "I will do everything in my power to catch this son of a bitch. You have my word."

"Thank you." This was all so surreal. Laz felt Red squeeze his hand, and it helped him breathe a little easier.

"I know it's frustrating, and you just wanna put all this behind you, but we still have a lot of work to do. I need you to recall any altercations you might have had with anyone recently. Is there anyone you believe might be out to harm you?"

Harm him or kill him? Laz worked in a creative industry. He was surrounded by a vast spectrum of personalities and plenty of drama. Many were good people who had a passion for what they did and loved to help those around them. Others preferred to crush whoever was in their way, using lies and manipulative tactics to climb their way to the top, not caring who they hurt along the way. There was plenty of rivalry, and even some nastiness, but enough to send a killer after him?

Laz shook his head. "There's no one I can think of who would do something like this."

"What about Bryan?"

"What?" Laz stared at Ace. "You can't be serious."

"Who's Bryan?" Mason asked, taking notes.

"My ex-boyfriend." The idea was ludicrous. "We're talking about a man who throws a fit when his sparkling water doesn't have enough bubbles. You really think he's capable of hiring someone to kill me?"

"He threatened you," Ace reminded him.

Mason lifted his gaze to Laz. "When was this?"

"A few months ago. Colton threw a party for me to celebrate my getting invited to Fashion Week in Paris next year. We got into a big fight."

"Tell him what happened," Red prodded gently. Laz worried his bottom lip, and Red nodded for him to continue. "It's important, Laz."

"Okay." Laz let out a sigh. "I know how this is going to sound, but I promise you, Bryan didn't send a killer after me. We were at the party, and we had a fight. I needed some space away from him, so I stormed off. Bryan followed me. He hates being ignored, especially when he has an audience. When he pushed me, I slipped on some wet tiles around the pool and fell, hitting my head before falling in the water. Red jumped in after me and pulled me out.

"The Kings took me inside, but Colton made sure Bryan didn't follow us. They took care of me, and while I was upstairs in one of the rooms, Bryan started to throw a fit downstairs about seeing me, so I told Ace to let him up. I was exhausted. I was hoping I could get him to back off for a while, but then he accused me of cheating on him with Red, who I'd met just before the whole pool incident. It was ridiculous. *He* was the one who'd cheated on me. Repeatedly. Anyway, I was done with him. We argued, and I broke up with him."

Mason nodded. "And how did Bryan take that?"

"As well as you can imagine. Not because he really loved me, but because *I* was daring to walk away from *him*. He threatened to ruin me, and I… I told him if he tried, I would take him down with me."

"Meaning?"

Laz sighed. "Bryan's ruined plenty of careers in his time, and I was afraid he might do the same to me one day, so I made sure I had insurance."

"What kind of insurance?"

"Photographs of him having sex with Elena Vicente's supposedly *straight* husband in an apartment he bought for Bryan with his wife's money."

"Who's Elena Vicente?"

"A fashion designer, and a big deal in our industry. She has a lot of influence. If those photos were leaked to the press, Elena would never work with Bryan again, and the fashion line he was hoping to launch with her would never happen. No one would want to work with him again."

"I'm guessin' that did not go down well with Bryan."

"No. Being the vindictive, spiteful human being that he is, he… revealed something very personal about me."

"Can you tell me what he said?"

Laz shook his head, horrified that another person would know what he'd done. It was bad enough Ace and Red knew, that Colton knew, but to have Mason and the rest of the Kings know? To have it documented? The thought made him feel sick to his stomach.

"Laz, if it's pertinent to this case—"

"It's not," Laz assured him, feeling his chest constricting. All he wanted was to forget it ever happened. Why couldn't he forget?

"Laz—"

"Coop," Ace said quietly. He shook his head, and Mason paused before nodding.

"Okay. What happened after he revealed personal information about you?"

"We got into it. It wasn't pretty. I punched him in the face, and he hit me back. We were pulled apart, and Bryan was dragged from the room. He yelled something like 'you're going to regret this,' or 'you're going to pay for this.' I can't remember exactly."

"Do you think Bryan told someone about the photos?"

Laz shook his head. "If anyone found out about his affair with Elena's husband, his career would be over. No way does he want those pictures leaked."

"Sounds like motive to me," Mason said. "Maybe he figures if he can't get rid of the photos, he'll get rid of you."

"That's just insane. Bryan may be a horrible human being, but he's not a murderer."

"He's a suspect. What about Elena Vicente and her husband? Do they know about the pictures?"

"No way. If Elena knew, the scandal would have been all over the internet. She'd have kicked her husband to the curb, and Bryan would be all over social media garnering sympathy and making himself look like the innocent party in the hopes of holding on to what scraps remained of his career. If you want to know every detail of his life, how he's feeling and what he's up to, just visit his social media accounts. It's all there."

"Okay. I'm gonna meet with my lieutenant and go over the details of the case with him, get this investigation moving. In the meantime, is there somewhere safe you can stay?"

Laz sat up straight. "Wait. What? I was going to go home."

Mason's expression turned sympathetic. "Laz, you can't go home. If someone is intent on hurting you, that's the first place they'll look."

"You can stay at our house," Ace said. "Colton's flying out to New York tomorrow, and I've got a case that requires me to be onsite, but I can drop by to check on you, and the rest of the guys will be around. With the new security measures we put in place during Colton's case, it's the safest place for you to be right now. One of our guys can stay with you."

"I can stay with him," Red volunteered, surprising Laz. It made the butterflies in his stomach go nuts. Him and Red under the same roof? Together? Alone? "I'm familiar with the house's security," Red added. "I know this is officially a police investigation, but I'm off duty for a few more weeks, so I can help out."

"Are you sure?" Laz asked. "You just finished a case where you were injured. The last thing I want is for you to get hurt because of me."

Red turned in his seat to face him and took Laz's hands in his. "Until the police catch this person and I know you're safe, I'm not going anywhere."

*Why?* Laz hated where his thoughts went, but he couldn't help it. Why did Red care so much about what happened to him? Were they friends or something more? Did Red expect something in return? Bryan was always going on about how all relationships were based on give and take. Sometimes the balance was skewed, but no matter the intent, humans were hardwired with expectations. Did Red have expectations?

"I can't afford to pay you," Laz told Red, searching his eyes. They were hazel green with amber around the pupils. The flinch was subtle, but Laz felt it as if someone had taken a knife to his heart. Red released Laz's hands, his expression hurt.

"I wasn't expecting you to."

King cleared his throat, getting Laz's attention. "You're family, Laz. We take care of family."

Laz stared at King. "But... we barely know each other."

"You mean a lot to Colton, and he means a lot to me," Ace pitched in, his voice full of sincerity. "That makes you family." He motioned to Mason. "Brokeback over here, also family."

Mason flipped Ace off, the two of them ribbing each other and making everyone laugh.

Red took Laz's hand in his again and smiled softly, his voice quiet so only Laz could hear while the others teased Mason. "You mean something to me too."

Was this what it was like to have a loving family? To have people who cared about you, supported you, protected you? For a long time, it had just been him and his brother, Gio, but even before that, when their father had been alive, it had been the three of them. When Colton came into their lives, for a little while, it had been four. Then Laz's father got sick and passed away, and they were back to three.

Laz swallowed past the lump in his throat. He didn't know what to say. When he was a kid, he envied his school friends. Envied their big families, the gatherings, barbecues, parties. The loving grandparents and mischievous cousins. Laz never had that. To this day, he had trouble understanding what the hell had happened with his parents' families.

How could they throw his family away? How could they disown his dad for loving and supporting his sons no matter who they loved? When Gio came out as bisexual in high school, their "family" had given their dad hell. His grandparents tried to take Laz away from his dad, from his brother. When Laz said he was like Gio—except for the part about liking girls—they blamed his father, said it was a good thing his wife wasn't alive to see what had become of her sons. His grandmother had said it in front of Laz. He'd been eight years old. What kind of family did that? Then his father got sick, and those bastards just let him die, with only his sons at his funeral to bury him.

"Laz?"

Laz snapped out of it. He moved his eyes up to Red, who was watching him worriedly. "Sorry. I, um, got lost in my own thoughts there for a moment."

"Are you okay?"

"Yeah." He dropped his gaze to his hand still in Red's. "I'm sorry if I offended you." His heart pounded in his ears. Red *did* care about him. Whether it was as a friend or more didn't matter right now. Laz was such an ass. He had to stop letting his horrible experiences with Bryan ruin whatever it was he had with Red.

"I wasn't offended," Red promised. "Just caught off guard."

And hurt. Red might not have said the words, but Laz knew.

"I'll feel better if Red is with you," King said before turning to Mason. "If there's anything we can do to help, just let us know."

Laz's head felt like someone was taking a jackhammer to his skull. He wanted to crawl into bed and sleep, except he couldn't because his bed, and his apartment, were off-limits.

Mason smiled sympathetically. "I think we're done for now, but if you think of anything, please call me." He handed Laz a business card, which Laz took and slipped into his jeans pocket, aware that his right hand was still in Red's. Was Red aware? He had to be. "When you get to Colton's, why don't you make a list of what you need from your place, and if it's okay with you, I'll stop by, pick up your things, then drop them off."

"I can do that," Lucky said. "You have enough to do at the moment."

"You sure?"

"Yes. If Laz is okay with it, I can do that. No problem."

Laz nodded. He couldn't go home. The severity of the situation was starting to sink in, which he found funny, considering a few hours ago he'd been running for his life. Either way, he was too exhausted to process it all.

"Thanks, Mason," Red said, releasing Laz's hand, then standing. "You've got my number. Keep me updated."

"Will do."

Laz sat staring off at nothing while Mason took notes, and the Kings stood together, talking quietly. It wasn't until Red put his hand on Laz's shoulder that he realized he'd zoned out again.

"Come on. Let's get you to Colton's."

Laz nodded. He thanked Mason again and followed the Kings out of the room and toward the front of the precinct. King and Lucky took position in front of Laz, with Red to his left, and Ace to his right. He thought it was weird, and it struck him then that they were shielding him, forming a tight circle around him.

Laz was surrounded by a wall of muscle, each King towering over him at six feet or taller. At five feet, eight inches, Laz wasn't that much shorter, but he felt eclipsed by these big men, not just by their size, but their confidence. They had no fear despite knowing the danger they were putting themselves in. This was what they did, what they'd been doing for years. It didn't stop Laz from being scared, not from the possibility he could be killed—though that did scare the hell out of him—but that one of the Kings would be killed or hurt because of him.

Red could have died. All because he'd been in the way when that madman had kidnapped Colton. Then on the beach when he'd put himself between Laz and the shooter.

"Guys, this isn't necessary," Laz said in the hopes they'd listen, but as expected, King would have none of it.

"It is. From this point on, no unnecessary risks. I'm assigning a small team to patrol Colton's property round the clock, just in case." King opened the door and addressed the others. "Stay vigilant." They escorted Laz to Ace's car that was parked between a huge black truck and Lucky's motorcycle, which Joker had dropped off earlier.

"Oh God, I just remembered my equipment." Laz raked his fingers through his hair, grabbing fistfuls of it. *Don't panic. Breathe.* Shit. His camera, all his lenses, his laptop…. "I'm so screwed." What if his insurance wouldn't cover the loss? Where the hell would he get the money to replace all of it? At least all his images were saved to the cloud, but the rest of it?

"You mean this equipment?"

Laz's head shot up at Ace's words, and he stared, dumbfounded, at the open trunk of Ace's car. His heart hammered in his ears. It was all there. Well, everything that fit.

"King's got the bigger stuff in the back of his truck." Ace said, pointing to the charcoal-gray truck with the covered truck bed. "He'll drop it off at Colton's for you."

"You guys are the best," Laz said, tears in his eyes. He threw his arms around Ace, squeezing him tight and making him laugh before he turned to Red and hugged him. "Thank you. You've done so much for me."

Red wrapped his arms around Laz, his cheek resting against Laz's head and his words soft. "You're welcome. You can always count on us, Laz." He squeezed Laz before pulling away. "Let's go."

"Don't forget to make that list," Lucky said, opening the back door of Ace's car for Laz. "Text it to me. Red will give you my number, okay?"

"Thank you, Lucky." Laz climbed into the backseat and buckled up as Red slid in beside him. He'd expected Red to sit up front with Ace but was grateful Red had chosen to keep him company instead. It was stupid. He'd been on his own for so long, he shouldn't be feeling so damned needy. Then he reminded himself someone was trying to kill him. He'd earned the right to feel a little needy and vulnerable. His brother's words echoed in his head.

*"You don't have to prove how strong you are all the time. It's okay to lean on others."*

Except Laz had been doing that for too long, depending on his brother, on Colton. Bryan's voice infiltrated his thoughts, and Laz closed his eyes, hating how deep the words cut because of their truth.

*"You were a nobody when I met you! You couldn't even afford the equipment you needed without big brother and his rich friends to help you."*

Despite working full-time and studying full-time, Laz would never have been able to afford his equipment, not without his brother and Colton's financial help. He'd tried to set up a payment plan with them to pay them back, but they'd refused. All they'd wanted in return was for him to follow his dream. Laz quickly shook those thoughts from his head.

Maybe he'd been a nobody in the industry when he'd met Bryan, and Bryan had certainly showed him a few doors, but Laz had been the one to open them and step through. He'd worked himself ragged getting his portfolio together, building his contacts, perfecting his craft. What about all the explosive situations Bryan had ignited that Laz had defused, saving both their careers? He could do this.

"By the way, I haven't told Colton what happened yet."

Laz's attention snapped to Ace, and his eyes widened. "What?"

"It'll be fine," Ace replied nonchalantly.

Was the man insane? How could he be dating Colton and make such a ridiculous statement?

"He's going to lose his mind," Laz said with a groan. He loved Colton. Had grown up around him. Admired him, respected him, and steered clear of him when he exploded. Colton was passionate and sometimes a little dramatic. He tended to overreact when his emotions got the better of him, especially when whatever was freaking him out had to do with someone he cared about.

"Yes, he is," Ace agreed. "There will be yelling. Lots of yelling. At me. Don't worry, you'll be fine."

"That really doesn't put my mind at ease," Laz muttered. He closed his eyes and let his head fall back, a small smile tugging at his lips when he felt Red pat his leg. Maybe Ace was right and everything would be fine. For all they knew, whoever had been sent to kill him had decided he wasn't worth the trouble now that the police were involved.

The ride to Colton's house—now also Ace's house, since Ace had moved in with Colton—took a little over forty-five minutes via A1A N. The mid-July sun was sweltering, and come August it was going to be even worse. The humidity made the temperature feel like it was in the hundreds. Thank God for air conditioning. Maybe he could make the most of a bad situation. Colton's house was amazing. It was huge, with an awesome game room, a pool, and a private walkway down to the beach just a few feet away.

"Why don't you two go on ahead," Red suggested when they pulled into the driveway. "I'll bring in Laz's equipment."

Ace peered at Red through the rearview mirror. "You're not fooling anyone."

Laz looked from Ace to Red and back. "What are you talking about?"

"He's trying to avoid getting yelled at."

Red's expression turned deadpan. "You're right. Good luck." He swiftly opened the door, got out, and closed the door behind him.

Ace shook his head in shame. "Do you see this? This is what I have to deal with."

"Well, Colt *is* your boyfriend."

"Of course you would take Red's side."

Laz snickered in amusement. "What does that mean?"

"Everyone always takes his side. It's those damned puppy dog eyes. So not fair." Ace climbed out of the car, ignoring Laz's chuckle. He opened the back door for him, grabbed some equipment from the trunk, then followed Laz up the set of steps to the front door where Colton was standing waiting for them.

"Laz, this is a lovely surprise." Colton froze, and Laz cringed. "What happened to your head?"

"It's just a graze," Laz replied calmly. "We'll explain everything inside."

Colton nodded and followed them into the house, heading for the living room after them.

"Babe, Red and Laz will be staying with us for a while. Starting today."

"Of course. What's going on?" When Laz looked to Ace and there was no response, Colton frowned. "What?"

Ace drew Colton into his arms. "First of all, I want you to know everything's going to be okay."

"That doesn't reassure me at all," Colton muttered, eyes narrowed. "What happened?"

"I don't want you to worry."

"Well, it's too damn late for that," Colton growled. "That's like starting a sentence with 'you can't get mad' when you know whatever you're going to say is going to cause that exact reaction. How many times have you done this?"

"Lots, but, babe, you have a tendency to get a little emotional, and—"

"I swear if the next words out of your mouth aren't what the hell is happening, my emotions are going to be the least of your worries!"

"Just calm down. I'm only—"

"Someone tried to kill me," Laz blurted.

"What?" Colton moved away from Ace to stare at Laz. "Oh my God. *What?* Oh my God."

"Thanks, Laz. That was… that was great."

"Sorry. It's been a long day." He was so, so tired.

Colton gasped, and in two steps had Laz wrapped up in his arms, a hand to the back of his head as he crushed Laz to him.

"Colt, I can't breathe."

"I'm sorry. I'm so sorry." Colton released him, then started to pace. "Okay, I need to call Nadine and have her reschedule the meeting, cancel my flight, hotel, and—"

"Stop. Colt, please stop." Laz took hold of Colton's arm, stopping his pacing. "I don't want you cancelling your trip."

"Are you kidding me? I'm not leaving this house knowing there's a killer out there looking for you. I need to call Gio."

"*No*," Laz snapped, startling Colton. "I'm sorry. I didn't mean to snap. I'm just really tired. Please, don't call my brother. He worries enough about me as it is. The last thing I want is for him to drop everything he's doing and run back home. He's done that enough for me."

"He's your brother, and he loves you. Of course he's going to drop everything and come home. Someone is trying to *kill* his little brother!"

"Colt, Gio is halfway across the globe helping people, helping others lift themselves out of poverty, saving lives. For all we know, I'll be causing him trouble for no reason. Whoever shot at me might be long gone."

"Laz…."

"It's fine. I'll be fine. I'll talk to my brother when he gets back from his trip. In the meantime, Red's going to be with me, and if we have any problems, the rest of the Kings won't be far. Mason's a detective now with major crimes. He'll be working on my case."

"Mason's working your case?"

"Yes? Is that, um—" He darted a glance at Ace before turning his attention back to Colton. "—okay?"

Colton put a hand to his chest and sighed in relief. "Oh thank God."

"You're… happy about that?" Laz asked, puzzled.

"Yes. Mason will keep me updated on the case, and unlike certain individuals," Colton said, casting Ace a sideways glance, "he won't hold back information to keep me from worrying."

Ace frowned. "Wait, you talk to Mason?"

"All the time."

"What do you talk about?"

Colton shrugged. "Lots of things."

"Like?"

"We're in the middle of something important, love."

Ace narrowed his eyes. "I don't think I like this."

"Oh, so you can be friends with your ex-boyfriend, but I can't?"

"I'm confused by that sentence. That's generally how it goes."

"No, I don't think so," Colton said, sounding amused. His smile fell away as he turned to Laz, his blue-gray eyes filled with concern. "How can you expect me to leave knowing the danger you might be in?"

Red walked into the living room, and Laz was immediately at ease. He smiled at Red. "I wasn't alone on the beach when it happened, and I'm not alone now. Besides, Red's getting pretty good at saving my life."

Red chuckled, shaking his head as he took a seat on the couch.

"There are better ways to end up in the arms of a big, strong, handsome man," Colton teased, arching an eyebrow at him.

"Again with the handsome," Ace murmured, ignoring his boyfriend's soft laugh.

Colton nodded. "Okay. I'll go on one condition."

"Anything."

"I want daily check-ins from either you or Red."

"Deal."

"Done. Our home is your home. I'll be back in a couple of weeks. Why don't you get set-up in one of the spare bedrooms? Do you need me to pick up some stuff for you from your apartment?"

"Thanks, but Lucky's going to take care of it for me."

"Okay, feel free to use my office if you need it, or set up your equipment wherever works best for you. I'm going to finish getting ready for tomorrow. I have to leave for the airport stupidly early, so I won't see you in the morning. If you need anything at all, you just call me or one of the Kings, okay?"

"I will. I promise."

Colton turned to Red. "This is your home too."

"Thanks, Colton."

Ace wrapped an arm around Colton and kissed his cheek. "I'm going to drop by King's place and pick up Red's stuff. I'll be back in a bit."

"Could you stop by my place and pick up my laptop?" Red asked. "He thought I'd try and work while I was supposed to be recovering, so I only had my tablet at his place."

"No problem. If you think of anything else you might need from yours, just text it."

"I'll come with you," Colton said, turning in Ace's embrace and wrapping his arms around Ace before giving him a kiss. Ace took it and ran with it, returning Colton's kiss. They were sweet together, and Laz was happy for Colton. He deserved to have someone who made him happy.

Leaving the two lovebirds, Laz turned to Red. "Would you mind helping me get my equipment to my room?"

"Of course." Red stood, and together they grabbed the bags and cases containing his gear.

Laz took the stairs up to the second floor where the bedrooms were, heading straight for one of the rooms at the end of the hall. It wasn't until he'd placed his laptop bag on the bed that he realized he'd picked the same room he'd slept in the night of the party. The room where Red had stayed with him all night. Red had slept on the couch, but Laz had felt his presence as if they'd been in the same bed. For the first time in a long time, Laz had slept peacefully. Now here he was again, in trouble, and again Red was with him, looking out for him, protecting him.

"How are you holding up?" Red asked softly, coming to stand beside him at the foot of the bed, his hand placed gently to Laz's lower back.

"How do you guys do it?"

"Do what?"

"Deal with people shooting at you. Even after King yelled for everyone to move, I couldn't wrap my head around what was going on. If you hadn't been there, I would have been dead. I had no idea what to do." Laz put a hand to his chest, feeling like his heart was going to beat out of him. He couldn't remember the last time he'd been so scared. No, he could. It was the day his brother told him their dad was dying.

"Most people don't know what to do, and that's normal. We have a lot of training behind us that allows us to do what we do."

"It's terrifying."

"It is."

Laz lifted his gaze to Red's. "Does it happen a lot to you? People shooting at you and the Kings?"

"Not all the time, but certainly more than we'd like. The Kings tend to handle more of the personal security cases, protection, kidnap, and extortion. Jack deals with designing and installing electronic security systems, consultations, cyber intelligence, that sort of thing, and Joker handles a lot of media and events. He's also in charge of canine contraband inspections."

"Canine? Like bomb sniffer dogs?"

"Yep. Joker was one of two engineer sergeants in our unit, so he knows his way around explosives and has lots of experience working with bomb-sniffing dogs. His best boy, Chip, is a gorgeous black Belgian Malinois that's trained for off-leash hunting, bomb hunting. Smart as a whip. We tease Joker that Chip's the brains of the operation."

"That's what I don't understand. You guys deal with multibillion dollar companies, wealthy clients, celebrities, people who have status. I'm a nobody."

Red placed his hand to Laz's cheek, and Laz found himself leaning into the touch. "Status doesn't make you somebody. Would your brother agree with the statement you just made?"

"No."

"Would Colton?"

Laz sighed. "No."

"Neither would I."

"Thanks." He was in so much trouble. Everything about Red pulled at him. Red's strength, those kind eyes, his tenderness, his warm smile. He was so different from anyone Laz had ever been with. Laz smiled when Red tucked some of his curls behind his ears, like Red couldn't help himself, and Laz liked it.

"Let me give you Lucky's number so you can text him what you need from your place. Then get some rest. If you wake up before dinner and you're hungry, just let me know and I'll whip you up something. If you need anything, I'm right here."

Laz handed Red his phone, and Red quickly added Lucky and the rest of the Kings, along with Jack and Joker to his list of contacts before handing it back.

"I really appreciate it." Laz stood on his toes and kissed Red's cheek. "I don't know what I'd have done without you."

"I'm here for you. Whatever you need."

"Thank you."

They stood facing each other, their eyes locked, neither moving. The air grew thick around them, and Laz felt a rush of heat go through him. Red was so close, Laz could smell his rich, musky scent, and it was doing all kinds of naughty things to Laz's insides. God, he smelled so good. A mixture of sweat, sunscreen, and….

"Is that lavender?" Laz realized what he'd said and dropped his gaze, mortified. "Not that I was smelling you or anything, or that you smell, I mean, you do, but it's a good smell, like really good. Oh God, I'm just going to shut up now."

Red laughed softly. "Yes, it's lavender. It relaxes me. I know a lot of people think it's a bunch of hippie nonsense, but aromatherapy helped me with my recovery."

"Recovery?"

Red nodded, his jaw muscles working as he averted his gaze. "When we came home."

"I'm glad it helped," Laz said gently, not wanting to pry.

"Me too." Red smiled at him then, and it was sweet but filled with sadness. Laz wondered what had happened. He knew The Kings had lost half their unit during an operation, but that was the extent of it. He couldn't find any information about the incident or the operation online.

Laz watched Red leave, his heart heavy for the loss Red and his brothers had suffered. He couldn't begin to imagine the kind of pain the Kings and their friends had endured. Whatever happened, Laz would try his best not to be a burden to Red. He'd somehow gotten himself into this mess; he'd find a way to get himself out of it.

# CHAPTER 5

"Hey, bro. I got everything he asked for," Lucky said as he rolled two large suitcases with duffel bags into the hall. "If he needs anything else, just let me know."

"Thanks." Red closed the front door, then headed back to the kitchen, where he was marinating flank steak for tonight's dinner. Lucky headed straight for the fridge to grab himself some sweet tea. He poured a tall glass and gulped half the liquid down, following up with a satisfying sigh.

"Mm, que rico. You make the best tea."

"Thanks," Red replied, amused, since he could easily recall a time when Lucky shunned all things tea-related.

The only teas Lucky had grown up drinking were part of the *cocimientos* his abuelita made for him when he wasn't feeling well, which although effective, were in Lucky's opinion, disgusting.

Naturally Lucky associated all teas with his grandmother's home remedies. It had taken a bet between Lucky and Ace for Lucky to try

Red's homebrewed sweet tea. Lucky might have lost the bet against his cousin, but he'd gained a new favorite drink.

"How's Laz doing?" Lucky asked, refilling his glass and popping a lemon wedge inside before he took a seat at the counter.

"He's not talking about it, but I think he just needs some time to process." Red gathered the ingredients he needed to prepare his homemade chimichurri sauce. Since Ace enjoyed cooking almost as much as Red, it meant the kitchen was stocked with their favorite ingredients, all fresh and organic. "I'm going to try and talk to him after he's rested, see how he's feeling."

Lucky nodded. He looked around. "It's too quiet. Where's Ace?"

"He went to grab some stuff for me from my place. Colton went with him." It was sweet how those two were attached at the hip, but then they both had very demanding careers, what with Colton running his family's worldwide shipping company and Ace being one of the Kings. It would make sense they'd want to spend as much time together when they had the chance.

"Ah, and how did Colton take the news?" Lucky's smile was evil, making Red chuckle. These two just loved winding each other up.

"As well as you think."

"Good. I bet Ace tried to play it down so Colton wouldn't worry. I'm glad Colton doesn't let him get away with that shit. Ace is always trying to do what he thinks is best for everyone without asking them what *they* think is best."

Red didn't have to ask. He knew Lucky was still mad at Ace for lying to him about his relationship with Colton during the case. Lucky had forgiven him, but still reserved the right to be annoyed about it for as long as he deemed fit. Mostly it was amusing. The cousins were loud, boisterous, and over-the-top. They certainly kept everyone on their toes. Red wouldn't have it any other way.

"So, uh, what's with you and Laz?"

Red paused halfway through chopping his oregano to glance up at Lucky. "Why don't you tell me? You obviously have an idea about it."

"You care about him."

"I do," Red said, returning to his chopping. "And?"

"And nothing."

Red peered at him. "Nothing." Did Lucky really expect him to believe that? He *never* said anything for the sake of hearing himself talk, and he didn't mince words unless he was digging for something.

"What?" Lucky shrugged. "I think if you care about him, and he cares about you—which is obvious he does—then you should go for it. He's a good guy."

Red put down his knife and leaned his hands on the counter. "Wait a minute. You almost had an aneurism when you found out about Colton and Ace, and now you're telling me to just go for it like it's no big deal?"

"That was not the same thing at all, and you know it."

"How?"

"Laz is not a client. He wasn't then, and he isn't now. Also, you're not on the job. You're here because you care about him. If this was a case, King would have assigned someone else to him."

"You're right. Laz isn't a client, and I'm not here in an official capacity, but that just means it's even more important I not let my guard down."

Lucky crossed his arms over his chest and narrowed his eyes. "Eso es un montón de mierda, y tú lo sabes."

"Lucky—"

"Fine. Whatever, bro. It's none of my business." He put his hands up, then returned them to the counter, drumming his fingers for several heartbeats before meeting Red's gaze. "You need to stop running away every time you meet someone you can see yourself falling for."

Red couldn't help his humorless laugh. "Are you kidding me? Do you hear how hypocritical you sound right now?"

"What are you talking about?"

"You do the same thing, Lucky."

Lucky's frown deepened. "No, I don't."

"Yes. You do. You just don't realize you're doing it." Was his friend really that oblivious? How could they all see it except Lucky?

Everyone who knew him thought him a player, and Lucky considered himself one as well. He left a trail of bed partners wherever he went. None of those men and women received his name, much less a phone number or second encounter. Repeat performances were not permitted, and although there was absolutely nothing wrong with a healthy sex drive, that's not what this was. Lucky was running from something.

"When do I do this?" Lucky demanded.

Fine. If Lucky needed Red to spell it out for him, then he would. "You do it every time you talk to Mason Cooper."

Lucky stilled, his eyes widening. He looked like he was about to pass out. "What?"

"Come on, Lucky. The way you two look at each other, the flirting, how he can't keep his hands off you? He's always manhandling you, growling at you about your damn motorcycle and how dangerous it is, and you're always poking him, winding him up. There's something there, but anytime he gets too close, you act the player, knowing he'll back off."

"No, no, no. This is not true."

"Really? Tell me what Mason said to you in the car on the way to the station. He did or said something that made you panic and had you flirting with the first person you saw to push him away. Except this time, it blew up in your face, didn't it? Because Mason didn't back off; he got pissed and called you out on it, which means you're getting to him, and that terrifies you."

"Nothing happened," Lucky replied through his teeth. "As for the flirting? I flirt with everyone. Mason is nothing special. I don't *want* a relationship, and neither does he. The guy couldn't even trust Ace. You think he's going to trust *me*?"

"Why are you so worked up?"

"I'm not," Lucky spat out, jumping from his seat. "Mind your own fucking business."

Red froze. Not because Lucky was telling him to fuck off—they cursed each other out all the time, gave each other a hard time, got in one another's business, because that's what family did—Red was stunned because seeing Lucky this upset confirmed Red was right.

It took a lot to upset Lucky. Sure, he ranted, bitched, and moaned. He cursed them out, got pissy, but truly upset? His face was flushed, his eyes dark, and he held himself rigid, fists at his sides.

"I had no idea," Red said softly.

"You have no idea what the fuck you're talking about," Lucky growled, spinning on his heels and storming off. Red watched him go, flinching when the front door slammed. Shit. This was bad, and of course now Mason was the lead detective on this investigation, which meant they'd be seeing more of him.

"Is everything okay?" Laz asked with a yawn as he walked into the kitchen, the disheveled hair falling over his brow, and just-woke-up look momentarily distracting Red. "I heard yelling. Did Ace scare Colton again?"

"It was Lucky. He was just dropping off your stuff. It's in the hall. I'll help you take it upstairs soon as I'm done here."

"Thanks. What are you making?" Laz took a seat at the counter across from Red.

"I just finished marinating some flank steak, and now I'm making some Chimichurri sauce for the tacos. It's Tuesday, so you know what that means."

Laz nodded, his eyes going slightly wide. "I have never met anyone as committed to Taco Tuesday as Ace."

"Yeah, he has a thing about food, and when it doesn't happen, he gets... intense."

"And pouty," Laz added with a chuckle. "Hey, do you mind if I do some work on my laptop while you work your magic? I know Colton said I could use his office, but I'd rather keep you company if that's okay."

"Of course. I'd like that."

"Be right back." Laz hopped off the chair, and Red continued to chop and mince. His mind went back to Lucky, and he tried not to worry about it. Ace hadn't given any indication he was worried about his cousin, so Red would leave it for now. Either way, there was more going on than Lucky was willing to admit.

Laz returned with his MacBook and got to work while Red finished up. The marinated flank steak was in the fridge, and now he was stirring the Chimichurri sauce before placing it in the fridge. As soon as it was time for dinner, he'd chop some radishes up, and the rest of the toppings. It was funny how just a few months ago he hadn't even known Colton, and now Red moved around his kitchen as if it were his own.

The house had become another home away from home for the Kings. They shared meals together every week, lounged by the pool, went to the beach, and had game nights in the game room. At first Red felt as though they were intruding on Colton's privacy, but the invitation had come from Colton himself. He'd confided in Red that he'd gotten used to having the Kings around and enjoyed their company. Being an only child, Colton liked the idea of having several annoying big brothers meddling in his life.

"What happens after you get the photos you need?" Red asked as he washed up the cutting board and knives.

Laz motioned him over, and Red quickly finished washing his hands and drying them before joining Laz at his computer. His laptop screen displayed photo-editing software and several images Red recognized from that morning's photo shoot.

"Now I go through all the images to narrow them down, selecting which ones I think will work best. The magazine editor who hired me for this job has a very specific look in mind, so now I need to make sure she gets what she wants."

"What if the client wants something you know won't work?"

"That happens more often than you'd think, which is why I also provide an alternative. Most of the time, once they've seen the two options, they tend to pick my sets. Even if I know their concept won't work, I'll try my best to give them what they ask for. In the end, all I can do is give it my all and hope I get paid for it."

Red frowned at that. "What do you mean hope you get paid for it?"

"When you're a freelance artist, especially at an entry-level, a lot of clients view payment as optional. You're lucky if you get paid on time, much less at all. You spend a good deal of time chasing up invoices, and sadly, sometimes you have to take the loss."

"That's horrible."

Laz shrugged. "Unfortunately, when it comes to the creative industry, there are people who believe art should be free, whether it's music, art, books, movies, or photography. If you can afford to give away your art for free, hey, that's awesome, but for the majority of us, although we're fortunate that we've been able to turn our passion into a career, our creativity is what pays the bills. It pays for food, rent, medical expenses, much needed equipment. For some it's the chance to use their passion and talent to forge a better future for themselves, to be able to put their kids through college, or pay for a much-needed medical procedure. In no other industry, do we expect people to work for free.

"And, yeah, to some what we do might be considered frivolous, or simply a way to pass the time, but where would the world be without the stories that transport us to another world? Without the music that inspires passion or lifts our mood, or the movies that make us feel like anything is possible. Art doesn't just happen, it's a part of us, a part we carve out of ourselves to share with others." Laz cleared his throat, his cheeks flushed pink from embarrassment. "Sorry, I get a little carried away sometimes. I've got a lot of friends who are part of the creative industry in some way. They struggle with this all the time."

Red smiled warmly at him. "No need to apologize. I love how passionate you are about your work, and I agree with you." He pointed to one of the images, and Laz enlarged it. Red recognized the model. The young man had been kneeling on the shore when Red arrived at the beach that morning, the waves crashing against him. Like the rest of the young men and women at the shoot, the model appeared flawless, with a slender, sinewy frame, sharp cheekbones, and perfectly pouting lips. "What's it like? Being surrounded by beautiful people all the time?"

"Exhausting."

Red chuckled. "Really?"

"It's all an illusion. Just minutes after this was taken, they were at each other's throats. You saw it yourself. Not that all models are like that. I know several who are amazing, but you don't often get a choice of who you work with. Each shoot involves several creatives with different personalities, and they don't always get along. Then you add ego and pressure into the mix, and it can get a little scary."

"So why do you do it?"

Laz clicked away at his laptop and an image opened, leaving Red speechless. He'd never seen anything so captivating. Most of the photograph was taken up by a stunning young man with pale pink hair, dark skin, and bright green eyes. Freckles were strewn across his nose and cheeks, his full pouty lips sporting glossy pink lipstick. The dress he wore had a white bodice that transitioned into a pale pink down into layers and layers of flouncy skirt. The top of the bodice was cut off, so it began beneath two prominent scars denoting where his breasts had been before his transition. He was draped on a white chaise lounge, one arm raised above his head, and although the contrasting colors and lighting made the image striking, it was the emotion in the model's face that had Red entranced. The running mascara, the one tear that had trailed down his cheek…. It was the look of heartbreak, but there was also hope, a sense of peace, and a light in his eyes that exuded inner strength.

"This is breathtaking, Laz. Who is he?"

"Thank you. Ky's a friend from college. He'd been struggling with his identity for a very long time, and his family didn't make it any easier for him. When he decided he couldn't hide who he was any longer, that he couldn't keep suffering to please others, he started to see a therapist, then socially transitioned before starting hormonal transition. His family insisted it was just a phase, but soon Ky was in for top surgery, and his family turned their backs on him completely. My friends and I were there to support him every step of the way.

"I was in the hospital with him when he woke up after surgery." Laz wiped a stray tear from his cheek. "The look on his face was something I'll never forget. His heart was broken because his family wasn't there, but when he cried, it was because he was finally beginning to feel like the person he was meant to be. I was so happy for him. One day we were talking, and I told him how I wanted to do high concept fashion photography, but I wanted more than beautiful people wearing beautiful clothing. I wanted to create gorgeous art with real people, people who had a powerful story to tell. He asked me if he could be my first model, and I was so honored he entrusted me to tell his story through my images. This is actually the final piece. It's a series."

"Where's Ky now?" Red asked, still riveted by the stunning photo.

"Getting ready for next year's Fashion Week in Paris. He's a highly sought-after model now, so I don't get to see him very often, but we keep in touch." Laz smiled softly at the image in front of him. "He says he has me to thank for launching his career, but I just provided the tools for him to share his story in a unique way. His success is all him, and everything he sacrificed to get where he is now."

"Is he happy?"

Laz nodded, smiling. "He finally has the life he always dreamed of."

Red was glad to hear it. He wondered what kind of life Laz dreamed of? What else outside of his career did he have his heart set on? "Thank you for sharing this with me," Red said sincerely. "I hope I can meet Ky one day."

"I hope so too."

It was only when Red turned his face away from the screen, did he realize how close he was to Laz. Their lips were inches apart, and he could feel Laz's warm breath on his skin. Red dug his fingers into the chair's polished wood backrest, his body seeking Laz's when Ace's voice boomed from the hall.

"Are you decent?"

Red let his head hang with a chuckle before straightening. "Yes," he called out. "Unlike you." With a wink at Laz, Red went to the fridge and pulled out the pitcher of tea, knowing exactly what Ace was going to say.

"Ooh, pour me a glass." Ace dropped down into a chair next to Laz and motioned toward the living room. "Your bag's on the couch."

"Thanks." Red placed the glass of cold tea in front of Ace. "Where's Colton?"

"He's taking a shower before dinner." Ace gulped down his tea in record time before jumping out of his chair. "And now I'm going to join him."

"Thanks, Ace. I did not need to know that," Laz informed him, shaking his head.

Ace laughed as he hurried off, and Red decided now was a good time to start the Mexican rice he'd be serving with dinner, along with some black beans. He removed a couple of cans from the pantry, chuckling at Laz's puzzled expression.

"Not that there's anything wrong with canned beans, I'm just surprised."

"Believe me, it's not my idea. Ace prefers the canned beans. He says he likes the taste better for some reason. I don't know. His Cuban family members think he's weird, and they're not wrong."

"Can I help with anything?" Laz asked, closing his laptop.

"Would you mind setting the table while I finish making dinner? Ace and Colton should be down by the time everything's done."

"No problem."

Laz moved around the kitchen as Red cooked the rice, removed everything he needed from the fridge to cook the steaks, and pulled the tortilla warmers from the cabinet. It was a little silly, but being in the kitchen with Laz felt… comforting. They moved around each other naturally, like they'd done it a hundred times.

"Have you always enjoyed cooking?" Laz asked as he removed dishes from the cabinets, and cutlery from the drawers. Tonight, it was just the four of them, though Red didn't anticipate it would be any less lively, what with Ace being here.

"I love cooking. Always have. My dads taught me from a young age."

Laz turned to him with a bright smile. "Your dads?"

"Yep. No one expects the Southern boy to have two dads, but I do. My dad always wanted kids, but he had no intention of marrying a woman. He was a flower child in the sixties, met the love of his life during the Summer of Love in San Francisco in 1967. Anyone who says there's no such thing as love at first sight never met my dads. They were just fifteen at the time, but from the moment they saw each other, that was it for them.

"They settled in Georgia after Pop's mom had a stroke. She knew about her son being gay and didn't care. She loved him, and my dad. They moved in with her, looked after her. Some people suspected my dad and Pops were more than best friends and roommates, but no one dared say a word against them to Grams. Anyway, my dad's best friend was living with her girlfriend a couple of hours away, and she offered to be a surrogate. She had no interest in having kids, but she loved my dad, so she was happy to do it. The four of them lived together for a while until I was born. After that, Alice and her girlfriend moved to San Diego."

"Did you keep in touch with her?"

Red shook his head as he popped the tray of tortillas into the oven to heat, then removed the cooked rice from the burner. "My dads explained everything to me from the moment I was old enough to understand. They never hid the truth. Alice may have given birth to me, but she wasn't my parent. My dads were. They loved me, provided me with everything a child needed. Alice loved my dad, and she loved me too, but not because I was her child, but because I was my dad's. My dads taught me that family is bound by more than just blood, and I really understood that after meeting King and the rest of the guys."

"Your dads sound amazing."

"I think they are," Red replied with a big smile. "They raised me to be compassionate and respectful of others, to look beyond race, gender, and sex to what's inside a person. Our lives haven't been easy by any means, and we shared some really scary moments, but I wouldn't change my family for anything."

"Where are your dads now?"

"Enjoying their retirement down in Fort Myers." Maybe one day Red would ask Laz to come with him when he visited his dads. They'd love Laz. Hearing Ace teasing Colton as they came down the stairs signaled it was time to get everything on the table. Soon as the table was set, Red got started on the flank steak.

"God, that smells so good," Ace said with a groan, coming into the kitchen to peek at the steak Red was cooking. "Where's yours?" Ace asked.

"Funny," Red laughed. "Grab me the cutting board and knife."

Ace went to do as asked, and Red turned the steak over. "Laz, how do you like your steak?"

"Medium-rare," Laz called out from the dining room.

Ace patted Red's back. "Same as you, big guy. You know what that means?"

Red arched an eyebrow at Ace. "That he likes his steak medium-rare?"

"No. It means it was meant to be."

Red rolled his eyes. "Sure. Let me base all my future relationships on how my partner takes their steak."

"Hey, Colton likes his steak cooked medium just like me. Mason likes his steak rare. Remember Ewan? Fucking disaster from day one. You know how he took his steak?"

"No, but I bet you're going to tell me."

"Well done."

Red cringed.

"Yeah. He ruined his steak like he ruined our relationship."

"Um, I'm pretty sure it was your finding him with his pants around his ankles and that dude's mouth around his dick in one of Frank's back rooms that ruined your relationship."

"That too, but if I'd paid attention to the steak that whole ugly incident could have been avoided."

"Yeah, okay. If you're done imparting your weird relationship wisdom, I'd like to get to eating dinner."

Ace leaned in, eyes narrowed as he whispered hoarsely, "Listen to the steak."

Sweet Jesus. His friend was a nut. But then that was old news. "Sit your ass down," Red told him as he carried the two iron skillets with the sliced flank steaks over to the table. Instead of sitting across from Colton, who sat next to Laz, Ace wedged himself between the two. Red took a seat across from Laz.

They talked as they served themselves and ate. Red was glad he'd decided to sit across from Laz, because every time Laz took a bite of something, he made the most decadent noise, and it went straight to Red's cock. Wonderful, because that's what he needed, to get a hard-on at the dinner table in front of Laz, and even worse, Ace.

"Oh my God, this is so good, Red," Laz said, following up with another moan. Red shifted uncomfortably, his gaze landing briefly on Ace, who waggled his eyebrows knowingly. Ignoring his meddling friend, Red took another bite of his taco. Thankfully Colton and Laz took the conversation from there, talking about Gio and how he'd be taking some vacation time soon. Laz was looking forward to spending some time with his brother. It seemed like the guy was perpetually away on business, but Red understood time off was a luxury you couldn't always afford when people were depending on you. Gio was the founder of a huge global charity that helped people all over the world start their own businesses, providing funds and loans otherwise unattainable to most of the people they helped.

"I can't wait for you to meet him," Laz told Red, catching him off guard.

"Yeah? That'd be great." Red hoped he didn't sound as nervous as he felt. He'd heard so much about Gio from both Colton and Laz, it was as if he knew the guy. Gio wasn't just Laz's big brother; he was Laz's hero. After their father passed away from cancer, Gio took over the role of parent, raising Laz and working two jobs so he could put his little brother through college.

"He's really looking forward to meeting you."

Red almost choked on his tea. "He is?"

"Of course he is. You saved my life, Red."

Red blinked at him. "He knows about that?"

Colton chuckled. "Gio may not be here, but there's nothing he doesn't know. We're his family. We don't keep anything from one another. Also, he has a way of getting information out of you without you even realizing it."

"I like him already," Ace said before stuffing the rest of his taco in his mouth. They finished dinner, all of them too stuffed for dessert, so Colton poured them each a glass of wine from one of his many expensive bottles. Red had worried for Ace after learning he'd fallen for Colton, uncertain how Ace would react to being in a relationship with someone who possessed the kind of wealth and status Colton did.

Red should have known better. Ace wasn't intimidated by Colton's wealth. He loved Colton, not his company, not his money or status, and as for Colton, he admitted that he enjoyed being able to spoil Ace when Ace allowed it. The two of them seemed to find a balance that worked.

"Why don't Ace and I clean up," Colton offered, but Red was having none of it. Colton was leaving for New York in the wee hours of the morning. He should be spending the evening with Ace.

"No, don't you worry. I've got this."

"Thank you. Well, I guess we'll turn in, then."

"So early?" Laz asked, checking his watch. "It's just after eight."

Ace nuzzled Colton's temple. "That was Colton's polite way of saying we're going to go boink like bunnies."

Colton dropped his head into his hands with a groan.

"I swear he has manners," Red promised. "Somewhere in there."

"What? We're in love." Ace threw his arm around Colton's shoulders, pulling him in to deliver a kiss to his temple. "Naturally there's going to be all kinds of hot, sweaty, man sex happening. Like, all the time. Don't worry, Red. I washed your sheets."

Red stared at him. "What? Wait, what sheets?" *No, way. He didn't.* Colton's face turned crimson, and he wouldn't look Red in the eye. "Please tell me you two didn't have sex in my bed. In my bed where I sleep every night."

"What?" Ace looked affronted. "Of course we didn't have sex in your bed. I would *never* have sex in your bed. That's just… wrong."

"Oh, thank God." He just never knew with Ace. Even after all these years, the only thing predictable about Ace was that he was unpredictable.

"We had sex in the guest room bed."

Laz had unfortunately been in the middle of drinking water when Ace opened his mouth, and now that water was dripping down Red's face. Ace all but fell out of his chair laughing.

"Oh my God, Red! I'm *so* sorry." Laz jumped from his chair, and ran around to Red's side with a napkin, his expression competing with Colton's for most mortified. "I'm sorry. So, so sorry."

"It's okay," Red assured him, taking the napkin to wipe his face. "It's not your fault." He glared at Ace. "I blame *him*."

"On that note. Time to go." Ace pulled Colton up with him. "Night. Thanks for dinner, Red. Awesome as always. We have to go now."

"Ace," Colton scolded, but his reprimand quickly gave way to a laugh as Ace pounced on him, kissing him, and wrapping his arms around him, manhandling him on the way to the stairs.

"Is he always like that?" Laz asked, smiling wide as he helped Red clear the table.

"Yep, and it's been nearly twenty years now. Man, how time flies. I remember my first day of training like it was yesterday." Red stood, and began stacking dirty plates to take to the sink. "You should have seen him then. Hell, both him and Lucky. Couple of scrawny ass teenagers with big ears and bigger mouths. If they weren't driving our drill sergeant nuts, they were getting themselves into all kinds of trouble, and dragging the rest of us with them."

They got everything off the table, and Laz wiped it down before joining Red in the kitchen. "How can I help?"

"It's fine. Don't worry about it."

"Okay, I'm going to take some of my equipment into the game room. I'll be right back."

"No problem." Red popped his phone onto the speaker dock, then tuned into his favorite digital music station. Cleaning up was a lot more fun when you had some good music to groove to. Ace loved to tease him about his taste in music, but Red didn't care.

Growing up, his dads were always playing their favorites from the sixties and seventies. They'd taught him to dance from the moment he could walk. A lot of people were surprised he didn't fall into the stereotype of white boy who couldn't dance, while others didn't expect him to be able to move the way he did because of his size and muscles, but he was pretty flexible, thanks to years of Yoga. He let the beat wash over him as he danced around the kitchen. A few minutes later and Laz was back.

"I didn't take you for a disco kind of guy."

"You kidding? Bee Gees, A Taste of Honey, The Trammps. Bring it, baby." Red danced around Laz, making him laugh.

"Oh my God, what's happening right now? What dance is that?"

"It's called the Bus Stop."

"Please tell me you have a white three-piece suit at home that you wear with an open-collared black shirt."

"I'm happy to announce I do not moonlight as John Travolta from *Saturday Night Fever*. I don't even own a pair of bellbottoms." He stopped beside Laz and grabbed his hand, pulling him beside him. "Come on. I'll show you. Start with your right leg, kick forward and clap, make sure your right leg lands back behind you. Good." Red did the moves slowly, step by step so Laz could follow along.

"Okay, we're moving back now. Left, right, left back then forward, right, and come to stand with your feet together. Now we're going to travel to the right, crossing your left leg behind your right, and end with your legs together. Perfect. Just like that. Now we're doing the same in the other direction, landing where we started. Tap your right leg out. Back to starting position. Tap your left leg out. Back to starting position. Click your heels together twice like you're Dorothy going home to Kansas."

Laz laughed, and Red's smile was stupidly wide. He loved hearing Laz laugh. He had the feeling Laz didn't get to do it enough.

"Tap your right toes, then tap back behind you. Tap twice in front, and twice in back."

"Jesus, how did Travolta do this?" Laz tripped, but Red caught him, and moved him back into position.

"With practice, I'm sure. Ready?" Red performed the steps, making sure to remember the clapping as he moved along with the beat. "Single tap forward and back again. Feet together, then turn to the left. Now repeat. Keep turning left until you end up facing forward again."

"Oh, is that all." Laz turned in the wrong direction, and they bumped into each other, stumbling and laughing. Red wrapped an arm around Laz to steady him, Laz's back ending up against the counter, their legs entwined, and their bodies pressed together. Laz placed his hands on Red's arms, and when he lifted his gaze to Red's, his smile was breathtaking. "Hi."

"Hi," Red replied softly. He should move away, but he couldn't bring his body to cooperate, not when Laz's hands were on him.

Laz slid his hands up Red's biceps to his shoulders, then down to his pecs, his eyes following the movement while Red kept his gaze on Laz's face. He was so damned beautiful with his soft, dark curls, thick eyebrows, and big blue eyes. Red brushed his fingers down Laz's stubbled jaw, stopping at his chin to run his thumb over Laz's plump bottom lip. For months he'd wondered what these lips tasted like. He hadn't been able to get Laz out of his mind. The man invaded his thoughts at all hours of the day, and sometimes at night. Laz tilted his head up, his eyes on Red's lips.

"We should probably—" Red's words died against Laz's mouth.

It was a tentative kiss, soft, uncertain, but when Red parted his lips, all uncertainty flew out the window on both their parts. Laz dove in, tongue dueling with Red's, soft lips demanding more as Red leaned into Laz, giving into his demands. Whatever Laz wanted, Red was willing to give. His left arm joined his right around Laz's waist as Red explored every crevice of Laz's sweet mouth. Damn, he tasted like heaven, and felt so good in Red's arms, like he belonged there.

Laz slid his arms up and around Red's neck, keeping him close as Lobo's "I'd Love You to Want Me" played quietly from the speakers.

They started to sway together, and Red smiled against Laz's lips, their kiss going from urgent to slow, sweet, and heartachingly intimate. Red loved kissing, loved all the ways his kisses could convey what he felt when words failed him.

"Hey, Red, I forgot—shit."

They gave a start and moved away from each other. Red's heart pounded in his ears, and he ran a hand through his hair in the hopes of getting his pulse to steady. He'd been so lost in Laz, he hadn't seen or heard Ace approach. Not good.

"I, um, I think I'm going to turn in. It's been a long day," Laz said, walking backward out of the kitchen, his cheeks flushed. "Goodnight, Red."

"Goodnight. If you need anything, you know where to find me."

Laz nodded. "Thanks for dinner, and, um, yeah. Thanks." With a shy smile, he spun on his heels, waving a quick hello at Ace as he darted for the stairs.

Red sighed and leaned against the counter, his arms crossed over his chest. He narrowed his eyes at Ace. "Has anyone ever told you, you have terrible timing?"

"Yes. Often." Ace winced. "I'm sorry. Can I just say one thing?"

"Not if that one thing is 'I told you so,'" Red muttered.

"Dammit."

"What did you forget?" Red moved across the kitchen to pluck his phone off the speaker dock and turn off the music. "You know, before you interrupted our first kiss."

Ace groaned. "Aw, come on, man. Don't guilt-trip me like that. I said I was sorry."

"You did." Red held back a smile. Yeah, he was being a dick, but it wasn't often he got to make Ace squirm. After several heartbeats of epic pouting from Ace, Red took pity on him. "It's fine. Really. What did you need to tell me?"

"I forgot to tell you that Quinn's getting married. We're all invited to the wedding. You know *everyone* is going to be there. It's in October, which I know is when your dads go to San Diego to visit Alice, so I wanted to make sure you let them know since the invites won't be going out for a few more weeks yet."

Red grinned widely. "Holy shit, Quinn and Spencer are getting married? That's amazing. Is the wedding in Miami?"

"Not sure yet. Possibly. Quinn wants his SWAT buddies to be able to pop in if they can't get the day off. Either way, maybe you can bring Laz as your plus one." Ace waggled his eyebrows, making Red laugh. He was such a dork.

"We'll see." They turned off the lights and checked the doors and the alarm before they headed upstairs. "Night, Ace. Tell Colton I said I hope he has a good trip."

"I will. Thanks, bud. Goodnight."

Red walked into his room and closed the door behind him, his thoughts going to the sweet and sexy man in the room next door. Warmth flooded through him at the thought of his kiss with Laz. Yeah, it had definitely been a good night. Maybe things would be different in the morning, but that didn't necessarily mean different in a bad way.

As he changed into a T-shirt and loose pair of pajama bottoms, he found himself smiling. Ace was right—not that Red was about to tell him so—there was something special between Red and Laz, and he was looking forward to seeing where things went.

# CHAPTER 6

Air. He needed air.

Red gasped, choking on the lungful of heavy smoke and dirt he'd sucked in. He gagged, then hurled, puking up water, saliva mixed with blood, and God only knew what else. His ears were ringing. Something warm trickled down his neck, and his body screamed in agony from the weight of his gear and something else crushing him. He was on his stomach, surrounded by rubble, the air so thick with black smoke he could barely see his hand in front of his face. A shadowy lump a few feet ahead took form, and he realized it was one of his brothers.

Gritting his teeth, Red pushed his gloved hands against the ground, shifting to move the chunk of wall off his back. It slid off him, hitting the ground with a *thunk*, and he was able to push himself onto his knees. He tried to get up, but a wave of dizziness had him losing his equilibrium.

*Get up. You have to get up.*

Pushing through the light-headedness, nausea, and pain, Red scrambled to get to his fallen brother. What the hell happened? One minute they were approaching their target, and the next an explosion had gone off. King yelled for them to fall back, and then the world around them ceased to be, a deafening boom sending bodies into the air, including Red. This wasn't how it was supposed to go.

Red reached his friend, his brother-in-arms, and rolled him over, all the while praying he was alive. Tears filled his eyes, and he wiped them away as best he could with his gloved hands. Deuce stared up at Red, green eyes that had once been filled with so much mischief now lifeless and empty, courtesy of the steel rod through his chest. A section of smoke cleared enough for Red to choke on his strangled cry. Three more bodies. *Oh God, no. Please.* He reluctantly left Deuce to check on Kicker. He was gone, and so was Spider. They were dead. They were all dead.

"Ace?" Red called out, his voice rough, his mouth so dry and scratched he tasted blood. "Lucky? Jack? Someone… please." A groan caught his ear, and he turned his head, his heart lurching to a halt, or so it felt like. "Oh God. No, no, no." Red scrambled over, dropping to his knees beside his friend. "King? King, open your eyes." Red checked his pulse. It was weak, but it was there. Jesus, he'd lost so much blood.

"Red," King wheezed, his breath coming out labored.

"I'm here. Stay with me. Come on, buddy." Red checked King over for additional injuries, cursing when he found the large piece of shrapnel speared into King's upper thigh. Thankfully it had missed his femoral artery. Red worked as quickly and efficiently as he could to stop the bleeding. King lay in a pool of blood. It had to be coming from somewhere else. "Shit. Where is it?" Red ran his hands up King's arms, and when his right hand slipped under King's vest to his shoulder, King cried out. *There it is. Fucker.* "Okay, just hold on." Trailing his fingers, he found another piece of shrapnel impaled into King's shoulder. He pulled it out, his heart splintering when King only groaned at the pain.

"King. Open your eyes."

King did as he asked, and Red went to work, aware of King shivering. His pupils were blown, his face pale, and he was clammy to the touch. "Who's going to keep Ace in line, huh?"

"I'm… not gonna make it, Red."

"Fuck you. Yes, you are." Red sniffed, blinking through his tears. "Bibi will kick my ass if I don't bring you home, and no offense, but your sister's scarier than you."

King chuckled before he started coughing, his brows drawn together, heartache marring his handsome face. "The others?"

As if they'd heard King, Ace materialized in the smoke, staggering toward them, Lucky's arm around his shoulder. Behind them, Jack had Joker in a fireman's carry. No one else followed. Half their unit, six of their brothers… gone.

"They're coming, but you gotta stay with me."

King smiled softly, his voice barely above a whisper. "Take care of them. They're… going to need someone to ground them."

"Stop," Red cried. "Just stay with me. Please." King closed his eyes, his head lolling to one side. "No, you're not going to fucking die!"

"Dustoff inbound," Jack called out through the thunder of the helo.

"Did you hear that? We're getting you out of here, so don't you dare fucking die on me. King? *King*!"

"Red, wake up."

With a gasp, Red scrambled back until he hit something hard. His eyes adjusted to the soft glow around him, but he couldn't focus. Where the hell was he?

"What's going on? King?"

"Red, it's me. It's Laz."

Red shook his head and shut his eyes tight. He had to control his breathing. *Fuck*! Why couldn't he breathe? Grabbing a fistful of his shirt over his heart, he pressed his fist down against his chest to keep his heart from exploding. He was dizzy and struggling to surface from the inky fog he was drowning in.

"King, where's King?"

"King? He's not here."

Red knew that voice, but he couldn't place it. His head was pounding, and his ears were ringing. He smelled smoke, felt the sand and dirt in his mouth. So much noise, so much blood.

"I need to see him," Red whispered. "I need to see him." Red covered his ears and drew his knees up. He closed his eyes, too afraid to move, afraid he was still there, that hell wasn't done with him and was dragging him back down.

"Hold on, Red."

Oh God, it was happening again.

"Shit. Ace and Colton are already gone. I'm calling King now, okay? King? No, I'm fine. Red, um, he's asking to see you. I think he had a bad nightmare or something. He's really distraught. Oh, okay. I'll do that."

The bed dipped, and Red jumped when a hand landed on his shoulder, but he couldn't bring himself to open his eyes.

"Red, it's me Laz. King's on his way, okay? It's going to be a little while, but he'll be here. He's okay."

"I need to see King," Red repeated, shrugging off the hand to his shoulder. He kept his eyes closed and focused on his breathing.

"Okay. Do you want to talk about it?"

Red pressed the heels of his hands to his eyes to keep the tears at bay. "No." He would, but not now. Not until he saw King. He knew he was supposed to talk about it. Avoiding it wasn't an option, and he didn't intend to, just... not right now. How much time passed since he'd heard King was coming, he had no clue. It seemed like forever, and in that time, he focused on his breathing, on running through what happened that day, acknowledging the loss of his brothers.

A phone buzzed somewhere, and the bed shifted again. "I'll be right back. It's King."

Red didn't respond. His entire focus was on not panicking.

"Red?"

The bedroom light came on, and Red's head shot up, his vision blurred from fresh tears. He hated that he couldn't control the sob that tore from him. King sat on the edge of the bed, drawing Red into his arms.

"I'm okay."

Red clung to King, his face buried in King's shoulder. "Is this real?"

King nodded. "Yeah, buddy. It's real. I'm here, and I'm okay."

Relief washed through Red, and he allowed himself to accept King's strength, to let his dearest friend hold him up, comfort him. When he was ready, he pulled back.

"I'm sorry I woke you."

"Don't be sorry," King said gently, cupping Red's face so their eyes could meet. It was so good to see the brightness in King's blue eyes, to see him so full of life. "You know I'll always be here for you."

"I know."

King released him and patiently waited.

"It's… it's been a while since I dreamed of that day," Red said quietly. His fallen brothers were never far from his thoughts, but it had been years since he'd been triggered this badly. Sometimes certain sounds or textures brought back memories of his time in the service, not all of them bad memories either. It had been years since he'd dreamed of that day, and so vividly. Like he'd been back there.

"I could feel the smoke choking me, my throat raw from the sand and dirt." He swallowed hard. Movement to his left caught his attention.

"I should go." Laz stood awkwardly to one side.

"You should stay," King said, his attention never leaving Red. How did King do that? How could he convey his thoughts with just one look? He knew what Laz was coming to mean to Red, and if

Red was going to have any kind of future with Laz, he had a right to know, even if it scared Laz off. Red nodded.

"Why don't you have a seat next to Red? If you're okay with that."

Laz nodded and quickly walked around the bed. He climbed up and sat cross-legged in the center of the mattress, facing Red and King.

King turned his attention back to Red, his voice quiet and soothing. "Why don't you tell us."

Inhaling a deep unsteady breath, Red started to talk. He walked them through his dream, from the moment he opened his eyes to his finding Deuce, Kicker, and Spider, then King. From knowing half his unit was gone, the smell of blood, of burning flesh, the heat, the fire, the fear.

"Then you passed out, and I thought you…. I thought you were gone too. I woke up after that." The tears rolled down his cheeks, and he didn't bother trying to fight them. He let out a shaky breath, but the pain in his chest had dulled to a small ache. Sniffing caught his attention, and he looked over to find Laz with his arms wrapped around his drawn-up knees, his face flushed as he cried quietly.

"Laz." Red didn't think. He drew Laz into his arms, wrapping him up in a tight embrace. He ran his fingers over Laz's hair.

"I should be the one comforting you, not the other way around," Laz said, his voice sounding off due to his stuffy nose.

"I've lived with this memory for a very long time. This is the first you're hearing of it."

"I'm so sorry you lost them. Both of you. I can't… I can't even imagine—" Laz pulled back, his expression horrified. "Wait. Was it what happened at the beach? Did that trigger your nightmare?"

Red wasn't about to lie. "Most likely."

"Oh God, this is my fault." Laz started to pull away, but Red stopped him.

"Laz, this isn't your fault. I was diagnosed with PTSD when I got back, but I spent a long time receiving PE and CPT treatment."

"What's that?"

"Prolonged Exposure and Cognitive Processing Therapy," King offered. "They're trauma-focused psychotherapies. When someone suffers from PTSD, it's natural for them to try and avoid anything that reminds them of the trauma, but that's not a long-term solution. Prolonged Exposure therapy had Red not just talking about his trauma in detail, but facing them through in vivo situations."

"In vivo? You mean like real life situations?" Laz looked horrified.

Red nodded. "It was gradual, a step-by-step process where I worked toward confronting situations that reminded me of my trauma. It was all safe, and yes, at first it felt like it was just making things worse, but the guys helped me stick with it, and eventually, it started to get better. It's why I can do what I do now as a King and not be triggered."

"Until now. Because of me, because of what happened on the beach."

"No, not you. Laz, PTSD isn't something that just goes away. Everyone is different. The symptoms are different, the treatments, medication, the way they respond. It took years, but I was able to regain control of my life. There's always a chance of a setback, but it wasn't any one thing that triggered my nightmare; it was a combination of things. The gunfire, the guys all being there, the sand, the heat, the noise, someone I care about bleeding…." Red cupped his cheek. "It was not your fault. Do you understand that?"

Laz nodded.

"Do you need me to stay?" King asked.

"No, I'm good. Thank you for coming."

King stood and placed his hand on Red's shoulder. "Okay. Try and get some rest. If you need anything, let me know." He moved his gaze to Laz. "You too."

"Thank you, King. I'll walk you out." Laz made to get up, but King held a hand up.

"Don't worry about it. I'll set the alarm on my way out. You two rest." King turned off the bedroom light, leaving only the bedside lamp on. The house was plunged once again into silence.

Red had no idea what time it was, but he figured it was close to dawn, seeing as how Ace and Colton had already left for the airport. Otherwise Ace would have been the first one through his bedroom door after he screamed.

"Are you okay?" Red asked Laz, concerned how Laz was taking all this.

"Me?"

"It can be hard… to see someone like that, not knowing what to do to help."

Laz seemed to consider his words before meeting Red's gaze. "Maybe you can tell me how to help?"

Red smiled, and Laz leaned in to brush his lips over Red's. It was a butterfly kiss, but Red felt it down to his bones. He cupped Laz's face, stroking his cheek with his thumb. "Just the fact that you're still here means the world to me."

"Of course I'm still here. You were in pain. I wasn't going to just leave you to suffer alone."

Red swallowed hard. "Still. Thank you."

Laz looked like he wanted to ask, but thankfully he didn't. Red was far too exhausted and vulnerable right now to bring up his ex.

Laz dropped his gaze to his fingers, his gaze everywhere but on Red. "Can I… um, can I stay here with you? Until you fall asleep?"

Red's heart skipped a beat. "I'd like that." He leaned over and turned off the lamp, then lay down with Laz lying beside him on top of the duvet. They were facing each other, and although the room was dark, enough moonlight came through the window for Red to see Laz. His beautiful eyes were on Red, and Red would have given anything to know what he was thinking.

"Close your eyes, Red. I'm right here if you need me."

Red did as Laz asked, his body finally losing some of the tension from earlier. It felt good having Laz beside him. He'd been on his own for so long he'd forgotten what it was like to share his bed with someone. Before he realized it, he'd fallen into a deep, dreamless sleep.

Heat flared through Red's body, the delicious pressure to his cock stirring him from sleep. Was he dreaming again? God, he hoped not. It felt too good to be a dream. He thrust his hips forward, a groan escaping him when he was met with a firm, round ass pushing back against him in response. Red dug his fingers into the soft flesh of hips before sliding his hand over and around where he found a hard cock straining against the soft jersey material of pajama pants.

"Mmm, feels so good," Laz murmured quietly, his voice laced with sleep as he continued to rub his ass up against Red's stiffening erection.

Red buried his face into the thick dark curls of Laz's hair and inhaled deeply, the mix of shampoo and Laz's scent making him punch his hips forward. Laz let out a decadent moan that went straight to Red's groin, and he wondered what it would feel like to be buried deep inside Laz. He wanted to run his tongue over every inch of Laz's body, wanted to bask in his scent, and feast on his most intimate parts. Laz took hold of Red's hand and slipped it beneath the waistband of his pants, drawing a groan from Red.

"Laz…." Red was curled around him, their bodies pressed together from head to toe, and it filled Red with such contentment. He was comfortable and so at ease. "We should stop."

"Why?"

"Because this will change our relationship, and I don't want this situation we're in to be the reason we do this." Red pulled his hand out from Laz's pants, hoping Laz understood. Laz meant so much more to him than a quick fuck. After everything Laz had been through, was still going through, Red didn't want to rush him into something he might not be ready for. Then there was everything that happened last night. Laz turned to face Red, the clarity and intensity in his eyes catching Red off guard, forcing him wide-awake.

"You think whatever's going on between us is a result of my life being in danger? Because we're stuck together?"

"Isn't it?"

Laz narrowed his eyes. "My life wasn't in danger when we met. You called me gorgeous. Remember that?"

"Yes, but—"

"Tell me you didn't feel something between us the moment Ace introduced us, because I know I did, and I clearly remember the way you looked at me."

"How did I look at you?"

"Like I was the most beautiful thing you'd ever seen."

Red felt his face heat up. He placed a hand to Laz's cheek. "You're right. I was drawn to you the second I saw you."

"It was the same for me. You might not want to hear this, but you're part of the reason I broke up with Bryan."

Red stared at him. "What?"

"After you saved my life, all I could think about was how you had done more for me in a few minutes than Bryan had done in the *years* we'd been together. I've never been with a guy who's treated me like I was something precious."

"But you are," Red said, stroking his thumb over Laz's bottom lip. "When you care about someone, that makes them precious."

"See? After meeting you, spending hardly any time around you, I realized how fucked-up my relationship with Bryan was. I deserve better. When Bryan told me to kick you out, how he was the one who had a right to be there, it hit me how much I wanted you to stay instead of him. It was enough for me to tell him it was over."

"I agree that you deserve better than Bryan, but I didn't want to be the reason you broke up with him."

"I said you were part of the reason, but the real reason is, I did it for me. You helped open my eyes to the truth I'd been ignoring for a long time. So thank you."

"You're welcome." It might make him an asshole, but Red didn't feel guilty for having a part in Laz leaving Bryan. The guy was a manipulative, abusive jackass who only cared about himself, but it was knowing how little he'd supported Laz after what that son of a bitch photographer did that had Bryan on Red's shit list.

Laz moved his hand to Red's chest, and slowly slid it down to his abdomen then over the cock straining against his pants.

"Are you sure you want to do this?" Red needed Laz to be aware of what he was doing, of what they were starting. There would be no undoing whatever happened between them, and Red didn't want to lose Laz.

"I'm not sure of anything," Laz said breathlessly as he massaged Red through his pants, his lips curling into a wicked grin when Red sucked in a sharp breath. "But what I do know is that I want *this* very badly." He brought their lips together, and Red released a moan as Laz rolled him onto his back, then straddled him, his fingers slipping into Red's hair.

Red opened up for Laz, loving Laz's weight on him, how with every kiss Laz appeared to grow more frantic for him, like he was trying to consume Red. He bent his legs, drawing them up and widening his stance so he could get better purchase against the mattress. Gripping Laz's hips, he pushed Laz back until he was seated on Red's rock-hard cock. Red squeezed Laz's ass cheeks, and thrust his hips up, nothing but the thin jersey material of their pajama bottoms between them. Laz moaned and rutted against Red, the friction so damn good. If Red wasn't careful, he was going to come in his pants. Fuck, he couldn't remember the last time he'd been so turned-on, like his body was trying to set itself on fire.

Laz pulled away, and Red grunted his displeasure at the loss of those delicious lips. He cursed under his breath as Laz shoved Red's T-shirt up his torso, then began leaving a trail of scorching kisses across Red's skin. Red sucked in a sharp breath and arched his back up off the bed when Laz flicked a tongue over his left nipple, one hand moving back to Red's groin.

"Laz," Red groaned. He yanked his T-shirt up and over his head and tossed it to one side, his breath coming out labored as Laz licked, nipped, and sucked first one nipple, then the other, his hand slipping beneath the waistband of Red's pajamas.

This wasn't at all what he'd expected. Not that he was complaining. He was most definitely *not* complaining. Laz was clearly in control and determined to drive Red out of his mind, especially when Laz released him to take hold of his pants. Red lifted his hips so Laz could pull them down, caught off guard when Laz took them completely off and dropped them off the side of the bed to join Red's T-shirt. Then he lay between Red's spread legs and swallowed him down to the root.

"*F-fuck!*" Red's eyes all but rolled into the back of his head, and he grabbed fistfuls of the blankets as Laz expertly worked his mouth, alternating between sucking and licking. He moved fast and then slowed down before increasing the pressure around Red, then pushing his tongue into Red's slit. "God, Laz."

Laz stopped moving, his blue eyes dark with lust. He nodded, and Red cursed under his breath. Laz wanted him to fuck his mouth. *Oh, sweet Jesus.*

Red hesitated at first. He wasn't a small man, but Laz didn't seem concerned, and the way he'd swallowed Red told him Laz didn't have to worry about gag reflex. Slowly, Red started moving his hips, his bottom lip caught between his teeth at the toe-curling pleasure that was Laz's sweet mouth. He wouldn't be able to keep this up for very long, especially with Laz caressing his thighs, fondling his balls, and slipping his finger between Red's asscheeks.

"Laz, I'm gonna come," Red warned, but Laz didn't move. Instead, he used his lips to apply more pressure to Red's cock. If that wasn't enough to push him over the edge, the sight of Laz pushing his pants down and jerking himself off did it. Red's muscles tightened, and he cried out as his orgasm thundered through him. He emptied himself inside Laz's mouth, his breath labored and his skin flushed from the heat flaring through him. His body trembled as Laz swallowed every drop. Once Red was spent, Laz pulled back onto his knees, the want in his eyes unmistakable.

"Let me come on you, Red. Please."

Unable to find his voice, Red nodded fervently. *God, yes. Please come on me.* Laz quickly got rid of his pants and T-shirt before straddling Red's lap, his hand moving furiously, the other tweaking one of his own nipples.

"You're so fucking beautiful," Red said, breathless. Needing to touch him, Red grabbed hold of Laz's ass, and jerked him forward, until the tip of Laz's cock touched his lips. He opened his mouth and stuck out his tongue.

"Oh fuck. Fuck." Laz's body trembled, and he cried out as hot jets of come shot into and around Red's mouth.

As Laz pumped himself, he ran his fingers through the come outside Red's mouth, smearing it over his lips and chin, sending a shiver through Red. He'd never been so damned turned-on, or so he thought. Laz leaned in and licked Red clean. *Yep, just gonna expire right here.* He released a deep moan when Laz kissed him, and when they were forced to come up for air, Laz lay sprawled over him.

"That was…. Wow." Red wrapped his arms around Laz as they both caught their breaths.

"I've never done that before."

"What?"

Laz hesitated, his tone making him sound uncertain. "Gotten messy. You make me feel like my skin can't hold me, like I'm going to lose my mind."

"You do the same to me," Red admitted. "I guess we should get up and take a shower, huh?"

Laz lifted his head and smiled sweetly at Red. "Shower with me?"

"Okay."

Laz nodded. He really was absolutely beautiful. Red tucked a curl behind Laz's ear, caressing his cheek before finally making himself release Laz so he could get up.

The shower was big enough for the both of them, and after Laz set the temperature, he reached for the soap, but Red got to it first. He nuzzled Laz's temple, murmuring by his ear. "My turn." He smiled when Laz visibly shivered.

Red lathered Laz up, running his hands up his arms and over his shoulders, then down Laz's back, nails scraping ever so softly across his skin. He relished in the little noises that escaped Laz, and the way he arched his back, pushing his ass out toward Red. As much as Red wanted to push Laz up against the tiled wall and have his way with him fast and hard, he needed to take things slow. He didn't want to do anything Laz might regret. They still had so much to talk about.

Few people outside his family had seen him at his worst, and as bad as last night had been, it could be worse. If they were going to have something, he had to make Laz understand that what Red suffered from would never go away. There was always the possibility that he could be triggered, or relapse. No magic pill, no amount of love or good will would cure him.

"Red…."

The word was a soft prayer escaping from between Laz's full mouth, and Red wrapped his arms around Laz, bringing him back hard against his body, and turning his face so Red could capture Laz's lips in a sinful kiss. Laz rutted against him, and Red trailed his soapy hands down Laz's chest, one hand sliding down to his inner thigh, the other between them and up between Laz's asscheeks.

"Yes, please," Laz said breathlessly against Red's lips. He widened his stance, and placed a hand over the one Red had on his thigh, moving it to his cock. Gingerly, Red stroked Laz, reveling in the soft moans, in Laz's quiet gasps. He had his eyes closed, and he leaned into Red, allowing Red to carry his weight. Laz leaned his head back against Red's shoulder, and Red trailed kisses up his neck and jaw as he picked up his pace.

"Mmm, Red, you feel so good."

As Red pumped Laz's cock, he slipped a finger between his cheeks, the tip circling the rim of his tightly puckered hole.

"I can't wait to feel you inside me," Laz murmured softly, his hips moving a slow, sensual rhythm to match Red's strokes while Red continued to feast on Laz's skin. He kissed, licked, and nipped at all that smooth skin. Moving his finger away from Laz's hole, Red pumped his own hard cock before slipping it between Laz's asscheeks, rutting against him, moaning as his soapy member slid deliciously between those perky round globes. Laz moaned and began fucking Red's hand, their bodies pressed tightly together as they both writhed and rutted against each other chasing their release.

Red gently pushed a finger in, breaching his hole, and Laz bucked his hips, thrusting wildly into Red's fist while at the same time fucking Red's finger.

"I wish you could see how damn hot you look."

"Just think about what I'll look like being stretched by your gorgeous cock."

"Oh God." Red thrust his hips, rutting against Laz's thigh.

"Mm, I bet it's going to burn oh so good. We can do it on our knees, so you can watch my hole taking your big, fat dick inch by inch until you're deep inside me."

"Laz...."

"That's it, baby. Fuck me with your finger, imagine it's your dick."

*Holy shit.* He had no idea Laz could be such a little sex minx. Red released Laz, smiling at the little whimper he let out. He dropped to his knees, loving the way Laz cried out when Red swallowed his cock. He pumped himself, groaning as Laz's fingers slipped into his hair. It was sweet how he stroked Red's hair as Red worked his tongue and mouth around Laz's erection. Laz trembled like he was going to come apart, and he doubled over as he emptied himself inside Red.

The moment the salty come touched his tongue, Red came hard, his entire body shivering with pleasure. Laz let out a soft gasp, and Red pulled off him. He stood, and brought Laz into his arms for a kiss so Laz could taste himself. The little moan Laz let out was something Red could get used to. In fact, waking up next to Laz, showering with him, sleeping beside him were all things Red could get used to very quickly.

Rushing into relationships was not something he did. He was far too cautious and reserved for that. He took his time assessing whether the relationship he was considering would be worth it in the end. It sounded a bit cold, but he refused to risk his heart on someone he couldn't see spending his life with. Nothing was for certain in life, but that didn't mean he was willing to open himself up to heartache. Whoever he gave his heart to would have to be someone who could accept him and all his broken pieces, knowing neither they nor he would ever be able to completely mend them.

Laz smiled dreamily up at him, his gorgeous blue eyes filled with so much emotion, some of which Red couldn't decipher. There was trust in there, and the fact that someone like Laz, after all he'd been through, could trust Red spoke volumes.

"Good morning," Laz said with a sweet sigh.

Red chuckled. "Great morning." He kissed Laz, drinking in his soft lips, loving the way Laz opened up for him. Their tongues danced as they leisurely explored each other's mouth. Reluctantly he pulled away. "Let's wash up so I can feed you."

Laz opened his mouth, but his stomach rumbled. With a grimace, he glared down at his stomach. "Seriously? We have a super-hot naked guy in the shower, and you're just concerned about food. Traitor."

"You're adorable," Red said, popping a quick kiss on Laz's lips before turning him. "No funny business."

"Define 'funny business.'"

Red laughed and playfully smacked Laz's hand, which had started to wander up Red's thigh.

"Anything that's not getting washed up and out of this shower," Red replied, quickly washing himself up as Laz did the same.

Laz's sigh was very dramatic. "Fine."

They finished up in the shower and got out. Red handed Laz a towel and they dried themselves.

"Oh." Laz's gasp caught Red's attention, and he made to turn around, but Laz threw out a hand, stopping him. "No, wait. This is the first time I've seen your tattoo." Laz trailed his finger down Red's spine where the rod image of his tattoo was, and Red couldn't help the shiver that went through him.

"At first glance, I thought these were wings, except now that I look at it, they're not." Laz trailed his fingers over the lion heads in profile views on the back of his shoulders to each side of the snake heads, their manes looking like wings. His fingers moved to where Red knew the heart was that sat at the top of the rod, and then the crown above that. "What's this symbol called again?"

"It's the Caduceus, or the Rod of Hermes." Red stood exceptionally still as Laz traced the lines of his tattoo. It was a large piece, the lion manes behind each shoulder stretching from the center of his back out to his shoulders while the rod ended near his lower back.

"Wait, it's not the symbol for medicine?"

"Yes and no. It's sort of been adapted as the symbol of medicine because of all the confusion, which goes way back. The actual symbol of medicine is the Asclepius. It's a rod with one snake wrapped around it, not two, and no wings."

"Won't people assume your tattoo is connected to medicine?"

"Most likely, and it would make sense, considering I was a medical sergeant."

"But that's not why you got it."

"No." Red swallowed hard. He headed into the bedroom, Laz close behind.

"Why the Rod of Hermes?"

Red picked up his pajama bottoms from the floor and slipped into them while Laz pulled on his own pants. "Hermes was the god of many things, but what struck me was that he was the only god who could leave the Underworld without consequences. It was his job to carry the souls of the dead to Hades. With his wand, he put men to sleep and sent them dreams."

"And you're Hermes?"

Red sat on the edge of the bed. "By the time I got the tattoo, I was already carrying the souls of the dead. When I lost my brothers, I knew their souls would always be a part of me. I can't see the tattoo, but I know it's there. Just like them."

"Oh, Red." Laz stepped between his legs, and Red widened his stance so Laz could come closer. He closed his eyes, a sigh escaping him when Laz began stroking his hair.

"Sorry, not really what you need to hear before coffee."

"I'm glad you told me."

Red pulled Laz against him, wrapping his arms around him, and laying his head in the crook of Laz's neck. "I didn't mean to unload all this on you so soon. Everything with us is still so new, and… I understand if it's all too much for you."

"It's not," Laz promised.

Red straightened and met Laz's worried gaze. "Laz, what happened last night…. It could happen again. I mean, I've come a long way since I was diagnosed with PTSD, but I won't ever be cured. I've been through a lot of therapy. I was on medication. In the very early days, King didn't let me out of his sight because he was afraid I might hurt myself. My reactions to everything were explosive. I was in a real bad state and so damn angry. I took it out on Ace and the guys. King spent a good deal of his time breaking up fights between us, and although they'll deny it, I was the one who started those fights nine times out of ten. I loved them, but at the same time, I couldn't stop myself from hurting them, and that made me hate myself even more. I had nightmares, flashbacks, panic attacks. It was a never-ending hell."

"I'm so sorry you suffered through all that," Laz replied softly, caressing Red's jaw. "After you gave so much…." His eyes grew glassy, and he pressed his lips together.

"I'm sorry. See, I'm already upsetting you."

"You're not upsetting me, Red. I'm upset *for* you. I'm grateful to King and the others for being there for you, but I'm so damned proud of you too."

Red blinked at him. "You are?"

"Of course. My God, look at everything you went through, and look at you now." His smile was brilliant, and it brought tears to Red's eyes. Naaz had never wanted him to talk about his time in the military, especially not his time after. It hadn't been that way early in their relationship. She'd been supportive, compassionate, but soon it began to wear on her, and the cracks started showing. He never blamed her, but it had been difficult because it was a part of him. Bad or good, it played a part in making him the man he was today. Laz leaned in and placed a tender kiss to Red's brow.

"You came back and started fighting a different war," Laz said quietly. "You didn't give up, Red."

"I tried. During my PE sessions, after all that therapy, when it came time for exposure and I heard that first explosion, it triggered me bad. When it was over, I thought I was done. No way in hell I was going back, but King wouldn't let me." A small chuckle escaped him when he thought back on it. "He decided he was going to sit in on those sessions with me, for support and so I wouldn't storm out. Man, talk about if looks could kill." He shook his head with a laugh. "You should have seen my face when I looked at him. It would have made the toughest soldier retreat, but not King. He'd just narrow his eyes that way he does when he's daring you to try something." Red demonstrated, making Laz laugh. "'Course it's way scarier when he does it."

"See? You're thinking back on that time and found something to smile about. I can't begin to imagine what you went through, Red, but I can see that you put up one hell of a fight. You've come through the other side, and no, you're not cured, but you *are* a changed man. You're a far cry from the man who returned with so much anger in his heart. The Kings and the guys didn't give up on you, and neither will I."

It was very sweet of Laz to say, but it was one thing to hear about the effects of PTSD and another to experience it. King had known how to deal with Red, the same way he knew how to deal with the rest of their brothers. The man just had this sixth sense when it came to people. He had an innate talent for assessing people and situations, then taking the appropriate action.

King was also physically strong enough to subdue Red, and had on more than one occasion. Yet, Laz was the first person Red had been with who'd been so open and honest with him about his condition, who acknowledged that he wasn't perfect, that he wasn't completely whole, and that was okay.

"Thank you." Red kissed Laz, enjoying his warmth and affection. He'd never known anyone like Laz, and he hoped that whatever this was between them would continue to flourish into something wonderful. Red would certainly do his damned best to be everything Laz needed. When they came up for air, Red brushed his fingers down Laz's jaw. "But promise me that if it gets too much, you'll tell me."

"I promise." Laz took Red's hand in his and gave it a tug. "Come on. This time, *I'll* make *you* breakfast."

"Are you sure? I'm happy to cook." Red followed Laz's lead and pulled on his T-shirt before heading out of the bedroom.

"And I'm happy to have you cook your amazing food, but not this time. You're going to sit that fine butt down at the counter and let me cook for you for once."

"Fine butt, huh?" Red growled playfully as he nipped at Laz's neck, making him laugh. Yeah, he could easily get used to that laugh and the sweet open smile that followed. In truth, he could get used to all of Laz pretty quickly and happily.

# CHAPTER 7

Red's playful poking had Laz squirming, and when Red slid his fingers under Laz's T-shirt as they walked, Laz couldn't stop his snort-giggle. Normally he didn't like anyone tickling him, but Red was just so damned loveable that not only didn't he mind it, but Laz welcomed his touch.

"Oh my God, quit it."

Red let out a mock gasp. "Are you ticklish, Lazarus?"

"What gave me away?"

"Ooh, you're just full of sass, aren't you?"

They reached the kitchen, and Laz turned to face Red, stood on his toes, and nipped at Red's bottom lip. "I'd much rather be full of something else."

Jeez, what had gotten into him? Well, he knew what he wanted to get into him. He really needed to get ahold of himself, but being around Red made him feel kind of giddy, and now that he'd tasted Red, he wanted more. Something about Red made him feel so bold and confident. Was it because he felt safe with Red? Because he knew that Red would never purposefully hurt him or make him feel bad about himself?

Red groaned and made a grab for Laz, but Laz slipped from his grasp with a laugh, walking backward into the kitchen.

"Nice try, *Russell*."

"Little smart aleck."

"Sit that fine butt down while I whip us up some eggs Benedict. Do you like avocado?"

Red took a seat at the counter. "You kidding? Lucky would disown me if I didn't eat avocado. His mom serves it at every meal; I kid you not."

"His family's in Miami, right? Along with Ace's?"

"Yeah, they have a cousin who lives down there too. He's a SWAT officer. Actually, he's getting married in a few months. Maybe if you're not doing anything around that time you'd like to come?"

Laz paused halfway through opening the fridge door, his heart skipping a beat. "That depends."

"On?"

"Whether I'll be going as a friend or your date." Laz glanced at Red, holding back a smile at the way Red toyed with the fruit bowl in front of him, his cheeks flushed. Unlike Laz's skin that was a natural tan thanks to his Greek roots, Red's skin was exceptionally fair, which meant when he blushed, it was very evident, and gorgeous.

"I was, um, hoping you'd like to go as my date. If you want. No pressure. I don't want you to think you have to just because, um…. Crap. My God, could I be any more awkward?"

He really was too sweet. Laz smiled wickedly. "You mean because we got each other off?"

"Yeah, that," Red replied with a cough.

"Red?"

"Yes?"

Laz closed the fridge door, and Red swiveled his chair as Laz rounded the counter. He visibly braced himself as Laz put his hands on Red's knees and spread them before stepping in between his legs. He loved the man's strength, but mostly he loved how despite

Red's impressive physique, he was gentle and often uncertain, like he wasn't aware of how amazing he was.

"Were you under the impression I was all sweet and innocent?" Laz asked, slowly running his hands up Red's thighs. Red swallowed hard, and Laz slid his hands up and under Red's T-shirt.

"Well… not gonna lie, it kinda crossed my mind."

"Sweet, yes." Laz leaned in to brush his lips over Red's. "Innocent, not so much. Are you disappointed?"

"Disappointed?" Red's eyes darkened with want, and he slipped his fingers into Laz's hair, grabbing a fistful of it, his other hand taking hold of Laz's right hand and moving it over to the hard cock tenting his pants. "Does that feel like disappointment to you?"

Laz groaned. It most certainly did not. He loved how Red seemed incapable of not touching him, particularly his hair. "You know, at this rate we're never going to get anything done."

"Yeah, but on the other hand, sexy times."

"You make a very *solid*"—Laz stroked him through his pants, making Red release a growl that went straight to Laz's groin— "point." He pulled away and smiled at the little whimper Red let out.

"That's just mean."

"Aw, your pout is so cute."

"And yet…." Red motioned to his groin before swiveling back toward the front.

"Sorry-not-sorry." Laz laughed. "And yes. I would love to go with you to the wedding as your date." He got to work making them breakfast, noting the extra bounce in his step. It was sweet how Red couldn't help but try and join in the cooking, whether it was by offering to slice the avocado, or toast the English muffins, or stir the hollandaise sauce. In the end, Laz gave into the puppy eyes Ace was always going on about. He was going to be in big trouble if he didn't develop an immunity to that look. "While I put together our Bennies, how about you whip me up a cappuccino on Colton's fancy coffee machine and make yourself one of those fruit smoothies."

Red was out of his stool so fast Laz let out a snort of laughter. It was like Red had been relegated to the naughty step or something and his sentence was finally over. They moved around the kitchen together, and Laz could see himself doing this every morning. Red would most likely be making breakfast for them while Laz made their drinks as they prepared for the day ahead. They'd eat together, wash up, and then kiss goodbye, wishing the other a good day as they headed off.

*Whoa, it's a little early to be thinking about living together.*

As he set their plates down, it struck him that he'd been in a relationship for years with Bryan and they'd never moved in together. Bryan claimed he needed to recharge in his own space not clouded by someone else's energy, and since being around Bryan the majority of the day could get pretty draining, Laz had never complained. Had they ever truly been a happy couple? Maybe in the beginning, but what did it say about them that Laz had always been happy to return to his little apartment alone? Moving in together had never appealed to either of them.

And yet with Red, it wasn't just easy picturing them living together, but the thought made Laz happy. The idea of sleeping in the same bed with Red, of waking up next to him, lounging around the house with him, making meals together in their shared kitchen, it all appealed to Laz a great deal.

"What are you thinking?" Red asked as he placed Laz's coffee in front of him.

"Thank you. I, um, was just thinking about how comfortable I feel around you." He wasn't ready to admit he was thinking about them living together. The last thing he wanted was to freak Red out. Their relationship had only just changed, and even if it all felt so right, things were moving quickly as it was. He needed to slow his roll and not rush into anything.

Red's smile was stunning, and Laz might have let out a dreamy sigh because Red chuckled. "I feel comfortable around you too." He leaned in and kissed Laz. "Thank you for making breakfast."

"There's extra hollandaise sauce if you want it. I kinda like to drown my eggs in it."

"I'll remember that," Red said before taking a big bite of his breakfast and releasing a moan. Laz narrowed his eyes at him, and Red swallowed his mouthful before speaking up. "What?"

"I would like to get through breakfast without a boner, if that's okay with you."

Red let out a bark of laughter. It was rich, warm, and lit Laz up from the inside out. Laz had just taken a bite of his breakfast when Red let out a deep, rumble of a groan that went straight to Laz's dick.

"Oh, mmm, this is so good."

Laz tried his hardest not to laugh. He took a sip of his cappuccino, doing his best to ignore Red and his very not-food-related moans and groans, each one more exaggerated than the last.

"Okay there, Sally. The hollandaise sauce is good, but it ain't that good."

Red moaned. "I don't know. The way it goes down my throat is just so satisfying." Another decadent moan followed.

"Oh my God, stop making those noises," Laz said with a laugh. "Seriously, you and that poached egg want to get a room?" He bumped his leg into Red's, and Red bumped his back, making Laz snort. They were ridiculous. It occurred to him then that he'd never had this much fun at breakfast before, and certainly not after fooling around with someone. Probably because before Bryan, the guys Laz slept with never stuck around long enough to have breakfast. Man, what a sad state of affairs his love life had been. *Had.* Was it too much to hope for that things would be different with Red?

They stopped horsing around long enough to eat and finish their drinks. When Laz got up to clear the plates, Red stopped him.

"No, you cooked, so I'll wash up. That's the rule."

"Okay. I'm going to go grab my phone. I left it on your nightstand. Be right back."

"Could you grab mine too?"

"Sure."

Laz went upstairs, unable to help his dopey grin when he walked into the bedroom and his eyes landed on the unmade bed. Oh my God, he'd actually made the first move. It was so unlike him. When it came to dating, he was pretty oblivious. Bryan had teased him that he wouldn't know someone was flirting unless they dropped to their knees in front of him and gave him a blow job. Yeah, his ex-boyfriend was a real gem. He needed to stop thinking about Bryan, but it was hard to eliminate all thought of someone who'd had such an impact on his life, and not in a good way.

It was like Laz was slowly starting to find himself again after a long period of becoming everything someone else had wanted him to be. He'd lost himself. Everything he'd become had been what Bryan wanted, what would make Bryan happy, what wouldn't upset him. After grabbing his and Red's phones, Laz frowned as he headed back toward the kitchen. Somewhere along the way, he'd completely lost himself. He'd forgotten how good it felt to be important to someone, to have his needs considered and addressed.

Maybe he was getting ahead of himself. Red cared about him, but did he see Laz as someone who was important to him after only a few months of knowing each other? *Okay, stop overthinking everything.*

Downstairs, Red was loading the dishwasher, so Laz placed his phone on the counter for him.

"Thanks." Red smiled brightly at him, and Laz all but poured himself into one of the counter chairs. He was like a lovesick puppy. All he wanted was to climb Red like a tree, kiss him, and do all kinds of naughty things to him. Red's loose pajama bottoms hung low on his hips, the thin material falling oh so perfectly over the roundness of his ass. A soft laugh caught his ear, and Laz's head shot up, his face about to spontaneously combust.

"I am so sorry."

The twinkle in Red's eye was evil. "Sorry you were staring at my ass, or sorry you got caught?"

"Definitely the latter," Laz admitted, making Red laugh.

"Well, at least you're honest. I like that." Red dried his hands and came to stand in front of Laz. He turned Laz's chair toward him, and placed one hand on the counter so he could lean in, their lips all but touching. "That's not the only thing I like."

"Oh?" Laz hummed. "What other things do you like?"

Red brushed his lips over Laz's. "I like your curls and how soft your hair is." He slipped his free hand into Laz's hair and ran his fingers leisurely through it. "I like your lips." A barely there kiss touched Laz's lips, and Laz sighed. "I like your body and how it responds to my touch." Red pulled his fingers out from Laz's hair, and trailed them down Laz's arm, sending a shiver through him. Red's lips tugged at the corner in a smile. "I like the feel of your hands on me."

Laz didn't hesitate. He slid his hands beneath Red's T-shirt, caressing the muscles of his chiseled abs, loving the tremor that went through Red, and the little huff of air he released. Laz widened his legs so Red could step between them, and he melted against Red as Red brushed his lips first over Laz's cheek, delivering a feathery kiss before he placed a kiss to the tip of Laz's nose. He moved his lips back to Laz's while Laz trailed his fingers up Red's torso, loving the feel of him, the softness of his skin, the contours of his well-defined muscles. Laz wrapped his legs around Red, keeping him close as Red brought their mouths together, their kiss quickly turning needy and hot.

Red tugged Laz's shirt off him, dropping it to the floor. Red's shirt quickly followed. Cupping Laz's ass, Red jerked Laz against him, their hard cocks rubbing against each other through the thin fabric of their pajama bottoms. Laz couldn't get enough of Red, of his taste, his touch, the feel of that hard body against his own.

Red's mouth tasted like the fruit smoothie he'd had with breakfast, and Laz kissed him as if any minute now he might take his last breath, as if he were trying to imprint the taste of Red in his memory. Their bodies were pressed together, and Laz wrapped his arms around Red's neck, arching his back, offering himself to Red. Whatever Red wanted from him, Laz was willing to give, because he knew Red would give as good as he got. Everything Red did seemed geared toward giving Laz pleasure, while Laz wanted nothing more than to please him in return. He wanted to make Red feel so damned good he'd forget everything but the pleasure he was experiencing at that moment.

Laz squeezed his hand down between them and reached into Red's pants to pull out his big, thick cock. His thoughts went to earlier that morning when he'd had his lips wrapped around Red's gorgeous length. He used the pearls of precome at the tip to aid in the glide as he slowly stroked Red.

"Laz," Red gasped against Laz's mouth as their kissing grew more urgent, matching Laz's hand movements as he pumped Red's cock. Laz groaned when Red pushed Laz's pants down, and pulled his cock free then took them both in hand.

"Oh, yes. Make us both come, Red." It was like his body was on fire. A blazing inferno raged within him, all for Red. He couldn't remember the last time he felt like this, like his body couldn't contain the need. It was a little terrifying how powerful these feelings were. He kept telling himself to take it slow, not to let himself get swept up in a man who appeared to be everything he ever wanted, but couldn't possibly be. He was scared the bubble would burst. Scared he was right, and that Red was too good to be true. That it was all hot sex and sweet kisses now, and then later—

"Stay with me," Red breathed against his lips, and Laz sucked in a sharp breath. He let his head fall back, exposing his neck to Red's talented mouth, his body shivering with pleasure. He let himself get lost in the sensation of Red's firm grip on his dick, on the friction of their erections being stroked together. It was like he was going to crawl out of his skin with desire. Red thrust his hips over and over, and Laz dug his nails into the back of Red's shoulder, his breath hitching at the low growl Red released.

"Oh Fuck. I'm going to come, Red."

"Do it. Come for me, Laz. Come *with* me."

Red nipped at Laz's earlobe, and Laz thought he would shatter. He cried out as his orgasm flooded through him, his come forming a sticky mess over their abdomens. Red muffled his own cry against Laz's mouth, his release adding to the mess between them. He continued to stroke them until they were too sensitive. Little tremors shook Laz, and he let his head rest against Red's shoulder as his breath steadied.

"Are you okay?" Red asked softly.

Laz nodded. He felt boneless. "Can we just get back into bed and, like, never leave?"

Red chuckled. "We could, but then King would send Ace and Lucky to find out what happened to us, and that might get a little awkward. Also, Colton might wonder why I've suddenly taken up residence in his guest room."

Laz snickered before sitting back with a sigh. "You're right. Darn our meddlesome and loving families."

With a quick kiss to the lips, Red cleaned them up before swiping their shirts off the floor and handing Laz his.

"You know, if you wanted to keep yours off...." Laz shrugged nonchalantly. "I'm not against it. Just saying."

Red looked down at himself, then flexed, his pecs doing a little bounce. "You like?"

*Oh, hell yes.* He liked *a lot.* Laz nodded and trailed a finger down one of Red's bulging biceps. "I want to lick you like a Popsicle."

Red let out a bark of laughter, and Laz groaned.

"And I said that out loud, didn't I? Will you excuse me? I need to go into the living room and crawl under the couch or something until I have brain function again, so yeah, maybe you should put on your shirt because clearly all this," Laz said, motioning to Red's general muscleyness, "short circuits my brain."

"You're cute."

"I'm a weirdo."

"Then we'll be weirdos together." Red leaned in to murmur in his ear. "I would love for you to lick me all over."

Laz was about to volunteer a demonstration of his Popsicle-licking services when his phone rang. Damn it. He must have huffed or pouted or something, because Red chuckled as he put on his shirt. He stepped back into the kitchen to wipe down the counters.

"Hello?"

"Is this Lazarus Galanos?" A woman's voice chirped cheerfully from the other end of the line.

"Yes, speaking."

"Mr. Galanos, this is Ms. Vargas's assistant. I'm calling from *Único Lifestyle Magazine* about the editorial shoot you applied for. I'd like to apologize for taking this long to call you back. We had some scheduling issues with the designer we're interviewing for the article, but everything is back on track. Ms. Vargas was very impressed with your portfolio, and she'd love for you to come in for an interview. Really, it's more of a formality. She's interested in hiring you for the job, but she always has to meet the photographer first to get a feel for them and what it will be like to work with them on the project. Are you still interested?"

Laz didn't even think about it. "Yes, of course! When would you like me to come in?" He was aware of Red's gaze on him, and when he glanced up, he was surprised by the worry he saw. He offered Red a reassuring smile, and Red visibly relaxed, returning Laz's smile, then resumed cleaning up.

"How does next Thursday at 10:00 a.m. sound?"

"I'll be there. Are you able to tell me who the designer is that I'd be working with?"

"I'm sorry. The designer is very adamant we keep that information confidential until the shoot is over. They're hoping to avoid being hounded by the press."

"Of course. I understand. I'll see you Thursday. Thank you so much." Laz hung up, and Red laughed at the happy dance Laz did before he let out a loud whoop. He couldn't believe they'd called him. After not hearing back from them for several months, he figured he wasn't what they were looking for. It was hard to know whether his style would be a good fit when the magazine was keeping the name of the designer under wraps, but he'd submitted his portfolio anyway.

"Good news?" Red asked, drying his hands on a dish towel.

"Great news!" Laz ran over and hugged him. He was so excited. "I got called in for an interview with the editor of *Único Lifestyle*

*Magazine.* I applied months ago for an editorial shoot. The magazine is doing an article on a huge fashion designer, and although I didn't know the designer, whoever it was would be important, since the magazine was keeping it all under wraps. Anyway, the editor loved my portfolio and thinks I'll be a great fit for the shoot. They want me to come in next Thursday." He needed to calm down. "I mean, it's not a done deal. There's still the interview, and after talking with me, Ms. Vargas might decide I'm not a good fit after all."

"Would a lot of photographers have applied?"

"Oh God, yeah. The magazine's one of Florida's biggest fashion magazines. The number of applicants must have been huge. Why the hell would they have picked me?"

"That's just it, Laz. Out of all those photographers, they called *you*. That's fantastic!"

Laz's smile was so wide, his face was starting to hurt. He probably looked like a crazy person, but he didn't care. They'd called him back. "I can't believe it."

"I can," Red said, smiling at him. "You're incredibly talented. Congratulations. I'm very proud of you." Red squeezed him tight, and Laz felt his cheeks flush hot. It was stupid, but hearing those words come from Red made his heart so happy, because he knew Red meant it. He was genuinely proud.

"Thank you."

Red hugged him tight, and Laz allowed himself to bask in Red's warm embrace. They hadn't been like that very long before Red's phone went off. It would seem the outside world had found them once again.

"I better get that." Red released him and picked up his phone, the smile dropping from his face. "It's Mason."

Which meant possible news on Laz's case. For a moment, he'd forgotten about the reason they were here together under the same roof.

"Hey, Mason, how are you? I've got Laz here. Okay, one sec." Red tapped his phone, then rounded the counter and placed the phone between himself and Laz. "Mason, you're on speaker with me and Laz."

"Hi, Mason," Laz greeted. "How are you?"

"Could be better, to be honest. How are you two doing?"

"Good. I'm guessing you have news?"

"Yeah, I wish it was better news, but we keep hitting a load of dead ends. We questioned everyone who was at the beach and got nothing. Colton gave King permission to forward the list of Bryan's friends who were in attendance the day of the party when you both argued, and we brought everyone in for questioning. Now, I'm gonna say this to you because we're friends. Those boys are all hats and no cattle."

Red snickered, and Laz snorted out a laugh. He didn't know exactly what that meant, but considering Mason was talking about Bryan's friends, it wasn't difficult to figure out.

"Most exhausting four hours of my fucking life. Pardon my French. If Bryan is anything like the gaggle of airheads he hangs around with, then you are better off without him. One of them asked me if he could touch my gun. I shit you not. I swear, I have never seen anything like it. Anyway, sorry, getting off topic there. I'm still a little traumatized by the whole experience. We were hoping to have questioned Bryan and Mr. Vicente by now, but unfortunately that's going to have to wait as they're both out of the country."

"That's some coincidence," Red drawled.

"My guess is Bryan and Mr. Vicente are still having an affair, and you know what that means."

"Either Mr. Vicente isn't aware of the photographs," Red offered, "or he isn't threatened by them."

"The fact those two are out of the country isn't looking good for them," Mason said.

"Yeah, but Bryan had that shoot in Madrid booked months ago, back when we were still together." Mason's words sank in, and Laz gritted his teeth. *That fucker!* "Wait, you said Paolo's out of the country as well. Let me guess. They're in the same city."

Mason released a heavy sigh. "You would be correct. But even if Bryan booked his trip months ago, it does not negate the fact he could have taken the opportunity to make a move on you. I'm also concerned by Paolo's travel itinerary. Or should I say itineraries."

Laz's eyes went slightly wide. "Itineraries?"

"Paolo has travel arrangements for two cities during the same two-week period. He flew to Paris with his wife and will be flying back with his wife, but he has a luxury hotel booked in Madrid as well as other services. It would appear that those were paid for with his personal bank account, whereas the Paris trip was all paid for by his wife."

"They're still seeing each other." Laz had been right. He let out a snort of disgust.

"Which makes me think that neither man sees you as a threat. Now whether that's because they believe you won't go public with those photos or because one of them—or both—have decided to take you out of the equation remains to be seen. I'll be bringing them in for questioning the moment they get back. In the meantime, I'll keep looking into Paolo. If the man's hiding a secret lover, what else might he be hiding?"

"Thank you, Mason," Laz said.

"I'll keep you fellas in the loop."

"We appreciate that," Red replied. After thanking him, they said their goodbyes, and Red hung up. He turned to Laz. "Are you okay?"

Laz frowned. "What do you mean?"

"It looks like Bryan and Paolo are still involved."

"Bryan's not my problem anymore. If he wants to risk his career by continuing an affair with Elena's husband, then that's on him. I'm not surprised. It just confirms what I suspected all along. If I'd let him convince me to stay, believed him when he said he was going to change, he'd still be seeing Paolo behind my back, swearing he wasn't cheating on me." Laz shook his head. "I'm still not convinced either of them had anything to do with what happened on the beach, though." The idea that Bryan would somehow have found a way to hire someone to kill him was laughable.

"Well, we'll leave that up to Mason." Red stood and stretched, his muscles bunching and shifting beneath his T-shirt. "I think I'm going to hit Colton's gym for a while."

"I have those photos to finish editing." Laz looked out past the dining room and the wall of floor to ceiling windows. "It's gorgeous out there. I think I'm going to take my laptop out on the porch and do some work there. Do you think it's safe?"

Red nodded. "There's nothing but beach and ocean for miles, and we've got guys all around the property in case anyone tries to hide in the greenery on either side of the house. I won't be long, but if you need anything, just shout for me, okay?"

"Sure." Laz went upstairs to his room to change. He didn't want to lounge in his pajamas all day, so he pulled on a pair of long shorts and a T-shirt, slipped on some flip-flops, and grabbed his laptop. Colton's house was amazing. If Laz was going to be stuck indoors for a while, being relegated to Colton's beach mansion was hardly a chore. He loved Colton's house. It was huge, with two-and-a-half floors, wrapping verandas, tall ceilings, filled with light, wide open spaces, and most of all, it was wonderfully peaceful. The bedrooms were upstairs, while the game room, home gym, kitchen, dining room, living room, and movie room were downstairs. The pool and cabanas were located at the back of the house, along with a small helicopter landing pad, and beyond that, a private walkway led down to the beach. It was a far cry from Laz's cramped little studio apartment.

After college, Gio had tried setting Laz up in a one-bedroom apartment on the beach, knowing it was Laz's dream to wake up every morning, step out onto his balcony, and see nothing but miles and miles of ocean water shimmering beneath the Florida sun, but Laz wasn't about to live off his brother's hard-earned money. Gio sacrificed so much for his career. While guys his age were out enjoying their youth, getting drunk, going clubbing, getting laid, Gio had been building his life's work from the ground up, making a name for himself while also raising Laz. Gio paid for Laz to attend college and helped pay for half his equipment, while Colton paid the other half. The least Laz could do was pave his own path and make them proud of the man he'd become.

For Laz, Giovanni Galanos was his big brother. To the rest to the world, Gio was a rising star. When his charity work hit headlines, he'd been named one of the world's most influential philanthropists. Gio was also a private person. Despite his wealth, he wasn't flashy or frivolous. Instead, he used his money to help others, and he was always trying to help Laz, not because he didn't think Laz could take care of himself, but because they were family. Gio loved him and wanted him to be happy, but he'd already done so much for Laz.

Laz wanted to show his brother that everything he'd sacrificed had paid off. For now, Laz's dream of living on the beach would have to wait. He settled at the table out on the veranda and got to work touching up his photos, getting them ready for his client. He'd just finished touching up the last one when his phone rang. He smiled wide as he answered.

"Hey, Fitz."

"Hey, cutie. How are you?"

Laz hated the worry he heard in Fitz's tone, seeing as how he was the cause of it. The previous night, he'd called Fitz just before going to bed, and his friend had been beside himself with worry. It had taken Laz over an hour to calm him down and convince him that he was fine.

"I'm doing great. Sitting out on Colton's veranda, listening to the waves crash on the beach."

"That sounds heavenly. You sound better. I'm glad."

"Thanks. You know Colton's house is like a second home. Can't believe I stayed away for so long." Laz had loved coming to visit Colton, but it had been nearly impossible with Bryan, who behaved liked a spoiled brat whenever they visited. Bryan wouldn't allow Laz to come on his own, but then when he accompanied Laz, he spent the entire visit bitching and whining about how bored he was. Colton had put up with it for Laz's sake, but after several disastrous visits, Laz decided he couldn't put Colton through that anymore, so he'd stayed away.

"Me neither, but let's not talk about Miss Thing. What I want to hear about is you and your sexy redhead."

Laz laughed. "What about us?"

"Oh, no. Don't you even think about it. I want details. For example, are certain things in proportion to the rest of him?"

"He is… not a small man." The screech of joy Fitz let out made Laz laugh, and he loved to hear the excitement and happiness in his friend's voice. Fitz was the suffer-in-silence type. Unless he was angry, then there was nothing silent about him, but when he was deeply hurt, he preferred to act like it was no big deal when Laz knew that wasn't the case.

"Well, don't stop there. Come on. I want to live vicariously through you. Was the sex out of this world?"

"Who said we've had sex?"

Fitz snorted. "Please. You just said he's not a small man, so unless he flashed his junk at you, or you perved on him when he wasn't looking, you two got up close and personal."

"Did we get up close and personal?" Laz paused, knowing it drove Fitz crazy. After several frustrated grunts, and a little whine, Laz decided to put Fitz out of his misery. "Yes. This morning in bed. Then the shower. Then the kitchen." His faced flushed, and hurt from smiling so much. "I don't know what it is, Fitz, but the guy just presses *all* my buttons. I'm such a slut for him."

"Oh my God! Laz, honey, I'm so happy for you!"

Laz laughed at Fitz's enthusiasm. He hadn't realized how much he'd missed Fitz until now. Fitz had been another casualty of the destructive force that had been Bryan. Laz had been so stupid. He'd allowed himself to lose so many good friends. All for that selfish asshole. "It's just sex, Fitz, not a marriage proposal."

"Don't act like he's just some random dude you hooked up with in one of the backrooms at Sapphire Sands."

"No, of course not. Red's…."

"Special."

"You think so?"

"Honey, I know so. The way that man looks at you?" Fitz let out a dreamy sigh. "We should all be so lucky."

"Oh? And what about Jack? How did he look at you?"

The silence that followed went on for so long Laz thought maybe the call had been disconnected.

"Fitz?"

"Hm?"

Laz sat up with a gasp. "Oh no you don't, hussy. You don't get to 'hm' me like I don't know what I'm talking about. Lucky told me all about your little moment with Jack."

"It wasn't a moment," Fitz said casually. "He was nice."

"Nice? You know, I don't think I have ever heard that word come from your mouth."

"Shut up."

"Talk to me, Fitz. What happened?"

"Fine. I was freaking out because not only had some crazy person been shooting a gun, but apparently he'd been shooting at *you*. I didn't know where you were, and I kind of lost my shit a little bit. Lucky was trying to calm me down, but I was just spiraling. I thought I was going to have a panic attack. Then this guy steps out of the passenger side of this flashy convertible, and it's like everything stopped. I don't know what the hell was going on, but all I could see was him. He was beautiful, but a different kind of beautiful. I don't even know how to describe it. I mean, he looks just like a regular guy, nothing special, dark hair and stubble, but something about him…．

"It was his smile. It was just so sweet and genuine. He's got these amazing gray eyes, and when he saw me, he smiled, and it was like everything made sense. Everything about him is just…. God, I don't know. Even the way he walks, like he's so unassuming you would never guess he'd been a Green Beret, but the man was Special Forces, for crying out loud. Then he talked to me, and his voice, holy fuck, I thought I was gonna come in my pants right then and there. It was like the world slowed down and I could breathe again."

"Jesus, Fitz." Laz's jaw had all but hit the floor. He'd never heard Fitz talk about any guy the way he'd just talked about Jack. "What happened after?"

"He was so sweet and kind, Laz. You should have seen me. I was like a freakin' bobblehead. All I could do was nod. He probably thought I was like those vapid airheads. I couldn't string two words together to save my life." Fitz groaned. "It was so embarrassing. I bet he thinks I'm a moron."

"No. I'm sure he thought you were just shaken up by the whole thing, which you were. I'm sorry for worrying you. Are you going to talk to him again?"

"Why?" Fitz sounded startled.

"*Why*? Because of everything you just said. As far as I know he's single, so why not?"

"Please, a guy like that has no interest in a guy like me."

Laz frowned at that. "Why not? What's wrong with a guy like you? You're talented, gorgeous, smart, and successful. He'd be crazy not to be interested in you. I really hope you're not about to give me some silly spiel on how you're not good enough, because then by that account Red is too good for me, and we talked about this, didn't we? We both deserve better."

"But I turn into such a bumbling asshat around the guy. Will you stand next to me when I talk to him and, like, help me do the words and things?"

Laz chuckled. He could almost hear Fitz pouting. "Because I am such a smooth operator."

"Hey, you landed yourself some prime beefcake, so you gotta have some game."

"Was that a compliment, because I'm not so sure."

Fitz laughed. "So you'll be my wingman on Saturday?"

"What are you talking about? What's happening Saturday?"

"The 20th Annual Orlando Fabulous Fashion Charity Gala."

"Oh, I, um, didn't get an invite, and the tickets are out of my price range." The whole point of ticket sales to the event was to raise money, and as much as Laz would have loved to be a part of that, he couldn't justify that big of an expense right now. Mostly, because there weren't enough zeroes in his bank account.

"But you're going because you're my plus one."

Laz bolted upright. "What?"

"You heard me, boo. So dust off that sexy suit and get ready for a night of schmoozing and boozing."

"Oh my God, Fitz I don't know what to say. Wait, I can't leave Red." As excited as he was about the opportunity, there was no way Red would want Laz out there unprotected.

"Don't you worry, your man's already on the list."

"He is?"

"Well, yeah. He might not know it, though, since he's still off duty, but his company is the one handling security for the event."

"That's great!" It struck him then. If the Kings were handling security.... "Wait a second. Since when are you excited about schmoozing? Normally you just drink, people watch, gossip, and go home."

It was a great networking opportunity, and the event benefited a great cause, but neither he nor Fitz were big party people. They tended to mingle, chat, stay a while, then sneak away the moment everyone started having a little *too* much fun. Bryan would make fun of him for being such a "grandma," but he never complained about Laz leaving since it meant he could get up to whatever he wanted unsupervised, and that suited Bryan just fine.

"I'm trying to expand my horizons."

That had Laz cracking up. "Oh my God, you are so full of shit!"

"Whatever," Fitz huffed.

"You're excited because Jack is going to be there."

"Nobody likes a know-it-all, Lazarus."

Laz cackled. He loved teasing Fitz. Though in reality he was happy Fitz was moving on from that lying asshole, Jiles. Fitz was a good man. He deserved to find his Prince Charming, or in the case of Jack, a knight.

"I love you, Fitz. I know I don't say it enough, and I'm sorry I was away for so long, but I just wanted to tell you that."

"Aw, boo, I love you too. I'm glad to have you back. I missed my bestie."

"I missed you too." For the first time in forever, Laz felt truly happy. Like his life was finally on track after he'd taken that wrong turn and gotten so epically lost. He couldn't wait to see where this new path led him. Wherever it was, he hoped it included Red.

# CHAPTER 8

Red was torn.

On the one hand, he was extremely happy for Laz. The fancy charity event they were attending was a fantastic opportunity, giving Laz the chance to mingle with big names in the fashion industry who he might not have had a chance to meet otherwise, and it was clear from the moment Laz stepped into the room, that he was going to be a hit. He was gorgeous, charming, yet sweet, genuine, and kind. His smile lit up the room, and everyone he spoke to seemed enchanted by him.

On the other hand, the last few days with Laz had been amazing, and Red wished they were back in Colton's house making out on the couch while watching one of Laz's ridiculous movies or cheesy TV shows. After Red's workout at the gym on Wednesday, he'd showered, then joined Laz outside on the balcony. They'd talked for hours before going for a walk on the beach, a walk that ended in Red chasing Laz, and both of them stumbling into the crashing waves. They'd laughed and kissed. It had been perfect.

When Laz brought up the charity gala, Red hadn't been thrilled about him being out in such a public venue, but he understood what the event could mean for Laz and his career. When Laz explained the Kings would be providing security for the event, Red felt better about it, but he needed to speak to King first and let him know Laz would be attending. If the Kings were working security and Laz was going to be there, it would have an impact on whatever security plan had been devised for the event. King hadn't been thrilled either, and as Red suspected, the security would have to be reconsidered, what with the possibility of a threat following Laz. But King assured them he'd make the necessary changes. He would do everything in his power to make sure Laz was safe while at the gala. Of course no plan was a hundred percent foolproof, not when you were dealing with the public.

The Kings could put together the most sound security plan possible and have it all fall apart because one person decided to make a change they believed was insignificant. They always tried to have a contingency plan in place, and if all hell broke loose, they fell back on their military training to ensure everyone made it out safely.

Just recently, Joker worked personal security for a famous pop singer on tour, several stops of which were in cities around the state of Florida. She traveled with a stylist, which was common. However, on the day of the singer's Tampa concert, the singer's usual stylist—who'd been vetted and cleared by Joker—never showed up, but a replacement did. Joker instructed the singer to stay put in her dressing room and not leave until he looked into the matter. Protocol dictated that Joker keep the client and possible threat as far away from each other as physically possible until one or the other could be removed. Until the stylist was cleared, Joker had her placed in the farthest room away from the singer.

With only minutes until the singer was supposed to be on stage, she panicked, lied to the security detail outside her dressing room, and gave them the slip. She burst into the room with the stylist, demanding Joker release the woman because her hair needed attention immediately. While the singer threw an epic tantrum, called Joker names that would make a hardened criminal blush, and tried to sucker-punch him, the stylist—who was actually a crazed fan—tried to stab the singer. Had the singer gotten her way, or Joker not been there to disarm the fan so quickly and efficiently, things could have ended very badly. All because one person didn't stick to the plan or do as they were told. Sadly, that one person was often the person they'd either been hired by or for.

Once they'd gotten the okay from King for Laz to attend, the next two days had been just as blissful as the previous, and they'd fallen into a routine Red could easily grow accustomed to. Laz worked on a few smaller freelance jobs that involved photo retouching. He updated his online portfolio, and took some stunning photos of the beach at different times of the day, along with what he said was called macro photography, which Red found fascinating. He'd listened intently as Laz explained all the different pieces of equipment he used on a shoot at any given time. They'd spent the rest of the day cooking for each other, walking on the beach, or exploring each other's bodies, both enjoying the slow, delicious torture of getting to know every inch of each other. This was the first time in days where they'd had any interaction with the outside world.

The fashion charity event was taking place in a fancy studio in Orlando. Joker, Lucky, and Jack had been sent along with dozens of the company's armed and unarmed security officers. Thankfully, the layout made everyone's job easier as it was just a huge rectangle with a few smaller areas and only two exits, one on each side of the structure. Red could easily keep an eye on Laz as Laz and Fitz worked the room. The fashion portion of the evening had been in the main part of the studio, which was the largest, then the guests moved to the reception area where the party was. Other than those two areas, there was a private section for the organizers behind a white brick wall in the main area, and next to that, a green room. The equipment room, like every other space, had been checked and rechecked by the Kings, then locked.

Red tugged at the tie around his neck. "Stupid tie," he grumbled to himself. This was hardly the first occasion that called for him to be in a suit, but he preferred his work attire, or his T-shirts, and cozy yoga pants to a suit and tie, unlike Lucky who was making his way toward Red, strutting like he'd been born to wear Armani. Lucky moved gracefully and confidently, his head held high like he belonged there, and he fit in perfectly with the crowd of pretty people. Red had no idea how Lucky did it. The suit made Red feel boxed in, like his clothes restricted his movements.

"Hey, Red. You doing okay?"

"Yeah, thanks. Just feeling a little… crowded."

"If you want to go, I can look after Laz. It's not a problem."

"No, I'm good. If I change my mind, I'll let you know. I appreciate it, though."

Lucky nodded. He worried his bottom lip, then let out a sigh. "Listen, I'm sorry about blowing up at you like I did the other day. I got some things I need to work through, and I didn't mean to take it out on you. You know I love you, bro."

"I love you too. I'm sorry I got defensive and started poking you."

"Eh, speaking of poking…." Lucky waggled his eyebrows. "How are things with you and Laz?"

Red shook his head with a chuckle. "They're good. He's going to be my date to your cousin's wedding down in Miami."

"That's fantastic, Red! Good for you. I'm so happy for you, man. I really am." Lucky touched his ear piece, and Red knew he was about to be called away. "I have to go. There's a couple of drunk models trying to break into the equipment room. Probably trying to find a place to, you know."

"Resist the temptation," Red whispered loudly as Lucky walked away, earning himself the middle finger and making him laugh.

Big parties were never his thing. He preferred small intimate get-togethers to loud gatherings with hundreds of guests. He felt self-conscious standing in the large room filled with beautiful people. This type of event wasn't new to him. As a King, he'd worked security for even bigger events, but this time, he was seeing it through a different lens, one he would have to grow accustomed to if he wanted to be a part of Laz's life. This was Laz's world. These were the people he was constantly surrounded by. People with flawless skin, perfect teeth, and slinky figures, with legs that went on for miles.

Red felt a little like a bull in an antique shop. Every time he turned around, he was apologizing for bumping into someone. They weren't rude about it, but he just felt so out of place. He wasn't the tallest in the room, but he was certainly the widest. He'd also noticed he wasn't the only redhead with prominent freckles, but those redheads were stunning creatures. Not that he had a problem with his looks, it was just all so… intimidating. Maybe because they all seemed so comfortable in their own skin, and as he wasn't here on official duty, he couldn't hide behind his tactical uniform and the Four Kings Security crest.

Red had been nursing the same glass of champagne for over an hour now. Mostly, he just needed something to do with his hands. He wasn't a big drinker, much less a champagne drinker. He stood to one side, monitoring the room, his eyes always returning to Laz. He smiled to himself when he thought about how sweet Laz had been when they'd arrived. Red had told him he was going to check in with the guys and that Laz should do his thing. His pout had been adorable. He hadn't wanted to leave Red, but Laz was here to mingle and network, and Red didn't want to get in the way of that. It was childish, but a part of him thought he'd be forgotten once Laz started rubbing elbows with all the big names, but his stomach filled with butterflies when he realized that was not the case at all.

After conversing for a while, Laz would excuse himself and search out Red. Then he'd come over and stake his claim by kissing Red, not caring who saw. They'd gotten plenty of intrigued looks, but Laz didn't seem to notice. He'd say something sweet to Red, touch his arm, brush some nonexistent lint off his shoulder or smooth down his shirt, as if letting everyone know Red was his. Red *really* liked it.

As if sensing Red was thinking of him, Laz lifted his gaze, his eyes meeting Red's from across the room. He said something to Fitz and the women they were talking to before he headed straight for Red. In a room full of beautiful people, none of them could hold a candle to Laz. The slim-fitting, navy three-piece suit looked incredible on him, the color making his eyes pop, but it was his smile that stole Red's breath away. It was a smile that was just for him.

Laz stopped in front of Red and smiled up at him. "Hi."

"Hi," Red replied, breathless. Everything faded into the background—the hip music, the chattering, the people, anything that wasn't the beautiful man standing in front of him. "Having a good time?"

"I am, though if I'm honest, it's not really my scene. It's part of the job, though."

"Really?" That was a surprise. Laz seemed to be having a great time, but then the smile he had for those people was different from the one he had for Red. It was still friendly and warm, and he gave each person his undivided attention, but it couldn't compare with the smile he had only for Red. His eyes didn't light up with affection or need, the way they did when his gaze was aimed at Red.

"Don't get me wrong, I know how lucky I am to be here right now, and I'm grateful to Fitz for inviting me, but… do you want to know a secret?"

Red leaned in and smiled. "Always."

Laz moved in close, his lips inches from Red's. "I'd rather be home watching Netflix. Preferably with a big, strong, handsome redhead wrapped around me."

Red's smile couldn't get any wider. "As long as I get to be that redhead." He placed his fingers under Laz's chin, tipping his head up so he could look into his dazzling blue eyes. "What do you say? Netflix and chill with me?"

Laz threw his head back with a laugh, little creases forming at the corners of his eyes before he brushed his lips over Red's. "Only you. You look amazing, by the way. Is it wrong that all I want to do is get you out of this suit?"

"Either kiss already or go find a room before you turn into the next floor show."

Red straightened, aware of several pairs of eyes on them, some looking a little too interested. He turned his attention back to Laz and their newest arrival. Joker. His friend was stylishly disheveled as usual. Most people thought Joker worked hard to look like he'd just rolled out of bed, but fun fact: he most likely *had* just rolled out of bed. Joker did a lot of the evening and party events for the Kings, and once the event was over, the party usually continued.

Lucky might be the playboy of the group, but Joker was the wild child. Whenever King asked him if he ever planned on becoming an adult, Joker replied he was just living up to his namesake. Sacha "Joker" Wilder was the same age as Red, but he'd always been the smallest of the group at five foot seven and a hundred and forty five pounds. His face sported permanent scruff because the last time he shaved he got carded buying alcohol. He had the most expressive eyebrows of anyone Red had ever known, and his pale blue-gray eyes reflected a sharp mind that belied his aloof and unruly demeanor. Behind that wicked smile lay a fiery temperament many had tried, and failed, to tame.

"What is up with your hair?" Red asked with a laugh, tugging at a lock that had fallen over his brow. "You do own a brush, right?"

Joker playfully swatted his hand away. "It does what it wants, man."

Much like a certain disheveled someone.

Red shook his head in amusement before turning to Laz. "Laz, this troublemaker is Joker. Joker, this is Laz."

Laz smiled brightly and held his hand out to Joker, who shook it. "It's so nice to finally meet you. The guys are always talking about you."

"Uh-oh." Joker's wide smile turned wicked, and he waggled his eyebrows. "It's all true."

"Should have known you'd be here," Red teased.

"Of course. You know King hates anything frivolous and fun," Joker said, his gaze following a long-legged male model who sauntered by. He didn't say a word, but he didn't have to. It was written all over his face.

"You're on the job, remember?"

"Doesn't mean a man can't peruse the menu before the feast."

Red shook his head. God only knew who—or how many—he'd end up going home with this time. Joker refused to be defined by any labels. He did what he wanted, when he wanted, with whom he wanted, and if someone didn't like it, that was on them. He certainly wasn't going to lose any sleep over it.

"There you are, Laz." Fitz appeared, taking hold of Laz's arm and hiding behind him, or at least attempting to, since Fitz was several inches taller than Laz. "Please, save me from the Bennett twins."

*Here we go.*

"Twins?" Joker was suddenly on high alert as he scanned the floor for said twins. At hearing his voice, Fitz stepped out from behind Laz, his smile wide.

"Oh, hey. Joker, right?"

"That's right," Joker beamed brightly. "Nice to see you again, Fitz."

"You remembered."

"Of course. Jack was asking about you."

Fitz's cheeks turned a lovely shade of pink. "He was?"

"Yeah, he was worried. Wanted to know how you were holding up." Joker leaned in, talking quietly. "I'll make you a deal. You introduce me to the Bennett twins, and I'll give you the name of his favorite coffee place. If you should happen to bump into him one morning around 7:00 a.m. when he's getting his morning espresso, then…." Joker shrugged.

Fitz worried his bottom lip between his teeth when Laz nudged him with his elbow and motioned toward Joker.

"Deal." Fitz looped his arm around Joker's and winked at Laz before they took off in search of the Bennett twins, both whispering to each other conspiratorially. Something told Red that Jack was going to have his hands full with those two.

Someone waved to Laz, and he smiled cheerfully, returning their wave. They motioned him over, and Laz seemed reluctant to leave.

"Go on. Go be your awesome self. I'll be right here."

"Are you sure?" Laz asked worriedly.

"Positive. Knock their socks off."

Laz's smile was dazzling, and Red knew he'd done the right thing. With a quick but sweet kiss, Laz went off. Red would have loved to spend time with him, but that's not why Laz was here. Every event he went to was a step closer to his dream, and Red wanted to do everything in his power to help Laz achieve that dream.

Red checked in with Ace, Lucky, and Joker throughout the night in case they needed anything, but mostly he stayed close to Laz. Not enough where he was intruding or where someone would wonder why he was stalking Laz. He'd managed to swap his champagne for some water, and ate a couple of the very delicious appetizers on offer. It would seem Ace wasn't the only one with terrible timing. He'd just stuffed a caramelized onion and pear tart in his mouth when a young man in a long silk dressing gown of sorts, sauntered up to him.

"I remember you. You're one of the Kings."

Red nodded as he chewed, giving an apologetic smile. The guy didn't seem to notice. He smiled brightly at Red.

"I was at Colton's house the day of Laz's party."

Red swallowed and took a sip of his water. "Hi. Sorry, I had a mouth full of tart."

"Mm, lucky tart."

Red almost choked on his water. Was the guy flirting?

"I'm Adonis." He held out a slim hand to Red as if he expected Red to kiss it. With a bemused smile, Red shook his hand. The only models who had been at Colton's house the day of the party were Bryan's friends.

"It's nice to meet you, um, Adonis." Was that his real name? Didn't matter. Red needed to excuse himself. What he'd seen from Bryan's friends that day of the party had disgusted him. Although their loyalty to Bryan was commendable, they were mean, spiteful people. Red didn't understand it. How could someone live that way? Did hurting others truly make them feel good? He tried not to judge because everyone had their demons and one never knew the battle another human being was fighting inside, but he hoped that at some point they realized that taking their hurt and anger out on others wasn't good for their body or soul. He hoped one day they found peace within themselves.

Adonis was over six feet tall, slender, with high cheekbones, big green eyes, white hair, and pink pouting lips covered in lip gloss. He also seemed unaware of personal boundaries as he all but draped himself over Red. He ran a finger down Red's chest. "You were so heroic that day. The way you just dove in to save that clumsy Laz."

"He wasn't clumsy," Red said with a frown. "He slipped because he was pushed."

Adonis pouted. "Bryan was just upset. He's such a sensitive soul. His passion sometimes clouds his judgment."

*Is that what we're calling it?* Red was pretty sure Adonis was confusing passion for something far uglier.

"But he didn't mean to hurt Laz. He loved Laz. Did everything to help him, even got him invited to Fashion Week in Paris. And how does Laz repay him? He breaks up with him."

Red gently removed Adonis from his person. "I'm pretty sure there's more to that story." He was hardly about to talk about Laz or his relationship with Bryan while Laz wasn't around. "It was really nice to meet you, Adonis. I should probably—"

Adonis flung himself at Red and kissed him.

*What the ever loving....*

Red quickly moved Adonis away from him. "What are you doing?"

"Come on, handsome. Why waste your time with that boring nobody when you can have this?" Adonis brushed his fingers down his chest where his robe had come undone. He took a step toward Red, and Red took one back. "How about you take me into the green room, bend me over, and fuck my brains out? I *love* big cock. The bigger, the better."

"Um, how about no?" The last thing Red wanted was to cause a scene, but Adonis was very mistaken if he thought he could just waltz up to Red and get away with whatever it was he thought he could get away with. Red took another step back, coming up against a wall.

"Are you telling me you'd rather have sloppy seconds than this?" Adonis crowded Red and grabbed his wrists, intent on moving Red's hands to his ass. Red jerked his arms away.

"You need to walk away. Now," Red growled. He was not fucking around. "Whatever it is you're trying to get me to do is not happening. So you need to leave before—"

"Before what?" Adonis challenged before licking his lips.

"Before I kick your ass."

Red turned, his heart doing a little flip at the sight of Laz. Ooh, Laz was not happy.

Laz marched up to Adonis and put himself between Adonis and Red. "What the hell do you think you're doing?"

"Didn't take you long, did it?" Adonis sneered. "The second you kicked Bryan to the curb, you gave your ass to Big Red over here."

"What I do and with whom is none of your business." Laz shook his head in disgust. "What? So you thought you'd just throw yourself at my guy?"

*My guy.* A shiver went through Red at the declaration. God, he wanted nothing more than to be Laz's guy.

Adonis shrugged. "I was offering him an upgrade."

"Oh fuck off, *Richard.*"

Adonis stomped his foot, and Red couldn't believe it. The guy had seriously just stomped his foot.

"Wait, your name is Richard?"

Laz let out a cute little snort. "Yeah. His agent made him change it."

"Fuck you, Lazarus. You were never good enough for Bryan. What makes you think you're good enough for him?" Adonis— Richard—spat out, motioning toward Red. "He's just going to use you like every other guy until something better comes along, because you're the in-between guy. You're talentless trash, and the only way you can get anything in this industry is by giving up that ass."

Before Laz could lunge at Richard, Red pulled Laz behind him. He towered over Richard, his voice menacing. "You come anywhere near Laz again, and I'll have you arrested for harassment." Looking up, Red quickly caught Ace's gaze and motioned him over. Seeing Ace cutting through the crowd had Lucky joining them.

"Everything okay?" Ace asked, looking from Red to Richard and back.

"No. Escort *Adonis* here from the property and make a note of his details. If he comes near Laz again, I'll be pressing charges."

Ace turned to Richard. "Please come with us. We'll help you get your things and walk you out."

"Just how many Kings did you fuck, Laz?" Richard spat out. He continued to spit venom at Laz as he walked away. "Doesn't matter how much your suit cost or how well you clean up, you're always going to be gutter trash, Lazarus!"

"Hey, how about you be quiet and walk," Lucky growled. "Or I will personally call in someone much scarier to escort you away in handcuffs, and believe me, those cuffs you will not like."

When they were gone, Red pulled Laz into his arms, turning him so he faced away from the crowd. There was no way some of the guests hadn't heard the vileness Richard had spewed. Laz was so angry he was all but vibrating in Red's arms.

"Hey, look at me."

Laz's eyes grew glassy, and he shook his head, his lips pulled tight in a thin line.

"Talk to me, sweetheart. Don't shut me out."

"I really wanted to punch him in the face. You should have let me."

Red sighed. "I know, baby, but then we'd be letting him win. All people would know is that you punched him, and he'd spin that story to his advantage. I wasn't going to let him damage your reputation. You've worked too hard." Laz smiled up at him, his face lit up with joy. "What?"

"You called me baby."

Red blinked at him. "I did, didn't I?"

Laz nodded. His expression turned serious. "We need to go. Right now."

"Why?" Red looked around, searching for any possible threats. "Did you see something?"

"No. We need to go because I want to be all over you, and this isn't the venue for it."

"Oh. *Oh.* Okay." Red couldn't help his silly grin. He took hold of Laz's hand, and they headed for the exit. On the way there, they passed Ace and Lucky. Red thanked them, told them he and Laz were leaving, and then headed out. Red's Genesis G80 was parked just outside. He hadn't liked being without his car, so Ace and Lucky had been kind enough to pick it up for him.

Red scanned their surroundings, kept Laz behind him, quickly escorted him to the passenger side, and opened the door for him. Once Laz was in and the door closed, Red got behind the wheel. The drive out of Orlando and up I-4 was excruciating, because all he wanted was to have his hands on Laz. Once he hit I-95, he floored it, and then a thought struck him.

"Hey, do you want to go to my place?"

Laz's smile was radiant. "Yeah?"

"Yeah. And not just because it's half an hour closer." Red winked at him, and Laz chuckled. One night at his place would be okay. His condo was secure, and Red knew the building inside and out. Colton's house was definitely the better choice, but a few hours away wouldn't hurt.

Thank God there was little traffic on the drive up, because not long after he'd pulled into his parking spot inside his condo's parking garage, they were out of the car and all over each other. Laz flung himself into Red's arms, and Red had just enough time to lock the doors and set the alarm before he had an arm full of Laz. He hoisted Laz up, their lips crushed together in a sloppy, frenzied kiss. The security guys were certainly getting an eyeful tonight.

Laz wrapped his legs around Red's waist, his arms around Red's neck as he tried to steal the breath from his body. Either that or set him on fire from the inside out. Red somehow managed to get to the door of the garage without walking into anything, one arm wrapped around Laz, a hand cupping his ass as he returned Laz's smoldering kisses. They stumbled their way down the hall to the elevator, and Red threw a hand out, feeling around for the up button until he found it. They barely surfaced for air during the whole ride up to the fourteenth floor where his condo was. Laz writhed against him, his hard cock stabbing Red in the stomach, and Red squeezed Laz's left asscheek, desperate to feel the flesh of the soft globe in his hand.

He locked the door behind them, tossed his keys onto the kitchen counter, and headed for the bedroom, losing what items of Laz's clothing he could along the way. When he reached the bedroom, he managed to detach Laz and drop him on the bed. Moving quickly to the balcony doors, he threw the curtains open, flooding the bedroom with moonlight. He turned and released a groan at the sight of Laz naked in his bed. Red didn't wait for an invite. He tore at his clothes, yanking on his tie and throwing it to one side. Laz's blue eyes darkened with a raging desire, and Red's cock strained against his dress pants. There was no delicacy in undressing. He needed his clothes off. He kicked off his boxer-briefs and stalked over to the bed, his thick, painfully hard dick jutting up against his stomach and leaking precome. He stroked himself, loving the decadent, needy groan that Laz let out as he observed.

"You're so fucking gorgeous," Laz said, kneeling on the bed. He crawled to Red, who stood on the side of the bed, releasing a curse under his breath.

"And you look so goddamn good on your knees."

Laz hummed as he drew closer, those thick black lashes almost touching his cheeks as he dropped his gaze to Red's cock. He flicked his tongue against Red's shaft, and Red sucked in a sharp breath. He wrapped a hand around the base of his dick, and offered it to Laz, who sucked the tip into his mouth, his tongue pressing into Red's slit. Red groaned, the feel of Laz's tongue on him sending a shiver of need through him. He slipped his fingers into Laz's hair, curling his hand around a fistful of it.

"God, I love your mouth. I love to watch my cock slip between those beautiful lips."

Laz shivered, and he swallowed Red down to the root, making him cry out. Taking hold of Laz's head with both hands, he fucked Laz's mouth, his body ready to fly apart from the delicious heat, but he needed to taste Laz. Red stepped away, smiling at the whimper Laz released at the loss. Laz sat back on his heels, waiting, and the thought of him waiting to be instructed ignited a blazing inferno within Red.

"Get on your back," he ordered.

Laz scrambled quickly to lie on his back, his legs bent. He let out a little surprised yelp when Red grabbed his ankles and dragged him over so his ass was hanging off the edge of the bed. Red knelt, and wrapped his arms around Laz's legs, jerking him forward so he had access to Laz's pretty puckered hole. Laz cried out when Red speared him with his tongue. He writhed on the bed like he couldn't get Red deep enough inside him. Red feasted on him, loving the taste of him, his musky scent, the way he gasped and moaned Red's name.

"Please, Red."

Red had no intention of letting up the sweet torture. He nipped at Laz's thigh, relishing in the sweet sounds Laz made and the way his body trembled beneath Red's touch. Red licked and laved, fucking Laz with his tongue. He slicked a finger, then replaced his tongue with the slick digit. He stroked Laz's cock with his other hand, studying Laz's face as his lips parted in ecstasy. He groaned and pleaded, pushing his ass down against Red's finger, trying to get Red in deeper. Red moved his mouth to Laz's cock, swallowing him whole while he finger-fucked Laz.

"Oh God!" Laz arched his back up off the bed, and Red put a hand on his hip to hold him down. "Red, please, I need you to fuck me. Please fuck me."

Red popped off Laz, moving up his body to kiss him. "Don't worry, baby. In a minute you're going to be so full." Red kissed him, taking as much as Laz was willing to give him. He loved kissing Laz. Loved the feel of his body beneath Red's, the way he reacted to Red's ministrations, like he was all but ready to fly apart.

Leaving Laz for a moment, he fetched lube and a condom from his nightstand before quickly returning. Laz was a vision, lying in the center of the bed, cheeks flushed, chest rising and falling in rapid pants, his lips swollen from their kisses, and those gorgeous curls a mess.

"You're so beautiful," Red said softly, placing two lube slicked fingers to Laz's hole. "I can't wait to see how you look when you ride me."

"Fuck." Laz palmed his stiff cock, stroking himself as Red stretched him, pushing his fingers deep down to the knuckle. Laz gasped then moaned, the sound music to Red's ears. He changed his angle, and crooked his fingers, and Laz almost shot up off the bed.

"Oh my God, oh God, yes, Red. *Please*."

Red added a third finger, his movements careful but quick as he readied Laz. They were both shaking, desperate to feel the other, to fill and be filled. When Red couldn't take any more, he pulled his fingers free, and climbed up onto the bed. He sat with his back against the headboard.

"Come here, sweetheart. I want to feel that tight, greedy little hole around me."

Laz moved quickly, straddling Red's lap, the bottle of lube in one hand, condom in the other.

"I want you to put it on me," Red said.

Laz tore at the condom packet and moved off Red. He rolled the condom down Red's cock, giving it a squeeze as he did, the little minx. Red sucked in a sharp breath, grabbed Laz's arm, and dragged him back to sit across his lap. He nipped at Laz's bottom lip.

"Show me how much you want my cock. Ride me."

Laz lifted up, and guided Red's achingly hard shaft to his hole before slowly sitting back. Red hissed at the pressure, and Laz winced at the pain of being breached. He paused, adjusting himself to Red's thickness before he started moving again. Red was going to tell him to slow down and take all the time he needed when Laz plunged down the rest of the way.

"Holy fuck!" Red wrapped his arms around Laz, who lay against him, his face buried against the crook of Red's neck. "Are you okay?"

Laz nodded. He let out a huff before undulating his hips, and Red groaned.

"You're so damned tight."

Sitting back, Laz slid his hands up and over Red's shoulders, then down to his pecs, tweaking Red's nipples, and making him buck his hips with a low groan. He certainly hadn't been expecting that.

"I'm going to start riding you now," Laz said, voice dripping with sex. "And you're going to jerk me off."

"Well somebody's a bossy bottom," Red teased.

Laz arched an eyebrow at him and tweaked his other nipple, making Red hiss at the pleasurable pain. "I believe what you meant to say was 'yes, love. Whatever you say.'"

Red felt his dick twitch inside Laz, and he moaned. *Love….* He certainly wasn't opposed to hearing that word when connected to the fiery man on his lap. "Yes, love. Whatever you say."

"Good. Then what are you waiting for, handsome?" Laz leaned in and sucked Red's bottom lip between his teeth, giving it a little nibble before releasing it with a hum. "Later, I'll get on my hands and knees and you can fuck me until I scream out your name, but right now? I'm in control of this ride."

Red wrapped a hand around Laz's cock and sucked in a sharp breath as Laz started to move, slowly at first, rotating his hips, and caused a low rumble of a growl to rise from Red's chest. The fluidity with which Laz moved his body, the natural tan of his skin, the wild curls falling over his brow, filled Red with an animalistic need to possess and be possessed. Then Laz started to move in earnest.

Their kisses grew sloppy and desperate as Laz fucked himself on Red's cock, his fingers digging into Red's shoulders as he used Red to chase his release. Red loved every second of it. He loved seeing all of Laz's insecurities slip away as he sought out his pleasure. Laz kissed, licked, and nipped whatever part of Red he could get a hold of, all the while murmuring dirty promises. There was no question who was in control, and Red couldn't get enough of it. Laz stopped moving and lifted to his knees. He cupped Red's face, and nibbled on his lips.

"Fuck me, Red. I want you to fuck me so hard and deep that I'll feel you for days."

"Fuck, Laz."

"Exactly." Laz tweaked Red's nipples hard, his mouth devouring Red's as Red grabbed hold of Laz's plump asscheeks and split them open, thrusting his hips, and plunging his cock deep inside Laz, making him cry out.

"Yes!"

Fueled by Laz's loss of control, Red did as he was asked, pounding Laz's sweet ass, his fingers digging into Laz's flesh to the point he'd probably leave bruises. Sweat dripped down the side of his face, and when Laz licked a bead of sweat, Red lost his rhythm. He drove himself in and out of Laz wildly, the bed shaking and squeaking beneath them as Red wreaked havoc on Laz's hole, the sounds of Laz's pleas for more spurring him on. Laz frantically jerked himself off, a decadent moan escaping those glossy lips.

"Fuck, Red. Oh fuck, I'm gonna come!"

Red pulled Laz off him, and pushed him onto his hands and knees before plunging inside him with one thrust. Laz cried out Red's name, and Red folded himself over Laz's back, one arm holding him up while he wrapped the other around Laz's neck so he could hold Laz in place while he pounded into him. His muscles strained, and he gritted his teeth at the mind-numbing pleasure.

"Tell me I'm the only one who gets to do this," Red demanded. "Please, Laz. No one else."

"No one else," Laz promised. "Just you. Tell me I'm enough for you."

"Oh, darling, you're more than enough. You're everything."

Laz sucked in a sharp breath, and Red slammed his hips against Laz's ass. The sound of their bodies coming together over and over filled the room along with Red's name as Laz shouted it out. Red's muscles went rigid, and his orgasm exploded through him. He thrust in deep and fast as he roared his release, his come filling the condom inside Laz's tight heat, their bodies trembling. When he was spent, he released Laz, and sat back on his heels, stroking Laz's ass soothingly as he pulled out. Laz fell onto his side so he wouldn't lie in the pool of his come, his hair slicked to his head with sweat as he attempted to catch his breath.

Red carefully removed the condom, tied it up, and dropped it into the wastebasket across the room. He went to his en suite bathroom, grabbed a damp washcloth to clean Laz up and the spot on the bed before he lay behind Laz, curling around him protectively. He trailed his fingers up and down Laz's side. They were plastered together as they tried to catch their breath. The only sound in the room came from their quiet breathing and the waves. Laz suddenly jerked up.

"Is that the ocean?"

Red smiled, bemused. "Um, yeah. We're on the beach."

Laz scrambled off the bed, almost tripping over himself, and Red chuckled, wondering what on earth had gotten into him. He stood from the bed as Laz ran over to the balcony doors and slid one open before stepping outside.

"Why didn't I know you had a condo on the beach?" Laz asked in awe. He leaned against the balcony, his smile stretching from ear to ear.

"I don't know. It just never came up. You like it?"

"Red, I love it! This is amazing." Laz inhaled a deep breath and closed his eyes, listening to the waves crashing against the shore. When he opened his eyes, they were almost wistful. "I've always dreamed of living on the beach."

Red didn't ask why he wasn't. From snippets of conversations, he'd gathered money was tight at times and Laz's career was only now just starting to take off, what with his invite to Paris next year. Beachfront property was expensive, and depending on the area, out of most people's price range.

"I bought this place a few years ago. I don't know what it is, but we Kings seem drawn to the ocean. We've all ended up living on or near the beach. I guess it's not such a surprise for Ace and Lucky. They were born and raised Florida boys. I've always found it soothing. When I talked to my therapist about it, he thought it was a great idea. On the job, I deal with a lot of noise and crowds. Sometimes there's the threat of danger, at times actual danger. Being able to have somewhere peaceful to come home to after a hectic case, a safe place away from the outside world, is vital."

"I'd never want to leave," Laz said.

Red moved behind him and wrapped his arms around Laz. He rested his chin on Laz's shoulder. "You should see it in the morning when the sun rises."

"Can we?"

"Of course. I'll set an alarm. Want to see the rest of the place?"

"I'd love to."

Red turned, releasing a surprised yelp when Laz slapped his ass. He spun on his heels, and Laz laughed before taking off, swiping Red's shirt off the floor as he went. Red darted after him, chasing him into the living room. Thankfully, the kitchen light was on. He had a habit of leaving it on when he knew he was going to be home late or away for a few days. It cast a warm glow through the apartment, and left enough light so Laz wouldn't bump into anything.

Red easily caught up to Laz and scooped him up into his arms, loving the sound of Laz's laughter, but more importantly, loving the way it filled his home. Red popped a kiss on Laz's lips before putting him down, his heart swelling with joy when Laz slipped into Red's shirt, leaving a couple of buttons on the top and bottom undone. The sleeves were too long, so Laz rolled them up to his wrists, while the rest of the shirt fell to midthigh. Red turned on the lights, and Laz's smile was radiant.

"Oh my God, Red, your place is amazing!" Laz walked around the spacious living room decorated in soft hues of creams and grays with pops of blue-green. Did Laz realize he'd pulled the collar of Red's shirt up and was sniffing it? Like he couldn't get enough of Red's scent. "It's so bright and spacey."

Red winked at him. "I'm a growing boy."

"Don't I know it," Laz purred before he continued his tour.

Red loved his condo. It was a large three bedroom, two bathroom apartment he'd painstakingly decorated himself. His home was his lion's den, his sanctuary. It had taken years to get it exactly how he wanted it, and now he couldn't imagine himself anywhere else. He used one of the spare bedrooms as a guest room, and the second as an office, though he barely used it as he preferred to take his laptop out onto his balcony so he could face the ocean as he worked. He'd spent several nights out on his balcony in his comfy lounge chair with a blanket, often falling asleep. It was usually after being woken up by a nightmare. Not one of the bad ones, but enough for him to seek out the comfort the ocean provided.

Once they were done with the tour, they ended up back in the bedroom and out on the balcony. Red wrapped Laz up in his arms as they faced the beach, the moon casting its glow across the deep blue water, giving it a magical feel. The sky was clear, and beneath it, nothing but the miles and miles of ocean.

"Is it wrong that I love seeing you in my shirt?" Red placed a kiss to Laz's temple, enjoying the little hum that escaped Laz as he continue to nuzzle him.

"Not at all."

"What about if I said I love seeing you in my home?"

Laz turned in his arms, his cheeks flushed, and a shy smile tugged at his lips as he drew circles on Red's chest with his finger. "I'd say I love being in your home." He lifted his eyes to meet Red's. "With you."

"Maybe you could stay over sometimes," Red said, his heart pounding in his ears. God, they were moving fast, but it all felt so right. "And so you know, I don't invite anyone here who's not family… or someone I'm serious about."

Laz worried his bottom lip. He clearly wanted to say something but seemed unsure.

"You can say anything you need to say, Laz. I want us to always be open with each other. Trust is very important to both of us."

"Earlier, you said no one else." Laz lifted his gaze to meet Red's. "Did you mean that?"

"I did," Red replied, brushing his fingers down Laz's jaw. "I really care about you, Laz, and I'd like to see where this goes. I'd like to see you." He remembered Laz's words to Richard earlier that evening. "I want to be your guy."

Laz's smile was breathtaking. Then he leaned back, looking thoughtful. "Hm, on one condition."

"And what's that?" Red asked, holding back a smile.

Laz stood on his toes, wrapped his arms around Red's neck, and placed little kisses up his jaw as he murmured seductively, "You take me to bed and make a mess of me all over again."

"You drive a *hard* bargain, Mr. Galanos." Red pulled Laz up against him, his cock already filling at the thought of having Laz in his bed again. "I think I can make that happen."

"Then you've got yourself a deal, Mr. McKinley." Laz brought him in for a kiss, and Red hauled him up into his arms, enjoying Laz's legs wrapped around him. He carried Laz into the bedroom, intent on spending the whole night making a mess out of Laz, and if they happened to end up making love… well then, that sounded just fine with him.

# CHAPTER 9

Heaven.

A night of hot, filthy sex had turned heart-achingly tender, and the Sunday morning had been just as incredible. Red's alarm had gone off at dawn like he'd promised, and they'd sleepily pulled on T-shirts and shorts—Laz practically swimming in Red's clothes, but he hadn't cared—and they'd gone out onto the balcony to watch the sunrise. Red had wrapped Laz up in his arms, and they'd stood in companionable silence as the oranges, reds, and yellows of sunrise gave way to pinks and purples as the sky lightened. It had been absolute perfection. The only sound around, came from the ocean. It was like something out of a dream, especially since he'd shared the experience with Red. Or rather, his boyfriend.

A smile spread across Laz's face now as he thought about it, and he rubbed his foot against Red's, still unable to believe this was happening. Red was wrapped around Laz, like he'd been every morning for the last four days when they'd watched the sun rise over the ocean, except they were no longer in Red's gorgeous condo, but in Laz's bedroom at Colton's house.

As much as Laz would have loved to stay at Red's, he agreed the best place for him until this was all over was at Colton's. Even if it was farther from Four Kings headquarters, Colton's house had undergone a huge security overhaul during his case, which included everything from strategic exit plans to vehicles equipped with ballistic features. No other attempts had been made on Laz's life, but that didn't mean the threat was over, or that he could afford to get complacent.

The police were no closer to finding the shooter than they had been a week ago. Laz understood it wasn't like on TV. These things took time. Some sexy detective in a leather jacket didn't just walk out onto a crime scene and find *the* clue that would break the case wide open. In the meantime, he would enjoy the peace and calm while he could.

Laz was a little concerned at how quickly he was becoming addicted to Red, even if he couldn't wrap his head around the fact Red was his, that a guy like Red was happy to be his. When Red brought Laz into his embrace, whether in bed or watching a sunset together, Laz melted. He loved sleeping with Red at his side, waking up with Red curled around him, or finding himself half sprawled over Red, like he was making sure Red didn't escape. He tried to put off thoughts of what would happen when this was over. He'd miss waking up to Red's kisses and sleep-laced purrs, miss the warmth of Red's big, strong body pressed to Laz's as he fell asleep. He'd miss reading in bed, and hearing Red's soft snores when he fell asleep before Laz, usually a page or two into whatever he'd been reading.

Red kissed his temple, his voice a low rumble. "Let's get back into bed."

Laz hummed, then let out a soft laugh when Red walked them in together, his chest plastered to Laz's back.

"You're warm," Red murmured, squeezing Laz.

Colton was due to return from his trip in five days, and Ace would be back as well. Laz had a feeling Ace was purposefully staying away to give them time alone. The case that had required him to be on-site was over. Ace checked in with Red by phone, as did Lucky and King, but none of them came to the house. They really weren't as subtle as they thought they were, but it was sweet. Laz made sure to check in with Colton every day like he'd promised. He knew he'd have to call Gio at some point, but he was hoping to have more news on the case before he worried his brother.

Laz snuggled up to Red, releasing a happy sigh. Before he knew it, he'd fallen asleep and didn't wake up until his phone alarm went off. With a groan, he rolled over to shut it off, and when he rolled back, he realized Red wasn't in bed. Wide-awake, he got out of bed and brushed his teeth before he went in search of Red. Downstairs, as he drew closer to the kitchen, the mouthwatering smell of bacon filled the air, as did the sounds of some upbeat disco song. Laz bit down on his bottom lip so he wouldn't make a sound. He didn't want to disturb Red, who was dancing around the kitchen while he made breakfast. There was no doubt in Laz's mind that he was falling for Red. How could he not?

The more time he spent with Red, the more he wanted. He loved everything about the man. From his red hair and freckles strewn across his nose and cheeks, to his sinful body and boyish smile. Red was a warrior through and through. He was also the kindest, gentlest man Laz had ever known. Always thinking about others, putting their needs before his own. Laz felt an overwhelming urge to take care of him because Red was the kind of man who was always looking out for everyone else.

"Morning," Red said, spinning on his heels and winking at him.

"You knew I was here the whole time, didn't you?"

"Yep." Red popped a piece of bacon into his mouth. "Green Beret, remember?"

Laz ran his gaze over Red, from his broad shoulders and muscular chest encased in the snug T-shirt down to his powerful thighs and legs accentuated by the skintight boxer-briefs. "Believe me, I remember."

"I can see that," Red said with a chuckle as he closed the distance between them. He brushed his lips over Laz's before kissing him, sweet and deep, and Laz melted in his embrace, giving himself over to the strength that radiated from Red. Laz groaned in protest when Red pulled away. "No funny business this morning. You have an interview, remember?"

"Shit. You're right."

"Let's have some breakfast, and we can talk about it."

"Talk about what?" Laz asked, taking a seat at the counter as Red instructed. The smile had gone from Red's face, and Laz missed it already. Man, he was in so much trouble. Falling in love with Red wasn't a question of *if*, but a question of *when*.

Red fixed Laz a plate and placed it in front of him along with a frothy mug of heaven. He served himself and poured some coffee, then joined Laz at the counter.

"Thank you for making breakfast," Laz said, kissing Red's cheek, happy to see that smile again.

"You're welcome."

As they ate, Red confessed his concern regarding Laz's interview. Laz was supposed to be lying low, and he understood that, but he couldn't put his life on hold any more than he already had.

"I know you're not happy about this, and I'm sorry, but this is a big opportunity for me. The last thing I want to do is cause you problems, but I can't hole myself up in Colton's house until who knows when. I can't not work, Red." He didn't have that luxury. His rent and bills still needed to be paid. He had work expenses and a trip to Paris to save up for.

"I understand," Red said sincerely. "Who else knows about this meeting?"

"I don't know. The assistant who called me, I suppose. I mean, no one on my end. I don't know who else Ms. Vargas may have told."

"Is that the only person you're meeting with?"

"I think so."

"Well, at least we got lucky with the location. The building we're heading to is situated off Treasury Street and Cardova Street, just a couple of blocks over from Four Kings headquarters, so if there's an emergency, King can send reinforcements in a heartbeat. I've updated him on the situation, so he's prepared. I also did some recon work on the building, making note of the layout, number of floors, and exits. I need you to stay close to me at all times, and I'm going to need you to get me into the interview with you. I know that seems like overkill, but we're talking about your safety. I'm not taking any chances."

Laz blinked at him. "I'll try." How was he supposed to explain Red escorting him into his interview? He'd worry about it later. As they carried on with breakfast, Laz was both in awe of and concerned by the amount of prep work Red had done for his interview. It was a stark reminder of not only what Red did for a living, but why it was necessary. Every time he started to feel at ease, he was reminded of the dangers lurking out there, and he hated it.

Poor Colton. No wonder he'd lost it when his dad hired the Kings. One minute he was free, the next he had a small army following his every move, making sure whatever he did, wherever he went, he wasn't in danger. Laz was grateful he had Red, and touched that despite not being on duty, Red would go through so much trouble for him, but Laz also looked forward to getting his life back so he could start living it with Red without the threats.

After cleaning up, they showered and dressed. Laz went with a blue slim-fit, button-down shirt with quarter-length sleeves, the collar and upturned cuffs of his sleeves in white. He wore it tucked into a pair of navy dress slacks, a brown belt, and brown oxfords. He'd somewhat managed to tame his curls, and when he met Red downstairs, his heart skipped a beat at the stunning smile he received.

"You look amazing," Red said, pulling him in for a kiss but being mindful not to wrinkle him. "Ready?"

"I'm kinda nervous."

"It's just a formality, remember? You'll do great."

Laz nodded and took Red's word for it. He was secretly glad for the near-black tinted windows Red's car had so no one could see inside. It helped with Laz's nerves. Now that he was leaving the house and they were heading toward A1A and back to St. Augustine, he was starting to worry.

"It's going to be okay," Red assured him, taking Laz's hand in his and giving it a squeeze. "I'm going to be right beside you, and King will be a couple of blocks away. Mason won't be far either."

"Okay. I'm sure it's just the interview making me restless."

"Remember the breathing technique I showed you?"

Laz nodded. He breathed in deep through his nose and released the breath slowly through his mouth. He did it several times, his eyes closed as he concentrated on filling his lungs with air, on feeling the movement. They pulled into a parking spot just behind the building's entrance fifteen minutes early. Thankfully the building had plenty of parking to the side and back, otherwise Red would have had to drop him off and go find parking on the street, which was never fun. Under normal circumstances, they could have easily parked elsewhere if they'd needed to and walked, but that was out of the question when a killer could be lurking in the shadows. Okay, Laz really needed to not watch so many crime dramas.

Red scanned their surroundings before he climbed out of the car. He came around and opened Laz's door for him, keeping himself between the outside world and Laz as they headed for the main door of the building. Man, it was hot as hell outside. Just the few steps it took to get to the door had Laz's sunglasses fogging up from the humidity. It was in the nineties and wasn't even 10:00 a.m. yet. Inside, the lobby was wonderfully air-conditioned, and decorated in a subtle tropical theme with plaques and awards on the walls, along with elegantly framed photographs of all the celebrities and high-profile guests the magazine had featured. The receptionist was super cheerful, and Laz informed her he was there to see Ms. Vargas. She put in a call and then asked them to take a seat in the waiting area, that Ms. Vargas would be out shortly.

Before Laz could get any more nervous, a striking Hispanic woman in a white pantsuit and five-inch taupe heels walked through a set of glass doors, her smile wide when she saw Laz.

"Mr. Galanos?"

Laz stood and returned her smile. "Yes. Please, call me Laz." He took her outstretched hand and shook it. She was a beautiful woman in her mid to late forties, with long dark hair tied in a high ponytail and eyes so dark they were almost black.

"And you can call me Maria. It's so wonderful to meet you in person. Thank you for coming in."

"Thank you so much for having me."

Maria glanced over at Red and did a double take. "And who is this very handsome man. A new model?"

"Oh, um, no. This is my, uh—" Laz was about to say personal assistant when Red beat him to it.

"Private security," Red said, smiling brightly as he held out his hand to Maria. "I'm Russell McKinley, from Four Kings Security, but you can call me Red. Lovely to see you again, Ms. Vargas."

Laz was confused. Had Red and Ms. Vargas met before? Why would Red admit being a King? Laz might not be a client, but he supposed Red was sort of acting as security, but still. Why tell Maria? Some sort of realization dawned on her, and she smiled brightly.

"Oh, yes! Mr. McKinley, how good to see you too. I thought you looked familiar. Forgive me for not recognizing you right away."

"Not a problem. It's been almost a year since the Sunshine State Awards." Red turned to Laz with a smile. "Maria is a member of the board for the Florida chapter of the Society of Professional Journalists. The Kings provided security for the awards ceremony and reception."

*Oh shit.* Maria and Red *had* met. No wonder Red jumped in when he did. If he hadn't, Maria would have most likely remembered him at some point and caught Laz in a lie, and that was no way to start a business relationship. But why hadn't Red said anything earlier?

Maria's gaze turned concerned as she looked from Red to Laz. "I hope everything is okay."

"Nothing to worry about," Red replied, his smile sweet and reassuring. "Laz is a personal friend, so I'm helping him out. I hope you don't mind my being here."

Maria waved a hand in dismissal. "Of course not. The Kings are always welcome."

"Thank you."

"Come with me, please. Let's go to my office, and we'll get down to business."

They followed her through a set of thick glass doors, past several glass offices and cubicles, to the end of the floor, where her large office was. She stepped to one side and motioned for them to enter.

"Please, have a seat. I just need to check with one of my journalists on a column that's due today. I won't be a moment."

"Of course." Laz took a seat in one of the chairs in front of Maria's desk, while Red took a seat on the stylish white couch against the glass wall across from Laz. He waited for Maria to walk away before turning to Laz.

"Sorry, I didn't realize it was the same Maria I'd met at the awards ceremony. She was Mrs. Maria Vasquez at the time and looked very different. It was her eyes and the beauty mark over her lip that made me realize it was the same woman."

"That was a close call," Laz said, smiling when Maria approached the office.

"I'm so sorry about that. Deadlines wait for no woman." She closed her office door before taking a seat behind her desk. "Would either of you like something to drink?"

They both politely declined, and Maria tapped away at her computer. "You have a stunning portfolio, Laz. I was so excited when I saw it. Your lighting is exceptional, and your colors exquisite. I absolutely adore the way you use them to invoke emotion, but it was the use of lighting and color along with the model's expressions that captivated me. You have a way of drawing so much emotion and depth from your models. It's impressive. I think you would be perfect for this job, and the designer who you'll be photographing agrees."

Laz tried not to get too excited. The contract wasn't signed yet. "Who is the designer, if you don't mind me asking?"

"Well, we've kept it secret, but if you agree to take the job, I'll share that secret with you. But first, have a read through the contract." She slid the document to Laz, and he read through it, his eyes widening at the amount of money on offer, and it even included an advance, the other half to be paid upon completion of the job.

Laz didn't usually take jobs without knowing who he was going to be working with, but by the look on Maria's face and all the cloak-and-dagger surrounding the identity of the designer, he was clearly making the right decision by accepting.

"This look great," Laz replied. "I'd love to do the job."

"Wonderful!" Maria placed a pen in front of him, and he signed the contract where she instructed. Full confidentiality was required on his part before, during, and after the shoot, but that was nothing out of the ordinary when dealing with high-profile celebrities or industry professionals. He was so excited and couldn't wait to see who he'd be working with.

"Once the article is published, feel free to add whichever images you like to your portfolio."

"Thank you." If everything went well, this job could mean a big boost for his career.

"Would you like to meet the designer?" Maria motioned to a door on her right, and Laz's eyes went wide.

"They're here?"

"Yes. They wanted to wait until you signed the contract to meet you." Maria leaned forward, speaking quietly. "They're a little quirky that way."

Laz nodded, and Maria stood. "You can come out now."

The door opened, and a flurry of yellow tulle exploded into the room.

"Lazarus!" the woman squealed, rounding the desk and throwing her arms wide, bringing him into a big hug. "So good to see you!"

*Oh my God.* Elena Vicente.

Laz was momentarily stunned stupid, and he just stood there as she hugged him. Elena was boisterous, charming, and very eccentric. Her hair color seemed to change as often as her wardrobe, and she didn't believe in simple cuts, since her hair was an extension of her personality just like her clothes. This time her orange-blonde hair was pulled up high at the top of her head, her ponytail green so her head looked like a pineapple, which he believed was her intent, judging by the multilayered tulle skirt and gold sequin top. Pineapples were heavily featured in Elena's summer collection. Her ballet flats were a neon green, and her many bracelets jangled from her wrists. Her makeup was subtle, except for the pop of pink on her lips.

Snapping himself out of it, Laz hugged her gently. He'd been at a few of the same events as her, but never as a photographer, and he wasn't a big enough name to have been so much as introduced to her.

"When Maria told me who she had in mind for the article, I was so happy! I have heard so many wonderful things about you, and when I saw your portfolio?" She gasped dramatically. "Oh, bellissimo!"

"Um, thank you so much, Mrs. Vicente. It's a real honor to meet you."

"Oh, no, no, no. Call me Elena." She looked past Laz, her smile turning coy. "And who is your very pretty friend?" She raked her gaze over Red, no subtlety whatsoever.

"This is Russell," Laz explained quickly. "He's a close friend."

Red stood and smiled widely at Elena. "It's a pleasure to meet you."

"Hello, Close Friend Russell. Such a pleasure to meet you. Russell. It just rolls off the tongue, doesn't it? Rrrrrr. Rrrrrussell. I love it." Elena let out a gasp and swept her arms up and out dramatically. "Sea urchins!"

Laz startled at the sudden outburst. "I'm sorry?"

"Sea urchins. For next year's summer collection. It will be fabulous! Vintage colors. Very Victorian."

"That sounds really… interesting," Laz said, scrambling for the right words, but he had none. What words could he possibly string together that would be appropriate for this conversation? Sea urchins? Well, if anyone could make it work, it was Elena Vicente. He'd heard she was eccentric, but he wasn't quite sure that was the word he'd use to describe her. She started chatting to herself, as if she were mentally taking notes.

"No, mustard would be an ugly color. No sepia. Too cliché." She seemed to space out for a moment before shaking herself out of it and turning her attention back to Laz. "I think you will be perfect for this. Oh, there is someone else I want you to meet. He is very important to me and will also be featured in the article." She turned to the door, calling out, "Darling, come meet the lovely boy who will be taking our pictures."

A tall, handsome man entered the office, and Laz froze, a chill going up his spine.

"Lazarus, this is Paolo, mio amore. He is my husband. Paolo, this is Lazarus Galanos."

Paolo came to a sudden halt, his eyes going huge before he quickly pulled himself together. He smiled brightly and held his hand out to Laz, but his smile didn't reach his eyes.

"Laz, how nice to meet you. I have heard so much about you."

*Oh? From who? My sleazeball ex-boyfriend who you were fucking behind my back, and probably still are?* Laz felt terrible for Elena. She was obviously crazy about him. The way she looked at him, her arms wrapped around his. *The scumbag.* How could he do that to his wife? From the moment they'd married, rumors had circulated regarding Paolo, that he'd only married Elena for her money and status. He'd been a waiter at a luxury resort in Milan where they'd met, and shortly after, the two eloped.

At the time, Laz thought it unfair that Paolo was judged so harshly simply because he was younger. He'd been in his thirties while Elena was in her early fifties when they'd married, and even if Paolo hadn't worked a job since, whose business was it anyway? Elena preferred to have her husband at her side, and if he wanted to be there and it made her happy, then no one had the right to judge.

"It's nice to meet you," Laz lied, taking Paolo's outstretched hand. Laz had defended this man to countless people who'd sneered at his relationship, and now Paolo looked at Laz as if *he* was the asshole.

"This makes me so happy!" Elena clapped her hands gleefully. "This article is going to be marvelous!" She turned to her husband, who put his fingers beneath her chin, murmuring something into her ear that made her giggle and blush.

"I love you, my darling," he cooed as he gazed into her eyes. She melted against him, releasing a little sigh before whirling to hug Laz again, then turning to Maria.

"Please, whatever you need for this, you only have to ask. I must go now. I have a lunch meeting with a dear friend down in South Beach, and the drive will be long, but first, I must speak with your assistant to make arrangements for the day of the shoot." Elena fluttered around the office, talking to herself before heading for the door, stopping to boop Red's nose.

"Rrrrrussel. So good to meet you."

"Um, thanks. It's nice to meet you too," Red replied, amused.

She fluttered out of the office, and Maria chuckled. "Excuse me, Laz. I need to oversee this. I'll have my assistant send you the details of the time and place for the shoot. I can have someone show you out."

"It's okay," Red assured her. "I know the way."

"Thank you both so much. I'm so excited." She shook their hands before hurrying off after Elena, Paolo silently following.

It was only when the office was quiet, that Laz joined Red, whispering hoarsely, "I need to get out of here before I explode."

Red nodded. They left the office, headed back the way they'd come in, and thanked the receptionist on the way out. The lobby was empty, and so was the parking lot behind the building. Laz made it to Red's car before he exploded.

"I can't believe that lying bastard! How could he stand there, look into her eyes, and tell her he loves her, knowing he's fucking some guy behind her back? And the way he looked at me? Like *I* was the one who'd done something despicable."

"He clearly recognized you. Did you see his face when he realized who you were?"

"Yeah." Unbelievable. The urge to plant one in Paolo's face had been great, but the last thing Laz wanted was to upset Elena. It had nothing to do with the job and everything to do with that lying sack of shit. He felt for Elena, but it wasn't his place to get involved, which made him feel even worse.

"He was nervous," Red stated thoughtfully, "but I have no idea if that's because he was in the same room with the guy whose boyfriend he'd been screwing around with, or because he was surprised to see you alive."

*Shit.* "You think Paolo hired someone to kill me?" The guy clearly loathed him, but enough to want him dead?

"Maybe Bryan told him about the photographs, or somehow he found out, but the fact remains that not only is he in the same state as you, but that reaction was not the reaction of an innocent man. We need to let Mason know." Red unlocked the car when Paolo came bursting through the doors.

"Hey!"

Laz turned around, stunned to see Paolo marching toward him, his lips twisted in a snarl. Before he could get any closer, Red was blocking his path, putting himself between Paolo and Laz.

"Get the fuck out of my way."

"I don't think so. You need to step back."

Paolo craned his neck to glare at Laz. "You perverted little piece of shit. How dare you take photos of us!"

"Excuse me?" Laz's temper flared, and he moved around Red. "You have some fucking nerve!"

"I didn't take what did not want to be taken. You were obviously not enough for Bryan. He's always going on about how boring you were in bed, how you never wanted to do anything fun. No excitement at all. He needed a real man."

Laz's face burned with embarrassment. It wasn't bad enough Bryan had cheated on him repeatedly, but he'd badmouthed Laz to this jerk? And *while* they were still going out?

"You and Bryan deserve each other. You're both selfish assholes."

"I want those photographs."

"I bet you do."

Paolo made a move toward him, running straight into the wall of muscle that was Red.

"You lay one finger on him, and you're going to answer to me."

"Oh, I see." Paolo looked Red over with disgust. "So Bryan was right. The moment his back was turned, you were offering your ass to jolly Red giant."

"Don't you fucking dare. Also, it's none of your damn business who I'm seeing. I'm not the one who's a lying, cheating bastard. I never cheated on Bryan. How could you do this to Elena?"

"You stay the fuck out of my business!" Paolo stormed off, and Red pulled his phone out of his pocket.

Laz was fuming. God, he needed to calm down and get his shit together. He'd had just about enough of this. Fuck, even after they'd broken up Bryan was still causing him trouble.

"Mason? Hey. Yeah, you'll never guess who we just ran into. Paolo Vicente is back, and he happens to be right here in town. Yep. I'll text you the address. Oh, and he knows about the photos. Okay. Can you try and bring him in without tipping off his wife? She has no idea her husband is screwing someone else, and I don't really want her to find out like this. You sure? Okay, we can do that." Red hung up and ushered Laz to the passenger side of the car, then opened the door for him. As soon as Red was behind the wheel, Laz turned to him.

"What did Mason say?"

"He's going to send someone to tail Paolo and bring him in the moment he gets away from his wife, which considering he and Bryan are in the same town shouldn't be long. My guess is after the run-in he had with you, he's going to go see Bryan. Mason wants us to meet him at the precinct."

Laz pressed his lips together to keep from saying something nasty. What annoyed him most was Paolo's accusation regarding Red. Even if Laz had been attracted to Red at the time, and something had sparked between them, Laz wouldn't have screwed around behind Bryan's back. He'd made a choice. Even if Bryan hadn't been a toxic presence Laz needed to escape, Laz would never betray their trust the way Bryan had done to Laz.

On their way to the precinct, Mason called with an update. They had Paolo down at the station. It had gone just as Red predicted. The moment Paolo could get away from his wife, he'd headed to see Bryan. Unfortunately, Bryan wasn't home, which meant Mason was still trying to track him down without alerting Bryan that the police were looking for him, afraid of spooking him.

"I want to be there when Mason questions him."

Red pulled into an empty parking spot outside the precinct and turned off the engine before shifting in his seat to face Laz. "What?"

"You heard me. I want to be there when Mason questions them both."

"Laz, I don't think—"

"If one of them is responsible for trying to kill me, I want to look them in the eye when they get charged for attempted murder."

Red let out a heavy sigh. "I'll talk to Mason."

This time it was a little more like the movies. Mason came out to meet them and escorted them into a room full of what looked like security equipment. Cameras, microphones, and computers. There were several screens, one of which showed the interview room where Paolo was waiting to be questioned by Mason. He sat fuming, his arms folded over his chest, and his foot tapping impatiently, the expensive Italian leather loafers a stark contrast against the light gray floors. His whole outfit was a contrast to his surroundings. From the thick gold chain around his tanned neck and matching bracelet around his wrist, to the skintight white linen pants and short-sleeved button-down shirt with tropical pattern. His black hair was parted on one side, perfectly styled and gleaming. It struck Laz that he'd changed attire. He looked like he was ready for a night out clubbing on the beach. Back in Maria's office, he'd been dressed in a solid pale blue button-down shirt and gray slacks.

The interview room was clean but sparse, with only a table against the wall and two chairs facing each other, one presently occupied by Paolo. The room and everything in it was light gray, and set up to record both audio and video. Mason walked casually into the room and closed the door behind him. Paolo's eyes went huge, but then who wouldn't be worried when faced with the mountain of a man wearing a double shoulder holster with a gun tucked in each one.

Mason's shoulders were impossibly wide, his legs long, and his shirt stretched tight over his biceps, the sleeves rolled up his corded arms. The thick black leather band around his wrist added to his rugged appeal, and his all-black attire made him even more intimidating, if that was possible. His square jaw was full of stubble, and he seemed to fill up the room with his presence. Mason took a seat, his voice low and gravelly when he spoke.

"Do you know why you're here, Mr. Vicente?"

Paolo shrugged. "Because clearly you are offended by a man with good taste in fashion?"

"Mouthing off is not going to win you any favors."

The warning in Mason's tone was not lost on Paolo, and he let out a resigned sigh. Good to know the man had some kind of common sense.

"Speeding ticket? How should I know. Can we make this quick? I am meeting someone."

"Would that someone be the man you're cheating on your wife with?"

Paolo's face drained of color. He fidgeted in his seat and swallowed hard. "What, um, what are you talking about?"

"I'm talking about your lover, Bryan Burch. The man you were having sex with in Madrid while your wife was in Paris. Now tell me, did you and Mr. Burch plot together to have Mr. Lazarus Galanos killed, or was the idea solely yours?"

Paolo choked on air. "What?" His eyes bugged out of his head, and he started flailing. "Dio. What? Attempted… attempted *murder*?"

"You expect me to believe you don't know anything about the attempt on Mr. Galanos's life, when you clearly know about the photographs he has of you and Mr. Burch?"

The penny dropped, and Paolo leapt from his chair. "*What*? You think I tried to kill Laz because of some photos?"

"Not just some photos, Mr. Vicente. Photos that could mean the end of your pampered lifestyle and Mr. Burch's career. If your wife were to find out about your affair, it would be very bad for you, wouldn't it? You signed a prenup when you married Elena Vicente. If she kicks you to the curb, you're left with nothing. Not even the name Vicente is yours. You're a man accustomed to the finer things. Wearing the best designer clothes, dining at the most expensive restaurants, staying in luxury accommodations during trips around the world, all expenses paid. I bet the thought of losing all that makes you pretty angry."

"No. No, no, no. Look, I might *hate* Lazarus, don't get me wrong, but I would never try to kill him."

"That so. Sit down, please."

"I will stand."

"Sit. Down," Mason growled.

Paolo promptly plopped back down onto his chair.

Mason sat back and folded his arms over his broad chest. "And what about Mr. Burch?"

Paolo's head shot up. "What about him?"

"Has he mentioned harming Mr. Galanos in any way?"

"No." Paolo shook his head emphatically. "Bryan would never hurt anyone."

"Oh? And when *Bryan* pushed Mr. Galanos, causing him to slip on wet tile, injuring himself and almost drowning? What would you call that?"

"An accident," Paolo replied through his teeth.

"Or maybe a hint of things to come?" Mason shrugged nonchalantly.

Paolo shot to his feet again. "I want to speak to my lawyer."

"You mean your wife's lawyer," Mason said, pulling out his cell phone. "Would you like me to call him for you? Or would you like to finish answering some questions? It's up to you."

Paolo thought about it. A smug look came across his face. "Are you charging me with something, Officer…?"

"Detective Mason Cooper."

"Are you charging me with something, *Detective* Cooper?"

"No."

"Am I under arrest, *Detective*?"

Mason narrowed his eyes. "No, you are not under arrest, Mr. Vicente."

"Then I am free to leave?"

"Yes."

Laz dropped into the chair behind the desk, exhausted from the exchange. He watched on the monitor as Mason escorted a smug-looking Paolo from the interview room.

"So that's it, then?" Laz asked to no one in particular. What had he been expecting? If Paolo was guilty, did he think he was just going to confess? The man had everything to lose. He'd probably covered all his tracks.

"Let's see what Mason says."

Red's tone pretty much confirmed Laz was right. They had nothing.

A few minutes later, Mason entered the room, his expression saying it all. "I'm sorry, Laz, but we don't have any evidence that points to him hiring someone to kill you. I can't look into his finances or search his property without warrants, and to get those, we need probable cause. So far we haven't been able to find anything that leads us to believe the man is a threat to your safety. The photos on their own aren't enough, as the shots where they're being intimate have Paolo mostly turned away. *We* know it's him, especially with the photos you took of him just before and after, but Paolo can argue that it's not actually him in bed with Bryan, and that's enough for reasonable doubt."

While Red and Mason discussed the case, Laz's phone pinged. He pulled it out of his pocket and saw he'd received a new email. Slowly he got to his feet.

"Um, Mason?"

"Yeah?"

"Would an email from Paolo's email account saying, 'I'm going to make you pay for what you've done' be enough to get you a warrant?" Laz handed Mason his phone, and Mason's lips curled into a grin.

"How's about you print that out for me on that computer there."

Laz logged into his email account and did as Mason asked. He wasn't sure whether Paolo was just cocky or stupid. The man had been brought in for questioning regarding an attempted murder, and he was emailing threats the moment he walked out of the police station? Whatever the hell was going on, Laz hoped it was all over soon. All he wanted was to put Bryan and Paolo behind him so he could move on with his life, a life that included watching the sunrise with a fiery redhead wrapped around him.

# CHAPTER 10

Five days.

It had been five days since Paolo had been brought in for questioning, and four days since Mason had informed Laz he'd submitted his affidavit to a judge in the hopes of getting search warrants for Paolo's personal account, business account, and condo on the beach. There was a lot of law and police jargon involved, which confused Laz. When his head started to hurt, he'd thanked Mason and told him he was putting Red on the phone. Half an hour later, Red broke it down for Laz, and what it boiled down to was more waiting and hoping—*hoping* the judge agreed with Mason that there was reason to search Paolo's accounts and property, and *hoping* they found enough evidence to bring charges against him and arrest him. Laz still had no idea whether Paolo was guilty. What he did know was that he was done with all this. For now, he'd take comfort in the man he loved.

Laz's eyes shot open, and he sucked in a shaky breath as he stared at the ceiling.

Love? *Love?*

No way. He couldn't be in love, could he? It was too soon. Sure, he'd known Red for months, but they'd only just started dating. Then again, he'd felt a deep connection to Red from the beginning and had come to see him as someone important to him far longer than the short period they'd been together. Laz warned himself of the dangers of falling for someone so quickly, but what could he do? His heart had gone ahead and made the decision on its own. He'd had no say in the matter. And yet, he found he didn't care. He was ridiculously happy.

He was in love with Russell McKinley.

"Should I be jealous of whatever's got you smiling like that?" Red climbed back under the covers next to Laz, and they turned so they were facing each other.

"Only if you want to be jealous of yourself," Laz admitted. Could his dorky smile get any bigger? Red's expression was soft, and he leaned in to kiss Laz.

"I love that the thought of me makes you smile like that," Red murmured against Laz's lips. He rolled Laz onto his back, and Laz relished in the tender kisses Red trailed across his skin, from his jaw down to his neck. Laz closed his eyes and hummed at the pleasure of feeling Red's mouth on him. He drew in a sharp breath when Red sucked at one of his nipples, then teased and licked it before moving on to the next one.

Laz gave himself completely, spreading his legs so Red could lie between them as he continued his sweet torture. It was as if Red had familiarized himself with every inch of Laz's body, knowing exactly where to touch, where to kiss, or caress. Like he had a map in his head of all of Laz's sweet spots, all of which he exploited without mercy. Laz begged for more, shameless in his desire for the gorgeous man feasting on his flesh. With the flick of his tongue, he had Laz coming apart, and with a tender word, he rendered Laz breathless.

Red moved toward the drawer when Laz threw his hand out to stop him.

"Wait."

"Everything okay?"

"Yeah, I, um… I was thinking maybe we could ditch the condoms? I got tested a few months ago and have the results on my phone. They came back negative." Laz had no idea he'd been holding his breath until a brilliant smile spread across Red's face, a dimple appearing, because of course, the man had dimples. Sweet Jesus.

"I'm negative too. Everyone at Four Kings gets tested quarterly. I have my results from this quarter on my phone."

"So, is that okay?" The thought of having Red inside him with nothing between them had Laz achingly hard. He wanted to feel *all* of Red.

"It's more than okay." Red reached for his phone, but Laz stopped him.

"I trust you."

"That means a great deal to me, sweetheart. Thank you for putting your trust in me." Red pressed his lips to Laz's, kissing him sweetly before he let his head rest against Laz's.

Laz was placing more than his trust in Red's hands. He was placing his heart. Instead of saying so, he wrapped his arms around Red and thrust his hips up. "I need you inside me, Red." He felt the shudder go through Red, and Laz couldn't help the moan that escaped him. "Please."

Red pulled away long enough to grab the lube, and pour a generous amount into his hand. He stroked his hard length, his beautiful skin flushed, his lips slightly parted, and his hazel-green eyes burning with heat as he caressed every inch of Laz's body with his gaze. As if unable to help himself, Red shifted down the bed, took hold of Laz's foot, and placed a kiss to it.

Laz groaned, his cock hard against his stomach, the tip leaking precome as Red placed feathery kisses along Laz's leg. When he reached Laz's thigh, he licked at the crease where Laz's groin met his leg. Laz was going to lose his mind if Red continued his sensual torture. He needed to be filled by Red.

As if sensing his thoughts, Red took pity on him and lined the head of his thick shaft up with Laz's hole. He lifted Laz's legs to make the breach a little easier, and Laz hissed at the sharp pain.

"You okay?"

Laz nodded. "Please, don't stop."

The pain soon gave way to the most delicious pleasure, and Laz arched his back as Red sank into him inch by glorious inch. When his groin was seated against Laz's ass, Laz wrapped his legs around Red, and then Red started to move ever so gingerly. They kissed leisurely, as if they had all the time in the world. Laz could kiss Red forever. His soft lips, talented tongue, and heavenly taste had Laz panting before long.

"Oh God, Red."

Laz bit down on his bottom lip, afraid the words swirling around in his head would tumble out of him if he didn't. They were still so new. The last thing he wanted was to scare Red, or have him believe it was the circumstances they were in making him say the words, when the truth was he felt them down to his soul.

"You're so beautiful," Red whispered, almost reverently, and a part of Laz wondered if maybe Red didn't already know.

Red laced their fingers together and moved their hands up and above Laz's head as he undulated his hips, his thrusts slow but deep. A gasp caught in Laz's throat when Red changed his angle and punched his hips.

"Oh fuck! Red!" Laz shook, his body ready to come apart as Red pegged his gland over and over. His mouth opened in a silent cry as Red started to move faster, his thrusts short, deep, and hard. Red buried his fingers in Laz's hair, holding on to fistfuls of it, and Laz scraped his nails down Red's back, his orgasm exploding through him, his come hot and sticky between their joined bodies.

"Laz," Red groaned, his hips losing all rhythm. Sweat beaded his brow, his breath coming out labored, and his muscles tightening as he met Laz's gaze. "I'm so fucking happy that you're mine."

"Yes. I'm yours, Red. For as long as you want me," Laz promised.

"Always. I'll always want you," Red whispered before he let out a strangled cry and his release roared out of him, his come filling Laz's channel. His entire body shook, and Laz held on to him as he continued to pound into Laz until every last drop had been released inside Laz. When his flesh was too sensitive, Red carefully pulled out with a hiss before collapsing on Laz, his face buried in the crook of Laz's neck.

Laz didn't mind Red's heavier weight on him, in fact he loved it. He knew he wouldn't be able to stay that way for long, but he'd enjoy every moment while he could. He wrapped one arm around Red's expansive back, brushing his fingers over the defined muscles, while he stroked Red's hair. He inhaled Red's scent, a heady mix of sweaty man, sex, and lavender. With a smile, he closed his eyes, and drifted off until a familiar voice stirred him from sleep. How long had he been out for? God, his body ached so damned good. His heart skipped a beat at the memory of him and Red making love. There was no doubt in his mind that's exactly what they'd done. All he could think about was doing it all over again.

"I'm sorry to call you on this number, but it couldn't wait. I really need to see you."

Laz's heart dropped to his stomach, and a lump formed in his throat. Red was on the phone with someone. Maybe he was talking to King, and he was whispering because he didn't want to wake up Laz. Whatever it was, it wasn't what his silly brain was trying to convince him of. He wasn't about to start jumping to conclusions, and he certainly wasn't going to start doubting Red.

"I'm so sorry, but it can't wait. How about later today? Now? I can't. I'm… with a friend."

The back of Laz's eyes stung, and he quickly squashed his rising panic. Whatever it was, it was *not* what he thought. It couldn't be. They'd just spent the night making love. Red had told him he was Laz's. What the hell was wrong with him? He needed to stop. Now. He couldn't let himself go down this path. This was Red, not Bryan. Laz wasn't going to let that asshole ruin this for him. Red was an amazing man, and he'd never been anything but upfront with Laz. He'd never given Laz any reason to doubt him. If he wanted Laz to know what his conversation was about, he'd say so.

"Great. Thank you. I better go. Sorry? No, um, he's just a friend. Really."

Laz rolled onto his side, his eyes closed as the bed dipped and Red curled around him. Fuck, why couldn't he get the stupid idea out of his head? Why did his brain conjure up images of Red and some gorgeous woman? Not even another guy, but a woman. Was he that insecure? *Stop being an asshole.*

Red nuzzled the curls at the back of Laz's head, and Laz swallowed down the hurt. Maybe he should just ask? But what was he supposed to say? *Hey, I couldn't help but overhear your obviously private phone conversation, and it sounded like maybe you might be seeing someone else besides me.* Red wouldn't do that. *Right, because he's perfect? You know who else was perfect? Bryan.* Perfect Bryan who'd said he loved Laz and then slept his way across the globe behind Laz's back. *No. Stop. Just stop.*

Laz swallowed hard and forced himself to sound like his heart wasn't shattering in a million pieces. "We should get up and dressed. Colton and Ace will be here soon."

"Right. Shit. I forgot." Red placed a kiss to Laz's shoulder and brushed his fingers down his arm. "Want to join me in the shower?"

"Why don't you shower while I make us breakfast? I have a couple of invoices I need to check on this morning."

"Oh, okay." The disappointment in Red's voice was clear as day, but thankfully he seemed to recover quickly. "Thank you for your offer to make breakfast. I'll see you downstairs." With one final kiss to Laz's shoulder, the bed dipped and Red headed for the bathroom. As soon as he was gone, Laz jumped out of bed, grabbed some clothes, his phone, and ran to the end of the hall, where he ducked into Colton's bathroom to use his shower. He broke records with how fast he washed. Once he was dressed, he hurried downstairs and got to making them breakfast bagels, though the thought of eating anything made him feel sick to his stomach. Tears burned the back of his eyes, but he refused to give in. They were tears of anger more than anything, because he hated this familiar feeling. Hated that he was doubting Red, that after everything Laz had suffered he was once again doubting himself.

Laz didn't want to distrust Red, but the seed had been planted, and Richard's words echoed in his head as if to justify his shitty feelings. *What makes you think you're good enough for him? He's just going to use you like every other guy until something better comes along, because you're the in-between guy.*

Fuck Richard, and fuck this. He was *not* the in-between guy.

"You okay?"

Laz was so startled he dropped the glass of orange juice he'd been holding. It shattered into tiny pieces, juice going everywhere. "Fuck!"

"Don't move," Red instructed gently. "Your feet are bare. I don't want you to cut yourself. Let me get the dustpan and broom."

Laz did as asked, and Red was back a heartbeat later, brushing the shards onto the dustpan.

"I'm such a fucking idiot."

"No, you're not. It was an accident. I'm sorry I scared you." Red finished cleaning up, and it took everything Laz had not to demand Red tell him what the hell was going on. Why did he have to be so fucking insecure? What if he was wrong, and Red realized he'd made a big mistake with Laz, that he had his own baggage without taking on Laz's. He'd said there had to be trust between them, but then why hide the phone call? Laz mentally shook himself out of it. He had to give Red a chance. *Like you gave Bryan a chance? Over and over.*

"I think maybe this whole mess is starting to get to me," Laz said, pouring himself a new glass of orange juice. "The whole hurry up and wait thing."

"Maybe after breakfast you should get some rest. Get back into bed."

"No, I'm good," Laz said, mustering up a smile before he took a seat at the counter to eat. "Maybe I'll just go for a swim in the pool."

"I'll join you." Red kissed his temple as he took a seat beside him.

Laz's phone rang. He recognized the number but couldn't place it. "Hello?"

"Laz, this is Maria Vargas."

"Maria, how are you?"

"I'm good but in desperate need of your help."

"How can I help?"

"Elena had to move up the date of her interview as she's going to need to fly back to Milan sooner than expected. As you may know, the unveiling of her spring collection is next week down in Miami, and she'd been hoping to do the interview once it was over, but unfortunately she's going to have to fly out straight after the show, so she's asked if we could do the shoot today."

Holy shit. *Today*? "Yes, of course. Just tell me where I need to go."

"We had a lovely outdoor shoot planned, but it looks like we'll have to make do with the studio we have here. Everyone is on their way. I'm so very sorry to spring this on you at the last minute."

"Not a problem. I'll get my equipment together and head right over. See you soon."

"Thank you so much, Laz. You are a star." She hung up, and Laz started making a mental note of everything he needed to bring with him.

"Everything okay?" Red asked.

"I'm needed at the studio right away. The shoot's been moved up."

"Okay. Tell me what you need, and I'll load it into the car while you get ready."

"Damn it, I thought I'd have more time. I hate rushing into a shoot, especially one this important."

Red put a hand on his shoulder and gave him a reassuring squeeze, his smile sweet. "You're going to be great, Laz. You got this."

"Thank you." Warmth spread through Laz, and he allowed himself to fall into Red's hazel-green eyes. He was being an idiot. Red had been nothing but supportive, protective, and caring. Whatever that phone call had been was none of Laz's business, and certainly not the dire affair his head insisted on. He needed to stop letting his insecurities get the better of him before he ruined the best thing that had ever happened to him. This time, things were going to be different.

Something was wrong.

Red hated the ugly feeling in the pit of his stomach. His instincts were on high alert, and it had nothing to do with any physical danger. After he'd gathered all of Laz's equipment so Laz could get himself ready for the photo shoot, Red quickly got dressed. When they got into Red's car, Laz had been nervous but in high spirits, and although he'd been a little quiet on the way to St. Augustine, it was clearly from nerves. They'd arrived at the studio, and Red helped Laz carry all his equipment inside. Laz even sneaked a quick kiss when no one was looking while they waited in the lobby.

The moment they stepped into the studio, they were swept up in a flurry of activity as everyone prepared for Elena's arrival. After much reassurance that he was perfectly fine to, Red helped move equipment, especially the heavier pieces, and Laz teased him about his "manly muscles," which Red promptly flexed for him. Laz swooned dramatically across a chaise lounge Red had just moved, and they both laughed, everything seeming to go back to normal between them. At least until Lucky showed up.

"I need to step out for a little while," Red said, kissing Laz's cheek. "I'll be back later. If you need anything, Lucky's here to help."

Laz's smile faded, but he nodded. "Is everything okay?"

"Yeah, I just have an errand to run."

"Okay." Laz smiled, but it didn't reach his eyes. "See you soon, then."

Before Red could say another word, Laz hurried off. For the life of him, Red couldn't figure out what he could have done to bring this on. He was under no illusion that whatever was bothering Laz was connected to him, but no matter how many times he'd asked Laz, he received the same answer.

Nothing.

Red worried the entire drive over to Alexa's. Was it possible Laz knew? There was no way. Red had been careful. He'd made sure Laz was still deep asleep before taking the call after he'd texted her. Damn it, he should have left the room, but he'd been afraid of waking Laz. Before he could spare the matter another thought, Alexa opened the door, her lips pulled into a thin line the moment she saw him. She placed her hands on her hips and narrowed her eyes at him.

"Why do you look guilty?"

"I don't know what you're talking about." He smiled sweetly, but she wasn't having any of it. "Can I get a hug first?"

With a sigh, she allowed him to bring her into a tight hug. She was a tiny thing, the top of her head barely at eye level with his chest. He squeezed her, but not too tight, and she returned the gesture before pulling back and standing to one side to let him by. The place was as familiar to him as his own home, and the moment he reached the living room, he felt his tension ease. He sat down on the plush couch and sat back against the many comfortable throw pillows. The room was light and airy and filled with so many memories.

Alexa sat in the armchair across from him, her fingers laced together on her lap as she studied him. "I was a little surprised to hear from you." Her big brown eyes filled with concern. "Why the urgency?"

Red took a moment to gather his thoughts, to accept what was. He took a deep breath and said the words that had been taking shape in his heart. "I'm in love."

Alexa's eyes went wide before she seemed to gather herself and nodded slowly. "With your… friend?"

"Yes."

"Why tell me they were only a friend?"

"He," Red offered. "And he's my boyfriend. It's all very new." Red shrugged at her question, his face feeling flushed before he gave her a rueful smile. "I guess because I knew what you were going to say."

"And what's that?"

Red leaned forward, his elbows on his legs and his chin resting on his fists. "That I should be open and honest with him about the reason I called you. That if I felt the need to be here, then it's important, and if it's important, I should discuss it with him and not hide it."

"And yet you did none of those things, Russell. Why?"

"Because I'm scared. No, I'm terrified." He sat back and closed his eyes, inhaling the soothing scent of lavender. Centering himself, he met her gaze. "I'm terrified I'm going to scare him off."

"Like you believe you did with Naaz?"

Red nodded.

Alexa leaned forward, her gaze never leaving his. "We discussed this, Russell. You didn't scare Naaz off. She loved you, yes, but she wasn't as prepared for the challenges of being in a relationship with someone who has PTSD as she believed she was. It was neither your fault nor hers, but her insecurities and trust issues are what led to the end of your relationship, which she initiated by giving you an ultimatum with a predictable outcome."

Red sighed. "She knew I couldn't walk away from King."

Alexa nodded. "I believe in the end, it allowed her to walk away without guilt. She gave you what she believed was a very reasonable choice, and you chose Ward instead of her."

"No, I know." It had taken him a long time to come to terms with what happened between him and Naaz, but every once in a while, his insecurities reared up.

"What's his name?" Alexa asked softly.

Red winced. "Um, Lazarus. Laz." He knew what was coming. She arched a perfectly shaped brow at him.

"The young man you saved from drowning at Colton's party."

"Yes."

"That was some time ago."

Red rubbed the back of his neck. "Yeah, I know." He went back to the beginning, and told her everything, from Ace's little ambush, to the shooting on the beach, to the amazing days and nights that had led to Red giving a name to the fullness in his heart.

"It's clear that Laz has serious trust issues, and understandably so. He's only just come out of what sounds like an abusive relationship and is facing his own insecurities. Openness and trust will be crucial if you're both going to have a future together. I know it's a little early in your relationship, but if Laz is open to it, I would like for him to accompany you on your monthly sessions. I think it could benefit you both."

"I'd like that. Thank you. I'll talk to him about it."

They talked some more, and Red discussed his recurring nightmare, the reason behind his asking to see her so urgently, afraid he might be having a setback, but he was relieved to discover the nightmare was less about his PTSD and more about his fears concerning his relationship with Laz. By the time Red left Alexa's office, he could breathe again. No more hiding. He loved Laz, and if he was going to have a healthy relationship with the man he loved, he would need to be a hundred percent transparent.

When Red arrived back at the studio, he was eager to see Laz, to pull him into his arms and apologize for being such an idiot. He'd ask Laz to forgive him for not telling him about the nightmares and keeping them a secret from him because he'd been afraid Laz would walk away from him the way Naaz had. His heart was doing little flips, and he couldn't keep the smile off his face.

His smile was quickly replaced with something darker when he walked through the studio door to find a handsome man tucking a lock of Laz's curls behind his ears. The man said something that made Laz laugh and then leaned in closer than necessary to point out something on Laz's laptop screen.

Red took a step forward, but Lucky appeared, grabbed his arm, and pulled him to one side. "Bro, what the fuck is going on?"

"That's what I'd like to know," Red hissed. "Who's the guy hanging all over Laz?" And why was Laz allowing it?

Lucky shrugged. "Some art director or something." His deep brown eyes filled with concern. "¿Red, qué pasó? You two were all lovey-dovey and shit, and now he's acting like an ass. When I asked him if he's okay, he says he's fine, but his tone and eyes say he is not fine, you know? I am worried about him."

"Me too. Thanks for looking out for him." Red patted Lucky's shoulder and motioned to the door. "I got it from here."

"Are you sure?" Lucky asked, looking over his shoulder at Laz before moving his worried gaze back to Red.

"Yeah, thanks. I'll see you later, okay?"

Lucky nodded and headed off while Red took a moment to compose himself. Since neither Maria nor Elena were anywhere in sight, and the few people who remained seemed to be packing up, Red assumed the shoot was over already. Damn, it went quicker than he'd expected. That didn't explain Laz's behavior. Whatever game Laz was playing, Red was not happy.

Laz laughed, and Red's hackles went up, not because the man was obviously flirting with Laz, but because Laz was clearly flirting back. Laz poked the guy in the shoulder playfully, his smile wide as he said something that had the other guy in stitches. What the hell was going on? Red walked over, his eyes narrowed at the man, who glanced up and quickly straightened away from Laz when Red approached.

"Hey," Red said, trying not to growl out the words. Maybe he was just feeling a little sensitive after his session and overreacting, but then Lucky also believed something was up.

Laz muttered a greeting, but didn't even bother looking up from his screen. His smile had faded, and he pretended to concentrate on the images in front of him.

*The fuck?*

"You must be Red. Laz's security detail," the man said, extending his hand. "He said not to pay you any mind if you came over, but you're kind of a hard man to ignore. I'm Harold, the art director."

Red's eyebrows shot up near his hairline. Not to pay him any mind? Red shook Harold's hand. "Hi."

"We still have some work to do, but I can take Laz home if you have better places to be."

The way the guy said those words rubbed Red the wrong way, and he felt like maybe it was something Laz might have said to Harold. Red had needed to step out, and that translated to him having better places to be?

"Can I talk to you for a minute?" Red asked Laz.

"I'm kind of busy right now, but if you need to go do whatever it is you have to do, Harold can drop me off at Colton's."

Like hell he would.

"Laz." Red was trying to be patient, but the smugness in Harold's knowing grin, and the cold shoulder Laz was currently giving him without explanation, had him struggling to maintain his cool. When Laz didn't move, Red closed the laptop. The look he received was icy enough to freeze his balls off, but whatever snippy remark Laz had been prepared to throw his way died on his lips when Red narrowed his eyes. "I need to talk to you in private."

"Fine." Laz slipped out of the folding director's chair and walked with Red to what appeared to be a small office off the main area. Red waited until Laz was inside before closing the door and turning to Laz.

"What the hell is going on? What was that all about out there? Telling Harold not to pay me any mind?"

"Well, yeah," Laz said with a shrug. "As far as he knows you're just my friend, right?"

The way he said "friend" had Red's alarm bells going off. "What?"

"Forget it. I'm done here. Just take me home." Laz turned toward the door, and Red gently took hold of his arm.

A punch to the groin would have hurt less than the blow he received when Laz flinched and jerked away from him, but it was the look in his eyes that cut the deepest. It was the look of someone who expected to be struck.

"Don't touch me," Laz whispered.

Red swallowed hard, a mixture of painful heart-wrenching emotions flooding through him, everything from anger and hurt to regret.

What could he possibly have done to warrant such a reaction? The backs of his eyes stung, and he blinked away his tears.

"Wow, I have no idea what I did, but I'm pretty sure I didn't deserve that, Laz."

"You hurt me."

Red felt a tear roll down his cheek, and he quickly wiped it away. "I have never raised my hand to you. Ever."

"There are plenty of other ways to hurt someone." Laz remained turned away from him, curled in on himself, and the sight was too much for Red.

"I'll have Lucky take you home." Red left the room without another word. Somehow he managed to pull himself together enough to call Lucky. "Hey, I'm sorry to do this, but I need you to come back. Laz needs a ride home."

There was a pause on the other end of the line before Lucky spoke up, his voice soft and somber. "Okay, bro. Don't worry. I'm on my way."

Red waited until Laz was in Lucky's car before he climbed behind the wheel of his G80. He felt numb. Like his world was crumbling around him. He had the whole ride over to Colton's house to think about what happened. The only thing he could think of that could have caused all this was the phone call he'd made, but then why wouldn't Laz just say so? Why not simply ask? It didn't make any sense. By the time he got to Colton's, he was fuming. Not at Laz, but the whole goddamn situation. What the hell did it say about their relationship that it all fell apart at the first snag? Right now, he needed to hit something, so he changed into some loose yoga pants and a T-shirt before making his way to Colton's gym. Thankfully, he didn't run into Laz, but he did run into Ace.

"Hey, whoa, you look like a bull about to charge. What's going on?"

Red was about to say nothing, but stopped himself. "I need to blow off some steam."

"Going to hit the gym?"

"Definitely plan on hitting something," Red grumbled.

"How about a little sparring session?"

"I don't think that's a good idea."

"You're right, it's not a good idea. It's a great idea," Ace said with a decisive nod as he followed Red. "Then you can tell me what's got you stomping around like you're trying to bring the house down."

"Don't say I didn't warn you." Red walked into the large home gym, his body tight, and ready to let loose his frustration. The gym was impressive as far as home gyms went what with all the latest high tech equipment, but Red wasn't interested in the state-of-the-art treadmill or elliptical. Instead, he headed straight for the mat and the heavy duty MMA punching bag Ace had installed after he moved in. He pulled off his shirt, and dropped it on the bench before doing a few stretches. Then he swiped up a pair of boxing gloves, and pulled them on. Ace took position behind the punching bag, and held it for him.

"So what's going on?"

"I'm not ready to talk yet." Red rounded his shoulders before bouncing on his toes. When Ace nodded, Red let loose with a fierce right hook. Ace didn't say a word. He held on to the bag while Red unleashed all his frustration with a series of right and left hooks, jabs, and elbow hits, followed by several kicks. When he was sweating and panting, he nodded to Ace, who placed a water bottle to his lips and tipped it back slowly so he could take a few sips.

"Ready to talk yet?"

Red motioned toward the second pair of gloves, and Ace arched an eyebrow at him.

"That bad, huh?" Ace slipped on his gloves, and after some stretching, took position on the mat across from Red.

They went a few rounds, circling each other, but being mindful that not long ago Red had been recovering from gunshot wounds. Ace was quicker on his feet than Red, which helped him avoid Red's fists. He knew if he let Red get one of his right hooks in that he'd be on the mat. Red kept his gloves in front of his face and his elbows tucked against his body to protect his ribs. Ace liked to play dirty, but Red knew all his tricks. He blocked Ace's left hook when he faked a right.

Then he told Ace everything.

"You should have seen his face," Red said, dropping onto the bench. "Like I'd hit him."

Ace sat beside Red, his expression going pensive. "That seems a little extreme. It has to be more than him just overhearing your phone call. I mean, yeah, I can see how maybe he'd be pissed, but to react the way he did? Laz isn't so irrational. There's something else going on there, buddy."

"But how am I supposed to do something about it, if he won't talk to me?"

"I'll talk to Colton, see what he says. Maybe he can get Laz to open up a little. Don't give up on him, Red. He really cares about you. If he didn't, he wouldn't be so hurt about whatever it is he believes you did. Laz has been hurt badly in the past. Be patient with him, take things slow."

Red nodded. Ace was right. He had to be patient. Normally patience wasn't a problem for him. Next to King, Red was usually the one to show the most restraint, and in some cases—especially where Ace was concerned—he was even more patient than King, but when it came to Laz, Red was struggling to figure out which way was up. He just hoped that whatever storm was brewing, they could weather it together, or their relationship was doomed after just beginning.

# CHAPTER 11

How was it possible to have his heart broken twice in such a short amount of time? Did he have something written on his forehead that said "world's biggest sucker"? As if that wasn't enough, he still hadn't confronted Red. Every time he worked up the courage to have a calm, adult conversation, he'd think about the betrayal and picture himself punching Red in his stupidly handsome face. His heart told him not to leap to conclusions, but how could he not when the evidence was right in front of him? God, how could he be so stupid, letting himself fall in love with Red so quickly. He was such a fool, and a coward, hiding away in his room.

Yesterday, when Lucky pulled into Colton's driveway to drop him off, Laz thanked him and fled from the car like it was on fire. Thankfully Red hadn't been home, and Laz was able to get to his room without incident. He felt like such an asshole, but he'd even managed to avoid Colton and Ace. After locking the door to his room, he'd stripped and gotten into the shower, where he'd cried his eyes out like the sad, pathetic loser he was, and then he'd crawled into bed and stayed there.

The saddest part was his reason for not confronting Red, knowing when he did, it would be over. *They'd* be over. Laz was more afraid of losing Red than he was of having his worst fears confirmed—that Red had betrayed him. What did that say about his sorry ass that he preferred to suffer and know Red was still his than cut him loose like he should? It was like Bryan all over again. How long was he going to let Red string him along? Except unlike with Bryan, Laz couldn't pretend. He couldn't busy himself in his work and act like everything was fine, like he didn't know what was really going on.

Colton had been worried and tried to get Laz to open the door, but Laz lied, telling him he had a migraine and would talk to him tomorrow. This morning he'd showered and crawled right back into bed. Instead of doing something about the shitty situation he found himself in, he decided to torture himself by looking at the photo again. He stared at it, the image seared into his brain. They made such a beautiful couple. She was small and petite, with killer curves, dressed casually in a flowy mauve top, black leggings, and mauve ballet flats. Her dark hair was piled high on her head, and her smile was sweet. She seemed happy to see him. And *him.* He had her wrapped up in his arms, his chin on her shoulder as he hunched over due to their difference in height. His eyes were closed, and he looked at peace. They stood holding each other on the front steps of her house.

Once they were inside, had Red brought her into his arms and kissed her? Tears blurred Laz's vision, and he wiped them away with a sniff. He choked on a sob when his eyes landed on the text beneath the photo.

*I'm sorry you had to find out this way.*

Turning his phone off, Laz tossed it onto the bed before rolling over onto his stomach. He couldn't go through this. Not again. He wouldn't stay in another crushing relationship that left his soul bruised and battered. He hadn't meant to react the way he had when Red touched him, but it hadn't been long after he'd received the text with the photo, and it was still fresh on his mind. His reaction had been horrible, and he knew it, but all he could think about was Red wrapped around someone else, and the pain had washed over him in waves, the heartache trying to cripple him. Was he really so hard to love? Why wasn't he ever enough? He'd known Red was too good to be true. Damn it. Why hadn't he listened to the little voice in his head?

"Okay, that's enough." He'd had enough wallowing. He got out of bed and headed to the bathroom to wash his face. No more hiding. Colton was probably worried sick about him, and Laz wasn't about to bring his drama down on Colton. After splashing some water on his face, he changed into some cargo shorts and a soft T-shirt, slipped into some flip-flops, and headed downstairs. If he ran into Red, well, then it was time to face the painful truth.

It was over between them.

At least his career was moving in the right direction. The editorial shoot had been a success, and both Maria and Elena had been thrilled with his shots. Paolo's absence had been odd, and Laz had made sure to send Mason a text to let him know. Neither Maria nor Elena brought up the fact Paolo wasn't there when he was supposed to have been part of the shoot, but Elena was her usual cheerful, flighty self, so Laz didn't pry. He still had to retouch the photos, but Maria wanted to pick the shots she wanted for the article first.

Laz found Colton sitting at the kitchen counter with a cup of coffee and his tablet. No Red in sight. Or Ace, for that matter. Laz didn't know whether to be relieved or annoyed. When Colton saw him, he jumped from his chair and brought Laz in for a big hug, making Laz chuckle.

"It was just a migraine, Colton. No big deal."

Colton held him out at arms' length and looked him over. "Are you sure? How are you feeling? Do you need me to get anything for you?"

"I'm fine." With Gio being away so much, Colton had appointed himself big brother years ago, taking over Gio's fussing for him. Laz didn't mind. He knew how lucky he was to have two doting big brothers, even if one of them wasn't related to him by blood. "I'm feeling much better. I'm sorry I didn't come out to see you."

Colton waved a hand in dismissal. "You're feeling better, and that's what matters. Since the boys aren't around, I thought maybe you'd like to join me for a swim in the pool?"

"Ace and Red aren't here?" Laz was surprised by that. Was it possible Red was avoiding him? But then that didn't explain Ace's absence.

"They left about an hour ago." Colton looked like he wanted to say more but then thought better of it. "I don't think they'll be back until later today."

"Did they say where they were going?" Laz asked, as he heated up some milk for his latte.

"Ace said he had to help Red out with something."

"That's it?"

"Yes." Colton tilted his head as he studied Laz. He narrowed his eyes. "Why?"

Laz shrugged. "No reason." Not feeling particularly hungry, he decided to just make himself some buttered toast. What exactly was Ace helping Red out with? Covering up the evidence? Whoa, okay, he needed to slow his roll. He wasn't going to drag Ace into his mess either.

"You don't seem particularly satisfied with that answer," Colton replied, resuming his seat at the counter.

"It's none of my business, but you don't think that's a little… suspect?"

Colton frowned deep. "What's suspect? If it was important and something I should know, Ace would tell me."

"So you're okay not knowing what he's doing?"

"Laz, I trust Ace. And he trusts me. The moment we start demanding detailed explanations from one another for our every move, is the moment the trust in our relationship is gone. Did something happen with Red?"

"You know, I think I will go for a dip in the pool. That sounds nice." Laz smiled, but Colton wasn't buying it. Instead of questioning Laz, Colton let out a resigned sigh.

"Okay. When you're ready to talk about it, I'm here for you, you know that."

Laz nodded. "Thanks." He finished up his breakfast, then told Colton he'd be right back. He went upstairs to his bedroom to grab a pair of swim shorts and sunglasses, then joined Colton outside. It was a gorgeous day, and he was glad he'd decided to spend some time at the pool with Colton. An umbrella was open between two lounge chairs, and Colton had laid a towel down on each chair. He'd also placed a water bottle for each of them on the small table between the chairs. Laz changed in one of the cabanas, and when he came out, Colton was already sunning himself as he lay on a pool float, his blue-tinted sunglasses matching his swim shorts. At nearly six foot five, Colton's feet hung off the edge of the float.

"Mm, this never gets old."

Laz jumped into the pool, allowing himself to sink toward the bottom, the water heavenly, and nothing but quiet around him. He surfaced and smiled at the sound of Colton's deep chuckle. Colton was on his stomach now, his chin resting on his folded arms.

"Your hair is getting long."

Laz raked his fingers through his wet curls, his traitorous brain conjuring up images of Red grabbing fistfuls of his curls when they had sex, of the content little noises Red made when he nuzzled against Laz's hair. "Maybe I should chop it off. Get a buzz cut or something."

Concern filled Colton's silver eyes, his smile sad. "If that's what you really want."

What he wanted was to feel Red's strong arms around him, to have things go back to how they'd been just days ago when the two of them had been enjoying each other, caressing one another, mouths tasting, Red's lips against his skin. Their future together had looked so promising.

"You know what we need? Sangria."

Laz chuckled. "It's like ten in the morning, Colt."

"So what? It's cocktail hour somewhere in the world, right?"

"Why not." His life was in shambles, and his heart in tatters, so why not drown his sorrows for a while? Wow, bitter did not become him.

"Ace made a nice big pitcher of summer berry Sangria last night." Colton waggled his eyebrows.

"That sounds amazing."

Colton held his nose and rolled off the float into the water, making Laz laugh. Laz swam for the stairs and climbed out of the pool after Colton. They quickly dried themselves off, then went into the house, the cool air-conditioning nipping at his skin. While Colton removed the large plastic pitcher from the fridge, Laz took two plastic cups from the cupboard. The last thing he needed was his clumsy ass dropping glass around the pool. They placed everything on a tray, along with some snacks, and went back out to the pool. The morning was beautiful and peaceful, which was ironic, considering the turmoil inside Laz.

Colton carried the tray to the edge of the pool, carefully placed it down, and slid it close enough to the edge for them to reach easily. They filled their cups, and Laz gulped his down before Colton reached the bottom step. God, it tasted so good, the perfect mix of wine and berries. It really hit the spot. He refilled his cup before joining Colton inside the heavenly warm water.

"How are things going with you and Red?"

The mention of Red's name was enough to spear Laz's heart. He'd have to face the music sometime. His eyes welled, his heart wanting to confide in Colton, but Laz wasn't ready to speak his fears out loud. Not yet. He plunged beneath the water in the hopes of disguising the wetness to his eyes. He came back up and wiped the water from his face.

"I hope you've been getting some while I've been gone," Colton teased, picking up his cup, and taking a long drink of his Sangria.

"Colt!"

Colton laughed. "What? Red is very sexy. Why shouldn't you enjoy jumping the man's bones?"

"You have a boyfriend," Laz reminded him.

"I also have eyes. Just because I think Red is attractive doesn't mean I don't love Ace. Besides, Red may be handsome, but no one gets my engine revved like Ace does. God, the way that man moves. Mm, talk about a sinful body. I just want to sink my teeth into his gorgeous ass."

"TMI, Colt."

"Like you don't want to do the same to Red."

Laz ignored the comment, because while his mind was conjuring up ways to verbally eviscerate Red, his stupid body was pining for him like it had been sex-starved for years or something. "You're like my brother. I don't want to hear about Gio's sex life. What makes you think I want to hear about yours?"

Colton shrugged. "You never know. You might learn a few tricks."

"Oh really? You're a sex guru all of a sudden?"

"I will choose not to be insulted by your clear misconception of my sexual prowess."

Laz laughed at that, and it felt so good. "Oh my God, you sound like Ace."

"Shut up." Colton splashed at him, and Laz snickered as he splashed back. "You know, I saw it the moment Ace introduced you two. The way you looked at each other? I'd never wanted Bryan to be out of the picture so badly. I was one mimosa away from dragging him into the ocean with a garland of meat around his neck and hoping he got eaten by sharks."

Laz gasped before snorting out a laugh. "You are so evil."

"What? It's the truth!" Colton laughed, and Laz shook his head.

"I'm so glad you're home," Laz said, grateful to have Colton in his life. In truth, he was surrounded by loving people. It was important he not forget that, or take it for granted. "How did your meeting go?"

"Great. Fine. Boring business stuff. I ate *so* much pizza. So good. We should go down for a weekend. Watch a show on Broadway or something. Damn this Sangria is good."

"Someone's a little tipsy," Laz teased.

Colton shrugged. "Maybe, but not enough to not notice something's wrong."

"Nothing is wrong." Laz finished off his Sangria, then lay on his back to float. Above them, the sky was a perfect blue filled with white fluffy clouds. The sun was shining, and in the distance, the ocean waves rolled onto the shore. He closed his eyes and let out a steady breath. How long would it take before everything stopped reminding him of Red? He was surprised he didn't sink to the bottom of the pool with how heavy his heart was.

"Laz, talk to me. I've never seen you try so desperately to hide a broken heart, not even with Bryan."

"I think he's cheating on me." Why did he always bottle things up inside? It always went the same way. He'd try to bury it deep down until he just couldn't fight it anymore and it all came spilling out like word vomit. Ugh, he was hopeless. Laz straightened, amused by Colton's mouth hanging open.

"Wait, you're dating? When did this happen? Wait, never mind. We can talk about that later. Right now, tell me why you think he's cheating on you."

Laz told Colton all about the phone call he overheard and the photo he received. He waited while Colton mulled it over.

"Laz, I know the evidence seems pretty compelling, and I understand where your fear is coming from, but this is Red we're talking about. I'm not saying it's not possible for a man like Red to cheat, but Red isn't a coward. He's like the rest of the Kings, very upfront about things. He's been crazy about you from the moment he met you. I've seen how he looks at you, how protective he is of you. I think you need to sit down with him and have a conversation about what you heard and the photo you received. I mean, you don't even know who sent it. It's very odd."

"You're right." Laz poured himself another cup of Sangria. "I've been avoiding him, too scared to find out the truth. I can't keep doing that. I need to know." Red *was* different. There had to be a reasonable explanation for everything. *Just like Bryan had a reasonable explanation for everything.* God, he hated his brain sometimes. He really was his own worst enemy.

Laz enjoyed spending time with Colton. They talked about New York, Gio, the wedding in Miami later that year for Ace and Lucky's cousin. The Sangria was gone in no time, and they moved onto funny stories about Colton and Gio in college. Laz laughed at their schoolboy antics. They'd been such big dorks at the time. Then again, to Laz, no matter the cut of their tailored suits, they were still a couple of big dorks, and he loved them. After getting all wrinkly, they got out to hit the showers.

"Meet you downstairs for lunch?" Colton asked.

"Sounds great." They went to their rooms to shower, and once he was dressed in a pair of black cargo shorts and comfy T-shirt, Laz left his bedroom and smacked into a wall. Shit. No, wait, it was Red.

"Hey," Red said softly.

As much as Laz wished he could say he was prepared, that he was just going to come out and say, "Hey, we need to talk," he couldn't take the heartache in Red's gorgeous hazel-green eyes. Laz pointed behind him to his room.

"Sorry, I just remembered I need to go through some photos, and—"

"Stop. Please. Just tell me what I did to upset you, and don't say it's nothing because I know that's not true. I can feel it down to my core. It's breaking my heart."

Everything that had been bubbling inside him, all the pain, doubt, and fear came roaring to the surface, erupting like a geyser. "Breaking *your* heart? You son of a bitch! I can't believe you have the balls to say that to me after what you did!"

Red threw his arms up in frustration. "What did I do, Laz? How am I supposed to fix this when I have no clue what you're so pissed off at me for?"

"There's no fixing this, Red. I heard you. It was a really great way to be woken up, by the way, after what I thought had been the most amazing night of my life."

Red frowned. "What are you—" It seemed to dawn on him, and his eyes widened.

"There it is," Laz sneered, and Red narrowed his eyes, most likely at Laz's tone, but Laz was too hurt to care.

"The phone call. So you did hear me."

"Yes, I heard. I can't believe you! I poured my heart out to you, Red. I trusted you. I thought you were different. You made me believe I'd finally found the guy for me."

"That makes two of us."

Laz flinched. "What are you talking about?"

"I'm sorry you overheard that conversation—"

"I'll bet you are."

"Let me finish," Red said through his teeth. "I'm sorry you overheard that conversation and immediately jumped to conclusions."

"Oh really? You didn't say 'I really need to see you' or 'he's just a friend'?"

"I did say that. And you took that to mean what? That I was cheating on you and couldn't wait to get on the phone with my secret lover after a night of making promises to you? That I just had to call them right away with you lying next to me? I can't believe you would assume the worst of me like that. I'm not Bryan, and I don't appreciate the comparison. If you were worried, you should have just asked me."

Laz scoffed at that. "Like you would have told me the truth."

"Yes! I would have. I have done nothing to warrant being branded the cheat you think I am."

"Wow, I have to congratulate you on your performance. Maybe I would have believed you if I hadn't seen you with her!"

Red's brows drew together, his frown deep. "What the hell are you talking about? Her? Seen me with who?"

Laz pulled his phone out of his pocket, found the text, and opened the image before thrusting it at Red. He folded his arms over his chest as Red held the phone, staring at the picture. Laz expected shock or stunned recognition, guilt. He'd expected Red to deny everything, to start pleading it wasn't what it looked like. A cold shiver went through him when Red did none of those things. Instead, a coldness Laz had never seen in him before came into his eyes, and when he spoke, the iciness in his quiet tone had Laz second-guessing himself.

"Do you know who this is?"

"I don't care." Laz hated that his voice sounded so unsteady, but he'd never seen this side of Red, and it was a little scary.

"Well, you should. You should know how royally fucked-up this is. That phone call I made? Seeing this woman? I did that for you. For us."

Laz let out a snort. He should have known. "Oh, now I've heard everything."

"The woman in this photo—which you're going to tell me how you got in a second by the way—isn't my lover. She's my therapist, Laz, and has been for the last ten years."

Laz's arms fell to his sides, and his heart sank to his stomach, the blood draining from his face. It couldn't be true, could it? When he spoke, his voice was almost a whisper. "What?"

"This is my therapist, Dr. Alexandria Bradbury." Red shoved the phone back at him. "I called her because I needed to see her. I've been having recurring nightmares and waking up in a cold sweat in the middle of the night. I didn't wake you up because I was scared it would mess things up between us. I knew I couldn't keep hiding it from you, so I called her. Her schedule was full, and I wasn't due to see her for another two weeks, so I begged her to see me. My PTSD is the reason my last relationship fell apart, and I couldn't bear the thought of that happening with you, so I went to get help."

"Oh my God." Laz put a hand to his mouth, his body shaking involuntarily. Oh God, he'd... he'd fucked up. He'd fucked it all up.

"I don't cheat, Laz. If I want to be with someone and they want to be with me, then there's no one else. You said you thought I was different. Well, I thought you were different too. I understand what Bryan put you through, I do, but you should have *talked* to me."

Laz swallowed hard. "And when were you going to tell me about the nightmares or the call to your therapist?"

"I don't know, but it doesn't matter now, does it, because you didn't give me that chance."

"So it's okay for you to hide things from me? What happened to trust?"

"My choosing not to tell you in that moment is not the same thing as assuming the man in my bed that I have been losing my heart to is a cheating asshole because I overheard a few sentences of one half of a phone conversation and received a photo with a cryptic message. Who sent it?"

"I don't know. I tried calling the number, but it said it was disconnected." A multitude of emotions flooded over Laz, the strongest being shame. Red had been suffering, and instead of worrying Laz, he chose to get help, for them, for their relationship. Deep down, he knew Red would have eventually told him, and what had Laz done? Accused him of cheating. Jesus fuck, what the hell was wrong with him?

"So again, instead of asking, you took some stranger's word over mine and assumed the worst of me. Whoever sent you that was clearly hoping to get you to doubt me, and you did."

Laz swallowed hard. "You're right. I fucked up royally. That phone call was personal, and you didn't have to tell me about it. You should have had the chance to tell me when you were ready, and when I received the text, I should have just asked you. I let my emotions and insecurities get the better of me. I'm sorry."

"Sorry doesn't put the genie back in the bottle, Laz. It's clear you don't trust me."

Fear swept through Laz. Oh God, he'd ruined them. This was it. And why wouldn't it be? Why would Red forgive him, believing Laz didn't trust him, knowing what Laz thought of him? "I do trust you. I just got scared, and I'm sorry, please. What are you thinking?"

"I'm…. I don't know what I'm thinking. We should—"

Laz's phone rang, startling them both. Red let out a heavy sigh, turning away as Laz checked the screen.

"It's Mason."

"Put it on speaker."

Laz did as asked, holding the phone between them. "Mason, hey it's Laz. I've got you on speaker with Red."

"Thank Christ. Laz, I need you to come down to the station right away."

"What's going on?"

"We brought Paolo in for questioning after discovering something shady in his business account, but his wife showed up. Apparently the cat's out of the bag. Somehow someone informed her that her husband was cheating on her and that he was wanted for questioning by the police. Now she's down here losing her damn mind and asking for you, saying she needs to see you. Frankly, she's a little…."

"Eccentric?"

Mason let out a snort. "Nuttier than a fruitcake."

"We'll be right there," Red said.

Laz hung up and couldn't even bring himself to look Red in the eye. His heart was breaking all over again, knowing what he'd done. "I'm so sorry, Red," he said softly. "You deserve better."

"Why don't you let me decide what I deserve," Red said, sounding frustrated.

Bracing himself, Laz forced his gaze up, tears stinging the backs of his eyes at the hurt he'd caused a good man. "I'm so sorry, Red. I really am. You were the best thing that ever happened to me, and I'm so sorry I ruined it."

With a sigh, Red shook his head. When he moved his gaze to Laz, his expression softened. Laz's heart leapt in his throat when Red reached out to curl his fingers around a lock of Laz's hair, his voice rough with emotion when he spoke.

"You didn't ruin anything, sweetheart. We both made bad decisions, and we need to have a long conversation about this and why it happened, but it's not ruined. I promise."

Laz was almost afraid to ask. "So, you're staying?"

When Red brought Laz into his arms, Laz thought he might die from how good it felt. He wrapped his arms tightly around Red and buried his face against his chest, inhaling deeply. God, how he'd missed Red's scent, his arms, his warmth.

"Of course I'm staying. You mean too much to me, Laz. I won't give you up that easy. We'll work through this, like we'll work through every other bump that comes along." He pulled back and kissed Laz's brow. "We better go, but we'll talk when we get back, okay?"

Laz nodded, feeling some of the heaviness in his heart lift. He pulled back and nodded. "Thank you. For being so good to me."

"I'm not perfect, Laz. Neither of us is." Red lifted Laz's hand to his lips for a kiss as they walked down the hall together. "We both have baggage and our own demons to fight. We're going to make mistakes, get pissed at each other, and argue, but one thing we'll never do is betray each other's trust. Communication is going to be important for us."

"You're right. I know it's something I have to work on, and I promise I will." Laz had no intention of making the same mistakes again. He couldn't let his insecurities get the better of him. He wouldn't lose a good man like Red because of his past.

"I know it's a little early in our relationship," Red said somewhat hesitantly, "but Alexa suggested that maybe you come with me to my monthly sessions. She thinks it could help us both."

Laz beamed up at him. "I'd like that."

The smile he received had Laz's heart skipping a beat, and he knew he'd made the right decision. He was a little nervous about seeing a therapist, where he would undoubtedly have to talk about his past, but if it meant being able to help Red when he had a setback, or if it helped strengthen their relationship, he was happy to do it.

Downstairs, Colton and Ace had their heads together, and they were murmuring quietly to each other. When they spotted Laz and Red, they both turned, their expressions filled with hope. Laz was so very blessed to have such amazing people in his life. Maybe they weren't related by blood, but they were family.

"Everything good?" Ace asked, looking from Red to Laz and back.

"We're working it out, but yeah, we're good," Red said with a smile, and the way he looked at Laz had his heart swelling and the butterflies in his stomach going crazy. At least until Red told Ace they were headed to the police station, reminding Laz that Mason had found something. Was it too much to hope for that he'd finally be putting this whole mess behind him? Whatever happened, he wasn't alone. They'd get through whatever came their way together, and they had a whole family to support them.

# CHAPTER 12

It was a goddamn circus.

Except instead of parading elephants and trapeze artists flying through the air, it was a catty model, a blubbering playboy, a wailing designer, and a snarly detective. If Ace were here, Red was pretty sure he'd find a joke in there somewhere. The second Red and Laz stepped into the precinct and Red spotted Bryan in police custody, he knew all hell was about to break loose, and he wasn't disappointed. Good God, he could practically hear the cannons in Tchaikovsky's "1812 Overture" going off as Bryan struggled against the officers holding him as he shrieked at Laz.

"You spiteful little bitch! I should have known you'd open that big fucking mouth of yours! Because clearly the second it wasn't stuffed with his big dick you spilled your guts. You're a fucking slut, Laz! How long after you kicked me out did you wait to give him your ass? Not long I bet."

"Screw you, Bryan. You brought this on yourself," Laz spat out.

While Bryan and Laz screamed at each other, Paolo was begging his wife for forgiveness, stating he'd been weak, while Elena was screaming and sobbing, her mascara running down her face as she threw whatever she could get her hands on at her husband.

"How could you, Paolo?" Elena cried. "I gave you everything! I gave you my heart!"

The two broke off into Italian, and although Red had no idea what they were saying, it was clear Paolo was groveling, and Elena was… well, she was losing her shit.

"Goddamn it, Williams, get him out of here," Mason yelled at the officer struggling with Bryan. Another two quickly joined in as Bryan kicked and screamed at the top of his lungs. He was like a hissing, spitting kitten, all ninety pounds of him.

"You're a fucking whore, Lazarus! You're so fucking desperate to be loved that you give your ass to the first guy who pretends to give a shit about you, just like you did in London!"

*Oh Fuck!*

Red sprang into action, taking off after Laz as he bolted through the bullpen toward Bryan. He managed to grab ahold of Laz, hauling him off his feet and away from Bryan before he could land a hit.

"Oh for fuck's sake," Mason growled at the officers. "Get him the hell out of here!"

"Fuck you, Bryan," Laz spat out, flailing as he tried to get away from Red to launch himself at Bryan. "You should have been there for me! He raped me! He fucking raped me, and when I came to you, you told me it was all part of the job, you heartless son of a bitch!" Tears streamed down Laz's face as the precinct plunged into silence. Not one person moved or said a word, all eyes on Laz who choked on a sob.

"Mason," Red called out, needing to get Laz away from Bryan and his vitriol.

Mason snapped himself out of it, hurried over, and ushered them toward the far end of the room. "This way." He led them down the hall and opened a door to what looked like an office. "I'll be back in a few minutes."

The office had a small love seat, and Red pulled Laz down with him as he sat, his heart breaking when Laz started shaking. That bastard. Why did he have to keep throwing that vile incident in Laz's face? Because he knew how much it hurt. Fucking asshole.

Red drew Laz into his arms, murmuring comforting words and running a hand soothingly over his back as Laz buried his face against Red's chest to cry. As if the last few weeks hadn't been enough, that jackass had to claw at the scabs of Laz's barely healed wounds.

"I'm sorry," Laz said with a sniff. Red stood, grabbed the box of tissues off the desk, and handed them to Laz before resuming his seat. "Thank you."

"What are you sorry for? You didn't do anything wrong, Laz." Red ran his fingers over Laz's head, softly stroking his hair.

"I'm sorry I brought this whole mess down on you. This is all my fault."

"None of this is on you. Bryan and Paolo are the ones who brought this down on you. Bryan betrayed your trust multiple times, and when you had enough, you walked away."

"But if I hadn't taken those pictures…."

"Bryan would have found a way to ruin your reputation and your career. He's a shallow, vindictive, nasty piece of work. You were trying to protect yourself. Their affair is on them, and the fallout of their getting caught is also on them. If one of them is responsible for sending a killer after you, then they're going to answer for that as well. We're going to get to the bottom of this, and they're going to have to face the consequences."

Laz released a heart-wrenching sigh. "I'm so tired." He closed his eyes, his words almost a whisper. "Sometimes I see him in my dreams."

Red didn't need to ask who. Wherever that piece of shit photographer was, Red hoped justice would find him and make him pay for what he'd done, not just to Laz, but to who knew how many other young men. Young men who were new to the industry, eager to make a name for themselves, to learn from the best out there. They'd looked up to the guy, believed he was a mentor, that he genuinely wanted to help them, when the terrifying truth was that he was a predator. He lured them to his studio with encouraging words and false promises, then threatened to ruin their careers if they didn't give in to his sexual advances.

"For years I believed what happened to me was my fault," Laz said quietly, staring off at nothing in particular. "That because I didn't fight him, because I let him… do what he did to me, that I was just as guilty. How could I say that he… raped me when I didn't fight him?" A tear rolled down his cheek, and he absently wiped it away. "He wanted to fuck me, and I let him."

"Because you were scared. You told him you wanted to keep things professional, and when he told you what he wanted, you said no, Laz. When he made a move on you, you tried to leave, but he stopped you and threatened you. You were alone and scared, and that bastard took advantage of that."

"I was terrified," Laz admitted. He blinked away his tears, and when he looked at Red, his gorgeous blue eyes filled with anger and determination. "I'm not scared anymore. When this is over, I want the Kings to help me track that bastard down. I want him to pay for what he did and stop him from doing it again, because there's no doubt in my mind that sick son of a bitch is still doing it."

Red took Laz's hand in his and brought it to his lips for a kiss. "I will do everything in my power to make sure he ends up behind bars."

"Thank you." Laz stood, and Red followed him. "Now, I want to know what that dick Paolo has to say for himself."

Laz and Red were shown into the security room where they'd stood the first time Paolo had been brought in for questioning. This time, Elena was there. When she saw Laz, she flung herself into his arms in a flutter of glittery neon skirts.

"Oh, my dear Lazarus. You poor thing," she cried, her arms wrapped around his head as she petted him. "I cannot believe this is happening. You poor, poor dear. We have both been deceived so terribly by these awful men."

"I'm so sorry this happened to you, Elena." Laz said, hugging her and patting her back. They turned to the screen when Mason entered the interview room where Paolo had been pacing. He quickly took a seat, and Mason sat across from him. He handed Paolo several documents.

"Why don't you tell me about the four transactions highlighted on that bank statement."

A deep frown came onto Paolo's face as he studied the document. "I don't know what this is. What am I looking at?"

"This is your business expense account, correct?"

"Yes, but I do not know what these numbers mean."

"These numbers mean that three payments of twenty-five thousand dollars left your account via wire transfer to that company there."

"I do not know this company."

"No?" Mason pursed his lips and leaned forward, his elbows resting on his knees as he narrowed his eyes at Paolo. "I suppose that makes sense, seeing as how that company doesn't exist."

Paolo's brows drew together in confusion. "I do not understand."

"It's a shell company. It doesn't exist. Tell me, Mr. Vicente. Why are you transferring large sums of money to a company that doesn't exist?"

Paolo opened his mouth, but Mason cut him off.

"Unless this nonexistent company belongs to a killer for hire who doesn't want to be traced." Mason leaned over and plucked the documents out of Paolo's hands. "Lucky for Mr. Galanos, you didn't know what you were doing and ended up hiring a shitty marksman."

"This is madness! I did not hire anyone to kill Laz. That is absolutely ludicrous! I do not know anything about these payments or any shell company."

"Really, because you used this account while you were in Madrid. You expect me to believe you didn't notice seventy-five thousand dollars leaving your account?"

"No, I just use the card. I do not check how much is in there, what comes in or out. My wife's accountant takes care of everything."

"Yeah, about that. We spoke to Mrs. Vicente's accountant, and he says his access to your business account was revoked the day you flew out of the country. That's quite a coincidence, don't you think? That he loses access just before you leave the country, and at the same time, three large payments to a fake company leave your account, and shortly after, someone tries to kill Mr. Galanos."

Paolo's eyes were huge, and the severity of the situation must have started to sink in because his entire body began shaking. He was putting on one hell of a show.

"No, this is not right."

Mason handed Paolo another document, and Red recognized it to be the email Laz had printed out during their last visit to the precinct.

"How about the email you sent to Mr. Galanos, threatening him shortly after you left this precinct?"

The blood drained from Paolo's face when he read the email. His head shot up, panic in his eyes. "I did not send this."

"Really, because that's your email address." Mason took all the documents and stacked them neatly on the table. "I suppose you don't know anything about the photograph texted to Mr. Galanos of Mr. Russell McKinley and Dr. Alexandra Bradbury?"

"I have no idea what you are talking about!" Paolo jumped to his feet and started pacing. "I did none of those things. None! I want to speak to my lawyer. Not one more word."

"I cannot believe this," Elena said, lifting a shaky hand to her head. "It is not bad enough he is a lying cheat, but to go as far as to hire someone to kill for him?" She shook her head, her trembling hand going to her chest. Her bottom lip quivered as she turned to Laz. "Oh, Lazarus, I am so sorry. I will do everything in my power to keep your name from this. I will not let him drag both our names through the mud."

"It's not your fault," Laz replied, hugging her close when she started to cry again. "And we'll figure it all out. They're the ones who did wrong, not us."

"The scandal is going to be horrible, and with my spring launch in just a few days, what am I going to do? Paolo was supposed to be there to offer support." She pulled back, her eyes widening as an idea seemed to strike her. "Please say you will be there."

Laz glanced at Red before looking back to Elena. "Be where?"

"At my spring launch. I cannot do this alone. People will ask where Paolo is, and I'm afraid I will fall apart. There's so much to do, and it is too late to cancel or move it…." She broke off into another sob, and Red handed Laz the box of tissues he'd found on one of the tables. He felt for Elena. She was a little quirky but seemed like a lovely woman. She didn't deserve the scandal she was about to be thrust into. From what Laz had told him about Elena, she was a much beloved designer, a huge name in the industry, known for her charity work and never-ending cheer. The press would be merciless on their coverage of this story.

"Of course I'll be there," Laz offered sweetly. "Whatever I can do to help, Elena."

"Oh, thank you, Laz. You are such a sweet boy. Together, we will show those two jackals that we are strong. That they will never break our spirit." She gave a decisive nod. "Yes, we will show them. I will not let them win with their lies."

A knock on the door had them both turning, and a tall man in a very expensive-looking suit peeked in. "Elena?"

"Fausto. Thank you so much for coming. Laz, Red, this is Fausto, my attorney."

They exchanged pleasantries before Fausto escorted Elena from the room to give her statement. Before leaving the room, Fausto had asked Elena if he was to counsel Paolo, and Elena's reply had been a swift, "His boyfriend can find him an attorney."

Yep, she was definitely done with Paolo.

"I feel kind of guilty," Laz admitted, turning to Red.

"Why?"

"Because her spring launch is a huge deal, and my being there is definitely going to turn heads, but this wasn't how I wanted to get invited."

"I don't think you should feel guilty. Elena needs the support and asked you personally to be that support. You'll both do great."

"Thank you." Laz kissed him, heat spreading through Red, his body reacting to Laz's touch.

Red brought Laz up hard against him and released a moan as he deepened their kiss. God, how he'd missed the feel of Laz's body against his, the taste of him, his scent. Last night he'd barely slept, his bed feeling cold and empty without Laz. He'd learned his lesson, though. He should have known better than to be so secretive, hiding things from the man he'd lost his heart to so quickly and thoroughly. As Laz swirled his tongue around Red's, Red promised himself he would never take Laz for granted. A knock at the door startled them, and they quickly pulled away. Red chuckled at Laz's flustered appearance, and Laz shoved him playfully.

Mason stepped into the room, giving them a nod in greeting and a cheeky knowing smile before he turned his attention to Laz. "I thought it best to not have you witness my interview with Bryan. He is… not a pleasant man. Lord Almighty." He let out a whistle and shook his head in disbelief. "Anyway, I wanted to let you know that we'll be releasing him without charges. We've found no evidence suggesting he had anything to do with the attempt on your life, and quite frankly, the man doesn't have enough funds in his account to buy himself an ice cream cone much less hire a killer."

"What?" Laz was stunned. "But he just returned from a trip to Europe."

"Bryan freely offered us access to his bank account, and I can confirm there is nothing shady about his transaction. Terrifying, but not shady. The man spends more money on hair and beauty products than I make in a year. According to him, his expenses are taken care of by various 'benefactors,' many of whom he was visiting when he returned from Milan, hence why we were having trouble tracking him down. Although Bryan states he was initially furious about the photos, he decided if the photos were to get out that he'd use the publicity to boost his career. He provided us with several press release statements he'd composed not long after your breakup. He stated he was only concerned about keeping the affair a secret for Mr. Vicente, or as I suspect, for Mrs. Vicente's money."

"I wonder if Paolo knows about Bryan's 'benefactors,'" Laz asked.

"I doubt it." Mason's eyes filled with mischief. "But I have a feeling that's all going to change very soon."

"Oh?" Red asked.

"The lawyer Bryan called in for Mr. Vicente happens to be one of Bryan's so called benefactors."

Laz's eyes went wide. "Well, things are certainly going to be interesting around here."

"We've called Bryan a taxi and sent him on his way, but we've informed him not to leave the country. Mr. Vicente is still denying everything, but we have enough to arrest him and press charges. I'll keep you both informed."

"Thank you, Mason," Red said. "We really appreciate it."

On the drive back to Colton's, Laz was pensive.

"You okay?" Red asked.

"Do you think Paolo really did it?"

"People have done a lot more for a lot less," Red replied. "Paolo had the most to lose."

"You're right. Bryan may have lost the clothing-line deal with Elena, but there's no doubt in my mind he won't find a way to spin whatever story comes out in his favor. He has a huge social media following, many of whom are people just as spiteful and mean as he is. Whatever story he weaves, they're going to eat it up. They just love to jump on whatever drama he starts without sparing a second thought to whether there's any truth to what he's saying, or to anyone he might be hurting." Laz shook his head sadly.

Red took Laz's hand in his and gave it a squeeze. "This will all be over soon."

Laz smiled at him, but it was clear he was still worried, and Red understood. Sooner or later it would be all over the media. Until now, Elena had managed to keep a low profile, but with the unveiling of her spring line happening next week down in Miami and charges being brought against her husband, that was all going to change very soon.

"I'm going to have to testify in court, aren't I?"

"Yes, but I'll be right there with you. So will the rest of the Kings, and Colton." It was going to be a long, ugly battle, especially with Bryan involved, but Red would do everything possible to shield Laz from the ugliness as much as he could. "It's possible that we're going to be called in to testify as well."

Laz's head snapped up, his eyes wide. "What?"

"Well, me, Colton, and Ace were there when you and Bryan fought that night at the party. When you told him about the photos."

"Shit." Laz pulled his hand out of Red's to cover his face. "Oh God. I'm so sorry, Red. Fuck, the guys are probably going to hate me."

"Why?"

"Because now I've dragged them into this too."

"Laz, we own a private security company. Being called in to testify in court is nothing new to us."

Laz blinked at him. "Really?"

Red nodded. "We had to go to court for Colton's case, remember?"

Laz's pout was sweet, and Red couldn't wait to get him inside and pounce.

"That's right. I almost forgot about that."

"See? So don't worry. We've got your back." Red winked at Laz, and they had a pleasant ride down to Colton's despite the traffic. He even managed to make Laz laugh by putting on some of his disco tunes and doing a little boogie. Things were finally starting to feel like they were getting back to normal, and he couldn't wait to get Laz alone in bed so they could release some of the tension they'd been carrying.

At Colton's house, Laz apprised Colton of the situation while Red got Ace up-to-date as he helped Ace cook dinner. Ace was making his mother's famous carne asada with congrís and plátano maduro. Red loved plantains. If he wasn't careful he could eat a whole plate of them alone.

"Oh my God, that was so good," Laz said, patting his belly. "I'm so full. I can't believe how much I ate. And I had dessert." He shook his head as he looked down at himself. "I have no idea how I even had room for that rice pudding."

"There's always room for dessert. It goes into a special part of your stomach," Ace said, before shoveling another spoonful of rice pudding into his mouth.

"Or some people just have bottomless stomachs," Colton teased, motioning toward Ace.

"Hey, this body needs lots of fuel, especially with the kind of muscle pounding workouts I get." Ace waggled his eyebrows, and Colton gasped.

"Ace!"

"What?" Ace blinked innocently. "I was talking about gym workouts. What were you thinking I meant?"

As Ace teased Colton, Red met Laz's gaze across the table. Speaking of pounding....

"Okay, you two need to go get a room right now, because seriously," Ace said, shaking his head at Red.

"What?" Red asked, confused. "You're the one who started bringing up pounding workouts."

Ace thrust a hand at Laz, whose cheeks were a lovely shade of pink, his eyes wide and a little glazed. His breath seemed to be coming out labored, and oh God, the way he was looking at Red....

"If you don't get him out of here, I think he might spontaneously combust, and I just replaced the fire extinguisher."

"And why is that, love?" Colton asked, placing his hand on his chin as he arched an eyebrow at Ace.

"That's not important right now. What's important is that Red and Laz go have some makeup sexy times so they can stop making dinnertime weird."

"Yes, because they're the ones making dinnertime weird," Colton drawled.

Ace let out a bark of laughter and planted a sloppy kiss on Colton's lips. "God, I love you."

"I love you too," Colton replied with a chuckle before returning Ace's kiss.

Not waiting around for things to get any more heated up at the dining room table, Red swiftly got to his feet, rounded the table, and grabbed Laz's arm, pulling him to his feet. "Thanks for dinner. I'll do the cleanup for a week. Gotta go." He didn't wait for a response, but he didn't think he'd be getting one anytime soon, since Ace and Colton were currently going at it like they were about to run out of oxygen.

They hurried to Laz's bedroom, and Red had just closed the door when Laz launched himself at Red. The moan Laz let out when Red cupped his ass and hauled him up against him was raw and full of need. They attacked each other's mouth like they were starved for each other's taste.

"Oh God, Red. Let's never fight again," Laz said, rutting against Red. "Or if we do, let's have really filthy-hot makeup sex."

Red was so fucking turned on all he could do was grunt. They tore at each other's clothes, and Red didn't even wait to get Laz into bed. He dropped to his knees and swallowed Laz's cock down to the root, relishing in the sounds Laz made as Red sucked, licked, and laved. Laz dug his fingers into Red's hair, his hips thrusting wildly as he fucked Red's mouth. Red stroked himself, the beads of precome leaking from his slit helping with the friction.

"I want you to fuck me, Red," Laz pleaded. "Fuck me until all I can feel is your big, hard cock inside me, imprinting me, marking me. Leave your mark on me, so everyone knows I'm yours. Always yours."

Red popped off Laz, and picked him up, loving the gorgeous smile he got in return. He lay Laz on the bed and quickly grabbed the lube from the nightstand before returning to the beautiful man stretched out on the mattress, offering all of himself to Red, his body and his heart, because there was no doubt in Red's mind that he had Laz's heart. Maybe they weren't ready to say the words, but the love Laz felt for him shone brightly in his stunning eyes, and Red was going to spend the rest of the night showing Laz how deeply that love was returned.

# CHAPTER 13

Not long after Paolo was arrested, Elena demanded the event manager up security for her show. She'd suggested the Kings be brought in for additional support, but the event had an exclusive contract with a local security company. With Laz in attendance, King had spoken to the head of the event's security. The guy's condescending tone and arrogance made it clear he was an ass, but his second-in-command, Ignacio, was more cooperative. The information Ignacio had given King indicated adequate security, even with the pissing contest with his boss. But Red had no intention of letting Laz out of his sight.

A few hours before, King had called to inform Red that Paolo's bail hearing was moved up to the same day, and the Kings weren't taking any chances. They might not be providing security, but that didn't mean they were going to stay home. They'd be arriving soon. Besides, with them looking to open a branch of Four Kings Security in Miami, King figured he and the guys would do some location scouting later.

As much as Red wished their industry was filled with professionals who were respectful, had integrity, and were concerned with providing the best possible service, that was not always the case, especially when high-profile clients and multimillion-dollar contracts were involved. Until a contract was signed, anyone could come in, make a better offer, and lure the client away from a company. The Kings never resorted to such tactics. If a client wanted to hire them, no one could provide them with better terms of service, and if they were offered a cheaper deal, the Kings helped them understand what they were sacrificing for the cut in cost. With security, you got what you paid for.

Then there was the backstabbing, pissing contests, and posturing. Some security personnel not only took offense that a bunch of non-straight guys did the same manly job they did—and good God were those women they employed for personal security? Because apparently life on Mars was plausible, yet a woman security officer was inconceivable—but that the Kings had built one of the top security companies in the state. The Kings did their best to avoid dealing with those companies. In the end, their actions put any arguments to rest.

This was the first time Elena had done a show in Florida, so although Red knew she was a big deal, he had no idea just how big. The venue was a huge studio in downtown Miami with two indoor buildings and an outdoor area, all filled with guests. It was an impressive sight, everything decorated and lit up in colorful lights for the evening show, the buildings' white facades glowing pink and purple from the lighting. The unveiling would be held in the east building, but before that, a cocktail party was being held in the outdoor waterfall garden. After the fashion show, the after-party would move back to the garden.

Red stood in the waterfall garden next to Laz, the sun having gone down and the colorful paper lanterns casting a magical glow. Hammocks were stretched between palm trees, and waiters dressed in white linen suits offered the guests champagne and appetizers. There was an open bar, and one of the buildings housed a restaurant for guests who wanted to have a meal before the show began, or have a more intimate conversation.

A line of limousines and luxury cars stretched around the block as high-profile guests and celebrities arrived, everyone dressed in their finest summer evening wear. Event security personnel were all dressed to impress and blend in with the crowd. They had their earpieces in and microphones at the ready, including Red, who'd managed to sweet-talk Ignacio, the head of security's second-in-command, into giving him one, much to his boss's disapproval. Red might be here as Laz's plus one, but he wasn't about to be left out of the loop. The more high-profile guests that arrived, the more challenging the evening became. The arrival of celebrities, meant personal bodyguards, and with the security already in place, you had a hell of a lot of testosterone in one place. Too many cooks in the kitchen could lead to explosive results.

Elena was working the crowd and had been since she arrived. This was obviously not her first rodeo, and she was clearly a seasoned pro at deflecting unwanted questions by the media. Whenever someone tried to ask about her husband, she expertly managed to turn the topic of conversation around to her new and exciting spring collection. During interviews, she'd mention Laz and how he was a hot new talent to look out for. She gushed over him, telling everyone how she couldn't have gotten through this without his support.

"I can't believe I'm here." Laz smoothed down the front of his shirt for what seemed like the hundredth time, and Red gently put his hand to the small of his back.

"I know you're nervous, but you're incredibly talented. You deserve to be at this event."

"Thank you." Laz smiled at him, and stole a quick kiss. "I'm glad you're with me. I always feel so grounded when you're around."

The sweet confession had Red smiling like a dope, and he stole a kiss in return. "I'm glad I'm with you too."

The doors to the main building opened, signaling that it was time to go inside for the fashion show. Elena excused herself and joined them. She was very good about not going anywhere without Laz. Red pressed the PTT button clipped to his suit jacket cuff and spoke into his microphone. "Laz, Elena, and I are heading inside."

"Copy that," Ignacio replied. "Keep me posted."

Red followed Laz and Elena inside the main building toward the back of the huge room, past the runway set up against the huge stage. Security took position around the floor while the guests flooded in to take their seats. Backstage, models were running around in various stages of undress as Elena and two other men, one older and one younger, gave directions, making last minute adjustments. Frocks in various fabrics and colors bright enough to blind someone were tossed around, male models were strapped into heels, women stood getting their feet airbrushed in glittering metallic colors. Red had no idea what was going on or what any of it meant, but Laz seemed enthralled, and Elena was in her element.

Makeup artists and hairstylists ran around spraying, powdering, teasing, curling. Red had never seen such organized chaos. Despite the madness, everyone appeared to know what they were doing. If something went wrong, someone else came swooping in to fix it or provide an alternative. Fitz dashed out from what looked like a dressing room, and his smile was huge when he saw Laz. He ran over and gave Laz's cheek a big kiss, then surprised Red by giving his cheek a kiss too.

"It's so good to see you both! I need to go, but I'll see you at the after-party, right?"

Laz nodded. "Shine bright!"

"Like a diamond," Fitz sang, winking at him before blowing him a kiss and dashing off toward a model who was having some sort of hair crisis.

"Wow, is it always like this?" Red asked, jumping out of the way as a woman carrying a dress with so many skirts she couldn't be seen over them, whizzed by. He didn't usually do these types of events, and when he did, he often worked the floor, or if he was providing personal security, he would be with his client. This was his first time backstage at such a huge fashion show, and it was intense. Numerous security personnel stood at various posts keeping an eye on all the activity, checking credentials, and making sure that everyone who was backstage was supposed to be there.

"I've only worked small events, but yeah, it gets a little crazy backstage, especially in the dressing rooms, since at something this big you'll have a lot of models, all of whom have to share."

The music began and the models ran to line up on both sides of the curtain, then started to do their thing. Elena was scheduled to come out at the end once the showcase ended. Red stayed close to Laz as several people came up to him to say hello, to mention his portfolio and how they'd been hearing nothing but amazing things about him and his work. Laz exchanged business cards with nearly all of them, his smile wide. The longer he was there, the more comfortable he seemed to be getting. He pointed out people he'd worked with before, and those he'd like to one day work with. As people ran around, Laz pointed out what their jobs were and the tasks they performed. It struck Red that Laz was including him, sharing this part of his life with Red, wanting him to be a part of it, and it made Red incredibly happy.

Laz had been teasing Red about one of the outfits a male model wore, and how maybe Red should get something similar. It had been an extremely revealing piece.

"You think I could pull it off?"

"Oh definitely," Laz replied, his gaze turning sinful. He leaned in so only Red would hear. "I especially like those mesh short-shorts. Your ass would look amazing in those."

"Hm, it would definitely turn a few heads," Red teased, laughing when Laz peered at him.

"Who said anything about you wearing those outside? Those are for my eyes only."

Red laughed, loving the little growl that came out of Laz at the prospect of someone else seeing Red in the revealing shorts. He opened his mouth to reply, but his cell phone went off. "Hold that thought." He pulled his phone out of his pocket, his smile fading when he saw King's name on the screen. "Hey, everything okay?"

"No, we've got a problem."

"What is it?" Red asked.

"Paolo made bail this morning."

"What?" A chill ran up Red's spine, and he instinctively pulled Laz closer to him as he scanned the area. "How the hell did he make bail? Wasn't it set at, like, a million dollars? Where the hell did Paolo get that kind of money?" It certainly hadn't been from his wife. Just the mention of his name had her spitting at the floor and cursing him.

"The lawyer. I don't know how or why, but he got out this morning, which gave him plenty of time to get down here in time for tonight's event," King replied. "Let that asshat in charge know we're on our way. I don't want his guys giving us shit when we get there. It'll take a little time with traffic, but we'll be there as soon as we can."

"Do we know Paolo's heading this way?"

"Mason had a guy tailing him but lost him on some back road when Paolo got off I-95. He's definitely heading south. Mason's trying to get ahold of Paolo. Maybe he can convince him not to do anything stupid."

"Shit. He could be coming after Laz," Red said. "I need to move him somewhere safe until we know more."

"What?" Laz stared up at him, but he followed Red without question when Red started pulling him along.

"Where are you two?" King asked.

"Backstage. I need to find Elena. If Laz is in danger, she might be as well."

"Agreed. I had Ace send Ignacio a picture of Paolo, and ask him to send it to all his guys. Even if they've got all the exits and windows covered, they've got more area and bodies to secure than they have manpower, so be extra vigilant."

"Can you bring me a gun?" Red was a guest. No way they'd let him in here with a firearm.

"I've got you covered. I'll let you know as soon as we're onsite."

"Thanks." Red hung up, then quickly put in a call to Ignacio directly rather than use the earpiece. The last thing he needed right now was that dick Cohen throwing his weight around. Cohen might be in charge, but he was more concerned with trying to put Red in his place than listening to reason. Thankfully, Red managed to get Ignacio right away, and the man didn't question him when Red asked him to locate Elena and bring her backstage.

"Oh my God." Laz gasped, his worried gaze moving to Red.

"We don't know if Paolo is armed and what threat he might pose to you or the hundreds of guests in attendance," Red explained, "It's very unlikely that he'll get past the front door, but if by some chance he does, I'll do my best to detain him. The guys are on their way."

"I just don't understand. Why is he coming here?" Laz shook his head. "That makes no sense. He has to know the place is crawling with security, that you'll be here with me. Does he really think he's just going to walk through the door?"

"We don't know for sure that he's coming here, but until we know more, we can't take any chances. There's no telling what he's thinking," Red said gently. "Paolo could be facing time in prison. Who knows what's driving him right now."

Red's phone went off again, and he was relieved when Ignacio confirmed he had Elena. "Are you still backstage?"

"Yeah. Meet us by the first dressing room."

Two minutes later, Ignacio showed up with Elena in tow.

"What is happening?" Elena asked nervously.

"We've been informed that your husband made bail this morning and it's possible he may be heading this way," Red replied. "We need to get you and Laz somewhere safe until we have more information."

Elena gasped. "What? But how?" She shook her head. "It does not matter. He will not get through the door. There is security every-where, no?"

Ignacio nodded. "I have personnel guarding the exits and entrances, and the moment he's spotted, I'll be notified, but we have two buildings to cover and an outside area. Also, we only have armed personnel at the doors. Our people in here are not armed."

"Well, no," Elena said, eyes wide. "We have never had a problem before, and the thought of armed men everywhere made me nervous. Too many guns in your country."

"That's a debate for another time," Red said before turning to Ignacio. "Where's the safest place to move them to?"

Ignacio opened his mouth, but Elena snapped her fingers and spoke first. "The rain dress!"

They all exchanged glances before Laz asked the question they were thinking. "The what now?"

"The rain dress. It is the final piece of the show. It is made up of thousands of very small diamonds and crystals worth millions. It was designed to look as if the model is being rained down on. As you can imagine, the room it is kept in is very secure. No one is allowed in or out, and only two people have the key, myself and the event manager."

"Which room is that in?" Red asked.

"The final dressing room," she replied, pointing toward the other end of the backstage area where there was more security and less foot traffic.

"Okay." Red nodded and motioned for Elena to lead the way. "I'll stay in the room with you until the rest of the Kings arrive. They should be here soon."

They quickly escorted Elena and Laz past several dressing rooms until they reached the one that was closed at the very end. Two men in black suits stood guard outside the room, and they nodded when Ignacio greeted them. Elena removed the key from some hidden pocket in her dress and opened the room. Inside, the dressing room looked like a fabric factory had exploded. A long table was pressed up against one wall and it was covered in all manner of sewing supplies. The couch on the opposite wall was draped in various fabrics, and the rain dress Elena had described was on a mannequin in the center of the room, the diamonds sparkling beneath the lights.

"There will be guards just outside," Ignacio said. "Let me know if you need anything."

"Thank you. I really appreciate it." Red shook Ignacio's hand before the guy left and closed the door behind him.

"But my show," Elena said with a pout. "I am expected to be seen at the end. I must thank everyone for coming."

Red put a hand to her shoulder, his tone soothing. "And you'll make your appearance. We still have plenty of time. As soon as the Kings arrive, we'll assess the situation, and if it's necessary, we'll personally escort you to the stage, then stand guard."

"Thank you so much. Please, if Paolo does arrive, do not let the media see. I cannot stand another scandal. Everyone worked so hard on this show. I do not want his presence to ruin everything they have done."

"I'll do my best to keep things quiet, but you have to understand that I'm not in charge here, and neither are the Kings." Red carefully moved some of the fabric so Laz could take a seat on the couch. Elena dropped down next to him with a huff.

"So what now? We just sit here and wait?"

"That's pretty much how it works. If Paolo does show up, we need to keep you as far away from him as possible until he's detained." Red took a seat next to Laz and wrapped an arm around him as Laz leaned into him. He really hoped this was all over soon for Laz's sake. Anyone in his position would have had their nerves frazzled by now, but Laz was doing incredibly well.

"I'm very proud of the way you're handling all this," Red told him quietly. "I know you're exhausted and just want to get your life back."

Laz smiled up at him, and placed a feathery kiss along his jaw. "As long as you're with me."

Red's phone went off once more. It was King. "Tell me you have news."

"I do, but it's not good. Paolo's lawyer just called Mason. Paolo *was* on his way to the event, but not for Laz. He was going for Bryan. He was afraid Bryan was in danger."

"What? From who?"

"Bryan was supposed to be in tonight's show, but he got food poisoning and has been home puking his guts out all day. Paolo found out on the drive down and headed straight to Bryan's apartment in Miami Beach. Police confirm he's there now. Red, Paolo believes whoever tried to kill Laz is on their way to the event. His apartment was ransacked, and more money left his account while he was in custody. Paolo told his lawyer that his invitation to tonight's event was missing." King's words sent a jolt through Red, and he jumped to his feet.

"What is it?" Laz asked, coming to stand by his side.

"We're about ten minutes away." King sounded tense, and Red knew King hated the fact he wasn't here. He opened his mouth to reply when his earpiece came to life, and what Ignacio said turned his blood to ice.

"King, meet me in the garden as soon as you and the guys arrive. Something just went down. It could be him."

"Shit. Stay safe."

Red promptly hung up with King and let Ignacio know he was on his way.

"What's going on?" Laz asked.

"I need to go. Ignacio just called. They spotted someone behaving suspiciously in the garden, and when they approached the guy, he attacked one of the guards. There's blood, and it's a damn mess. It could be our shooter." Red opened the door and turned to one of the guards. He was a huge brick wall of a man, almost as tall and wide as Red with a stern expression that could stop someone dead in their tracks.

"Stay on this door until someone from Four Kings Security arrives. Got it?"

The guard hesitated but then nodded, and Red turned to Laz. He pulled him into his arms. "I'll be right back. If you need anything, security is right outside, okay? King and the guys will be here any minute, and I'll send someone over. If for some reason something happens, don't open the door for anyone that isn't one of us."

Laz nodded, his big blue eyes filled with concern. "Please be careful, Red. No more getting shot."

"I'll try my best," Red promised. His job as a King involved risks, and he couldn't pretend there wasn't any danger in what he did. Colton's case wasn't the first time he'd been hurt, especially when dealing with executive protection. He wouldn't lie to Laz about the dangers he faced, but he would also do his best to reassure him. They shared a quick but sweet kiss before Red took off. He closed the door behind him, making sure it was locked before hurrying toward the main floor. Running would arouse suspicion, so he walked as quickly as he could without drawing attention to himself, which wasn't always easy with his size and red hair.

Thankfully the fashion show was in full swing, so no one was paying attention to him as he scurried across the room near the wall until he reached the lobby. Then he did run. If someone *was* here to hurt Laz, Red was going to make sure they never got near Laz ever again.

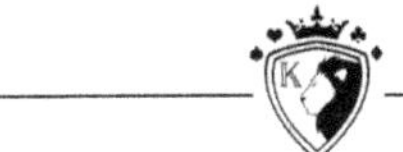

"Why would he do this?"

Elena was working herself into a frenzy. Red had only just left, but it felt like ages. Laz tried his best not to let his imagination run away with him. What if it was the shooter? Red wasn't armed. Not that he didn't believe Red was incapable of taking down an armed man, but that didn't mean Laz wasn't going to worry. Waiting to hear was the worst. It was going to be a challenge, being with someone who worked such a potentially dangerous job. He hadn't really given Red's position as a King much thought, seeing as how Red hadn't been on the job since Colton's case. Worrying about Red was something he imagined he'd always do, but he couldn't allow himself to think of the "what-ifs" or he'd drive himself and poor Red crazy.

"Do you think he really sent a killer after us?" Elena flailed her hands as she flitted furiously from one end of the room to the other like a hummingbird, her breath coming out labored.

"It's going to be okay, Elena." Laz tried to calm her, but she was working herself into a frantic state.

"How well do we truly know someone? I never thought he would hurt me, but what if he has sent that killer after me? Dio, no, no, no, this cannot be happening." She started to wheeze, and Laz tried corralling her in the hopes of ushering her to the couch.

"Why don't you sit down. I'll see if I can get someone to bring you some tea or water." Laz hurried to the door.

"Yes, thank you. Some tea would be very good. In my bag, in my dressing room. I have *tisane della salute* for when I travel and do not feel well."

Laz quickly went to the door where the guard stood, frowning deeply, concern written all over his face. "Mrs. Vicente isn't feeling well. She needs her tea. Can you bring it? It's in her bag in her dressing room."

The guard shook his head. "I have instructions not to leave this post." He motioned toward the tiny counter housing a sink, fancy coffee machine, and electric kettle. "There was a box of mint tea."

Elena fumed and stomped her foot. "No! I need *my* tea. You expect me to drink some rancid leaf water from who knows where? My tea comes from one of the greatest tea makers in Europe, not from some swamp in Jersey!"

Oh, dear God. Laz had no idea a human's voice could go that high in pitch.

"The pineapple," Elena shrieked.

"We need that tea," Laz said. "Either you go, or I go, but if I go and someone's waiting for me in Elena's dressing room, the Kings are going to be pissed." He hated using the Kings as a scare tactic, but he'd known them long enough now to know the kind of sway they had, and as a member of a private security firm, this guy wasn't about to piss off a King, especially *the* King.

"Okay, just stay in the room, close the door, and don't let anyone in. I'll be right back," he said gruffly before taking off toward Elena's dressing room. Laz did as instructed and turned back to Elena.

"Don't worry, he'll be back any minute now," Laz assured her, walking over to her.

"Thank you," she said, her voice hoarse as she fanned herself with what looked like a folded-up piece of pattern paper. "You are a good boy. Forgive me. I am very particular about what I ingest."

"I understand. Is there anything else I can do to help in the meantime?" He probably should have asked her what she meant by pineapple. He had a feeling that was probably what was holding up the guard. For all he knew she had a hollowed-out pineapple for a purse or something. Glancing over at the kitchen sink, he had a feeling tap water for her tea wasn't going to cut it, and he'd rather prevent another meltdown. "I should grab someone and ask them to bring you some bottled water to make your tea."

"Such a good boy." She pushed away from the table and turned to him with a smile. "It's a shame you must die now."

Laz dropped his gaze to the huge pair of scissors in her hand. His head shot up, and her smile faded, the look in her eyes turning his blood to ice. She'd taken the large scissors apart. After tossing one half onto the table behind her, she brandished the other half like a knife.

"Elena? What—" The truth slammed into him like a bullet train. "Oh my God, it was you. This whole time… it was you." It all made sense. Who else would have had access to Paolo's accounts, his email, his every move. "You've known about the affair, the photos, everything this whole time, haven't you?"

"You should have died on the beach, Lazarus, but it is not as if I have hired a killer before. It is not something you simply look up on the internet," she said, blinking innocently like she was discussing how hard it was to find a decent parking spot at the beach or something. "He was the brother of an associate of a friend of a friend." She shrugged. "Anyway, what is done is done. I should have known better than to trust a man. Lying, cheating, womanizing, bastardos, all of you!"

"Paolo didn't send anyone here to kill me. You did, didn't you?" Laz asked backing up slowly toward the door. Somehow Paolo must have found out, but how?

The quiet rage radiating off her had Laz's heart pounding in his ears. He wanted to know why the hell she was doing this, but he wasn't about to stand around waiting to get impaled by half a pair of scissors so he could hear her villainous monologue.

"I, um, I think I'm going to skip the whole dying thing today. Thanks." He shoved the mannequin with the rain dress at her, and as he suspected, she was nutty enough to try and catch it before it hit the floor, giving him just enough time to haul ass out of the room and into the backstage area, which was predictably in a frenzy now that the fashion show portion of the evening had ended. Behind him, he could hear Elena calling his name in a singsong voice, and it was creepy as hell. Holy shit, the woman was off her rocker. He needed to find Red.

Out in the main area, the crowd was huge as guests headed for the after-party. From the segments of conversation Laz managed to overhear, guests were told Elena would make her appearance and speech at the after-party since she didn't appear after the show. Laz moved through the masses of people as quickly as he could, occasionally glancing over his shoulder in the hopes he'd lost her. Part of him felt like an idiot for missing what was right in front of his face, but never once would he have believed Elena Vicente capable of doing what she'd done. The woman was eccentric, yes, but murderous? His phone rang, and he pulled it out, relieved to see it was Red. He didn't stop weaving through the crowds when he answered.

"Laz, where the hell are you? Where's Elena? Joker got to the dressing room, and you were both gone."

"She's trying to impale me with a huge-ass scissor!"

"*What?*"

"I lost her in the crowd, though. I don't see her. Red, she's the one behind everything."

"We know. Paolo's lawyer called us and told us everything. She's known about the photos from the beginning. I'll explain later. We apprehended the shooter, and he's in police custody, on the way to the station. Head for the garden. I'm on my way."

"Okay." He hung up, and tried to move as fast as he could, but there were so many people, and the closer they got to the doors, the tighter everyone packed together.

"Lazarus, darling!"

Oh shit. He could hear security radios going off around him, but if he shouted out to them, he'd give away his location, and if he could hear her, she was close by. He felt like one of those unsuspecting swimmers at the beach, naive to the fact that violins meant the killer shark was swiftly approaching, and oh my God, he was losing his damn mind. How did he get himself into these situations? At what point in his life had he taken such a wrong turn that he found himself fleeing a fashion designer on a murderous rampage? Okay maybe not rampage, but she was definitely not going to tailor him a new suit.

Finally he reached the doors to the garden, and he took off when he saw a blur of color whiz toward him. Someone screamed, and he skidded in the grass, turning direction just as she came barreling toward him, scissor raised high. With a yelp, he rounded a palm tree and headed for one of the many tables. Grabbing the centerpiece, he spun and gasped as her scissor plunged into the pineapple in his hands. He was never going to eat pineapple ever again. Ever. In fact he didn't want to see a damn pineapple for a good long while. She let out a shriek, jerking at the scissor, but he wasn't about to give her a second shot at him, so he tackled her to the ground, the garden erupting into gasps and shouts. Not that any of the guests came to his aid. Knowing Elena, they probably thought it was one of her screwy side shows.

"Laz!" Red called out from somewhere behind him, but Laz wasn't about to take his eyes off Elena. She fought fiercely, her nails scraping against his skin as he tried to restrain her, and then she kneed him in the balls. *Fuck!* He should have seen that coming. Stars filled his vision, and he fell onto his side with a groan as he cupped his boys.

"Holy shit," he wheezed.

"You're going to pay for this!" She lunged for the scissor, but Laz managed to snatch up the pineapple and swing it with all his strength like a baseball bat, smacking her on the side of the head, and sending her rolling on the grass. The moment she stopped, Ace was all over her.

Laz sat on the grass, trying to catch his breath when Red dropped to his knees in front of him. He pulled Laz into a tight embrace, and Laz wrapped his arms around Red, his eyes closed as relief washed over him. He soaked up Red's warmth, gave himself over to Red's strength, his face buried in Red's broad chest as the man he loved murmured sweet, comforting words at him and stroked his hair.

"Are you okay?" Red pulled away enough to look into Laz's eyes. "I'm so sorry I wasn't there, sweetheart."

The guilt in Red's beautiful hazel-green eyes had Laz on full alert, and he narrowed his gaze at Red. "No. You are *not* going to feel guilty about this, understand? None of us had any idea Elena was behind this, that she'd hired a killer and intended to frame her husband."

Red nodded and helped Laz to his feet, keeping him close as the media had a field day. Luckily for them, the cameras were all pointing at Elena, who was being taken away in handcuffs. Red ushered Laz to the end of the garden and a quiet spot away from the three-ring circus. Kings were coordinating with the event manager and security company to take care of the guests while additional police arrived on the scene.

"You were fierce out there," Red said, holding Laz close, and brushing his lips over Laz's. "I'm so proud of you."

"I think I kind of reached my limit of being pushed around. Also, I wasn't going to be killed by a woman who dressed like a pineapple."

Red chuckled and cupped his face, his smile fading as he stroked his thumb over Laz's cheek. "When Paolo's lawyer told us Elena knew about the photos all along, we realized she'd been behind everything, and all I could think about was how you were alone with her."

"How did he find out?"

"His lawyer did some digging around and discovered she'd hired a private investigator nearly a year ago. She knew about all of his affairs, and had been spying on him, listening to his conversations, which is how she found out about the photos. King thinks she was trying to save herself from a scandal by getting rid of all the guilty parties in some way or another and framing her husband for it, and it was working."

"I'm just glad it's over," Laz muttered, leaning into Red.

"Ready to go home?"

Laz worried his bottom lip, then let out a disappointed sigh. "I guess now that it's all over, we'll be going back to our own places, huh?" The way Red's smile lit up told Laz he'd made the right decision.

"Or, you know, I have this big condo apartment on the beach. There's an office I never use. You could make that room your office, studio, whatever. But you know, you'd have to come live with me."

Laz pretended to think about it. "Hm, live in a huge condo on the beach with a gorgeous man, waking up every morning in his arms and the sound of the ocean. I don't know."

"Maybe I can sweeten the deal a little bit." Red brushed his fingers down Laz's jaw, and smiled down at him. "How about if I throw in an 'I love you?'"

Laz's smile couldn't get any wider, and his heart felt like it might explode out of his chest. "I will accept your 'I love you' and counter offer an 'I love you' in return. I love you, Red."

"I love you too, Laz." Red brought Laz hard against him and kissed him within an inch of his life. Laz all but melted into a puddle of goo at his feet. Oh yeah, he was definitely moving in, and he couldn't wait to start his new life with the amazing man in his arms. Finally the nightmare was over, and his dreams could begin. Pineapples and all.

# *EPILOGUE*

"You guys are freaking hilarious."

Red hid his laugh behind the menu so his boyfriend wouldn't lump him in with the rest of the troublemakers, but Laz's arched eyebrow aimed his way said he wasn't getting away with it.

It had been months since Elena Vicente was found guilty of attempted murder. Apparently, she'd had enough of her husband's cheating ways, especially since rumors had begun to circulate about his many lovers, all of whom he loved to wine and dine on Elena's hard-earned dime. Discovering there were photos of him and Bryan in bed together had been the final straw, and she'd decided to get her revenge, planning to use Laz's murder to frame her husband while simultaneously destroying Bryan's career. There was speculation that Bryan getting food poisoning the night of the fashion show might have saved his life, considering the shooter and a murderous Elena were both in attendance.

The media coverage had been brutal, with the press looking into all parties involved. Bryan was splashed all over the media, and not in a flattering light. His nasty treatment of others came back to bite him in the rear, and the more people who were interviewed spoke of his backstabbing ways, the worse it got for Bryan. Last they'd heard, he was lying low in the hopes of salvaging what was left of his career.

The coverage for Laz had been mostly positive, and although some of it was no doubt due to the Kings and their reputation—seeing as how Laz was dating a member of the Kings—Red was certain it had more to do with the fact Laz was an honest, kind, and all-around wonderful man. It had been hard for Laz to see himself plastered all over the news, but more so to see coverage of Gio, who Laz was missing a great deal due to his return home being postponed for another six months. But Gio spoke to Laz every week and hoped to be back in the country soon. Red and Laz had gotten through everything together, and now Laz was busier than ever, each day getting closer to his dream job.

Any niggling concerns they might have had regarding how quickly their relationship was moving was obliterated for Laz the first morning he woke to the sound of the ocean, and for Red, at the sight of Laz in his bed. Red loved to tease that Laz only loved him for his condo, but it quickly became clear how much living near the ocean suited Laz. Whenever their schedules allowed it, they'd wake up, dress, and go for a run on the beach before getting ready for their day.

Laz was flourishing, not just in his career, but personally. He was more confident, bolder, and definitely sassier. With every passing day, Red lost more and more of his heart to Laz. He was beautiful, kind, and accepted Red as he was, broken pieces and all. Every month Laz joined him for joint therapy sessions, and Red suspected a good deal of Laz's newfound confidence stemmed from the help they were getting.

"So whose bright idea was it this time?" Laz asked, picking a chunk of pineapple out of his favorite Mahi fish taco and lobbing it at Ace.

"What? Why are you attacking me with your fruit?"

"Because I know it was you, smart guy."

Sunday brunch at Bibi's was quickly becoming a new tradition. Two large tables were pushed together, and this week it was the Kings, Colton, and Laz. Red's heart swelled as he took in the scene before him. He loved the sound of his brothers-in-arms' boisterous laughter as they teased each other, loved the way they'd embraced Laz as one of their own, as they'd done with Colton, to the point they'd taken to tormenting poor Laz with pineapples at every opportunity.

Lucky was in tears from laughing so hard. It was pretty obvious who the culprit was this time.

Laz gasped. "It was you! Damn it, Lucky!"

"You should have seen your face. It never stops being funny." Lucky let out a very indelicate snort when Laz chucked a piece of pineapple at him. It bounced off Lucky's shoulder, and landed in front of Ace. He picked up the pineapple chunk and showed it to Colton, a mischievous twinkle in his eye. *Uh-oh. Here we go.*

"Baby, if you were fruit, you'd be a fine-apple."

"Oh dear God, no." Colton shook his head, his eyes going slightly wide when Ace's grin turned wicked. He was just getting started.

"Olive you so much, Colt. You're one in a melon."

Colton let out a bark of laughter. "No. no, no, no. You're such a dork. Stop it."

"I think we make a great pear."

"No, really." Colton's expression turned deadpan. "I love you, but you need to stop. Like, right now."

Ace took that as a personal challenge to up his game. He turned his attention to King. "Hey, King."

King lifted his gaze from his plate, his mouth full of Bibi's famous BLT. He shook his head, and Ace turned his megawatt smile on Red.

"Hey, Big Red, what kind of dog doesn't bark?"

"Why me?" Red groaned. "I don't know."

"A hush puppy."

"Oh my God, that was so bad," Laz said with a snort.

Never one to give up, Ace turned back to King. "Hey, King. What do you call a fake noodle?"

Colton put his hands together and pleaded with King. "Don't kill him. We're flying to Hawaii next weekend, and I need him to make sure I don't pass out on the plane ride over. I don't fly well."

King grunted. "Fine."

Everyone laughed when Ace's eyes lit up and he did a butt wiggle in his chair before punching the air. "Yes! Okay, so, King, what do you call a fake noodle?"

With a heavy sigh, King sat back in his chair and crossed his beefy arms over his chest. "I don't know, Ace. What do you call a fake noodle. You're lucky I hold your boyfriend in such high regard."

"Wait for it." Ace paused for dramatic effect, then waggled his eyebrows. "An impasta!"

Everyone groaned and threw fries at Ace, which he attempted to catch with his mouth. He laughed with a mouthful of fries, and Colton glanced over at King, who shook his head.

"Nope. He's yours now. No take-backs."

The table erupted in laughter, and Red put his arm around the back of Laz's chair, sitting back to admire his little family. He was blessed, no doubt about it. Not only did he have brothers who he would give his life for, and who would give their life for him, but he had the most beautiful, amazing man at his side who he loved more and more each day.

"Hey," Laz said softly, getting Red's attention.

The love in those brilliant blue eyes stole Red's breath away every time. He leaned in and placed a kiss to Laz's temple, replying softly. "Hey."

Laz hummed and turned his face, brushing his lips over Red's, murmuring quietly so only Red could hear. "I love you. Thank you for letting me be a part of this."

"I love you too, sweetheart. Welcome to the family." Red brought their lips together for a sweet kiss, both of them laughing at the collective "Aww."

The little bell above the door announced a new arrival, and the table broke out into whistles and catcalls as Mason walked in wearing a snug black tank top, beach shorts, and sandals.

"Woo-hoo, look at those legs," Ace teased.

Mason did a quick scan of the café before flipping Ace off. He moved his aviators to his head. "Bunch of comedians."

"Beach bum looks good on you," Red said, his attention seized by Laz nudging him gently in the ribs. Laz motioned to Lucky, and Red held back a knowing smile. Lucky was blatantly checking Mason out, which was nothing new, but when his gaze landed on Mason's bulging biceps, he licked his lips. Lucky was practically drooling on the remaining half of his Cuban sandwich.

"Where are you off to?" Colton asked. The rest of them chuckled when Ace cleared his throat and Lucky snapped his eyes from Mason's chest to his face, his cheeks going pink.

Mason dropped his gaze to Lucky, who quickly sat forward and started to eat again. "The beach. I've finally got a day off, and I'm making the most of it. Well, damn, what's that?" He pointed across the room, and Lucky followed his finger, allowing Mason the chance to swipe a bunch of fries and stuff them into his mouth.

"¡Ay, Cabrón!" Lucky poked Mason's side, making the big man laugh around his mouthful of fries and twist his body to get away from Lucky.

"Mm, those are good." Mason pulled over a chair to the end of the table, angling it toward Lucky. "You gonna eat those, or you watching that pretty figure of yours?"

Lucky let out a snort. "You really think you can sweet-talk your way into getting my fries?"

Red had a feeling Mason could sweet-talk his way into more than Lucky's fries if Lucky let him. These two couldn't possibly be so oblivious. The attraction between them was palpable, yet neither man made a move.

"Come on, baby. Just one more," Mason said, his voice a low rumble.

Lucky smacked Mason's hand away from his plate. "No, get your own. And while you're at it, get some sleeves for that shirt."

Mason flexed his arm, a little smirk coming onto his lips when Lucky's eyes dropped to his bicep and widened. "But if I had sleeves, you couldn't see that muscle right there." Mason poked at his bicep. "You want to touch it?"

"No," Lucky scoffed before biting down on a French fry.

"Come on, Lucky," Mason purred, adding a wink. "You know you want to touch it."

"Do you want to maybe say that a little louder? I don't think the people across town heard you," Lucky hissed, shaking his head in shame at Mason, only to have Mason swipe another fry. He was pretty damn quick for such a big guy.

"What? I'm just talking about my arm."

"Sigue, que te voy a dar un cocotazo."

"I don't know what you just said, but it sounded like it might hurt, and not in a good way."

Ace snickered, and Laz leaned in to whisper in Red's ear while Mason continued to torment Lucky.

"Are they sleeping together?"

Red shook his head before replying, "No. I'm thinking they really wish they were."

Before Red could elaborate, Bibi came out of the kitchen, beaming brightly when she saw Mason.

"Hey, Cowboy!"

"Hey, Bibi." Mason got up and hugged her. "Nash around? He left me a message saying he wanted to talk to me about something, but when I tried calling him a few times, I got no answer."

Bibi rolled her eyes. "Mr. Smooth Operator dropped his phone in the fryer, so he's off getting a replacement."

Red cringed. "Ooh, how'd that happen?"

"Hm, let me see." Bibi put a finger to her lips in thought before turning and smacking Ace upside the head.

"Ouch! What the hell, Bibi?" Ace rubbed the back of his head, his eyes narrowed. "How is this *my* fault?"

"Oh, that's right. Nash dropped his phone because I walked in on him texting twinkle-tush over here about his next joyride on Lucky love-muffin's death machine."

Ace frowned up at her. "Why does Lucky get to be love-muffin, and I'm stuck with twinkle-tush?"

"Quiet, you. I can't believe you're still letting him go out on that thing."

"Still?" Ace gaped at her. "How long have you known?"

"Please. I knew from day one. Like you two can hide anything from anyone with your little man-giggles every time you get together."

The table erupted in laughter, and King held his fist out to his sister, receiving a fist-bump from her.

Ace turned to Colton, his pout fierce. "Aren't you going to defend my honor?"

Colton turned his head up to smile at Bibi. "Tell me more about these man-giggles."

"Ooh, my heart," Ace wheezed, putting his fist to his heart as if he'd been struck.

Red wiped a tear from his eye. He'd so called that one. Ignoring Ace, Bibi turned to Mason.

"Nash was calling because a cousin of his is going to Texas to spend some time on a ranch, and he knows you used to work on one, so Nash thought you could give his cousin some tips."

Lucky straightened suddenly. He looked like someone had just kicked him. Turning to Bibi, he asked. "Is that Oscar?"

Bibi nodded. "Yeah, that's right. Why?"

Lucky stood so fast his chair made a loud screeching sound across the floor. "I need to go. Ace, your turn to pay." He marched off, slamming through the door so hard the little bell smacked the wall above it.

"What just happened?" Bibi asked, confused and concerned.

"I'll go check on him," Mason said, hurrying off after Lucky, who'd snatched his helmet off his bike.

"Shit." Ace shook his head. "Goddamn it."

"What is it, Ace? What did I say?"

"Oscar."

Bibi shrugged. "Yeah, so what?"

"Oscar and Mason hooked up in one of the back rooms at Frank's. They ran into Lucky on their way out after doing whatever they got up to. Oscar seemed really interested. My guess is Nash is trying to set Oscar up with Mason. That's why he was calling. He's just using the whole ranch thing as an in for Oscar."

Bibi's eyes went huge. "Oh my God, I had no idea. Oscar was in here last week. We were hanging out, and he was talking to Nash a lot. I thought it was about his trip."

Outside, it suddenly got loud, and they turned their attention to the window. Mason had just grabbed Lucky's arm and jerked him around to face him. It didn't take a lip reader to know that Lucky was giving it to Mason with both barrels, and Mason was giving it right back. Both of them were flushed, their hackles obviously up, and Lucky was so pissed he was practically vibrating.

Mason thrust a finger in Lucky's face and growled something that made Lucky flinch. Ace was out of his chair, his protective instincts clearly kicking in.

"Sit down, Ace," King said firmly but gently. "Lucky's gotta work this out for himself."

With a heavy sigh, Ace dropped back down into his chair.

It was painful to watch. Lucky shoved Mason away and said something that had Mason pressing his lips together in a thin line, his muscles bunched, and his hands balled into fists at his sides.

"I don't understand," Laz said. "They clearly want each other. Why are they fighting it so hard?"

"It's never going to work out," Ace said, his frown deep and his green eyes filled with worry. "I know them. They're both a couple of explosive hotheads with serious commitment issues."

"But how long can they keep this up?" Laz asked worriedly. "It's got to hurt."

Red squeezed him close and kissed the top of his head. "All we can do is be there for them."

The thunderous roar of Lucky's motorcycle filled the air, the tires kicking up dirt as he turned that beast of a machine and took off, leaving Mason standing in a cloud of dust, staring after him.

Colton put his hand on Ace's shoulder. "Go check on him."

"I'll be right back." Ace kissed Colton before heading outside to Mason. At least both Lucky and Mason had friends and family to support them through this mess. Whatever the hell was going on between those two, it had been building for months, and Red was growing concerned, because at some point, all that steam would erupt, and when it did, Red feared the fallout.

Ace spent some time outside with Mason, and when he came back in, it was just to apologize and say his goodbyes. He was clearly worried about his cousin, and his friend, and that made everyone else worry, because no one knew Lucky and Mason like Ace did.

They all sat around chatting some more, and then everyone went their separate ways.

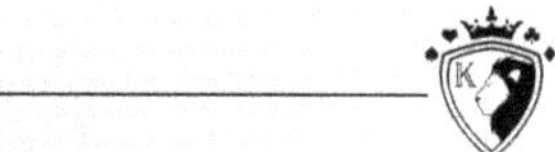

Red drove himself and Laz home, and later that evening they stood out on the balcony together to watch the sunset.

Red wrapped his arms around Laz from behind and nuzzled his temple. They watched the blues of the sky turn to golds and oranges. Other than the sounds of the waves and occasional seagull, stillness surrounded them. Peace washed over Red, and he let out a contented sigh.

Like the ocean outside their balcony, Red's life would always be filled with storms and rough waters. It was part of who he was. He'd never thought he would find the person for him, that special someone who would take his hand and stand on the pier with him, facing the darkness and turmoil until the clouds parted and the brilliant sun shone once again.

Until Laz.

Now he had Laz in his arms, he had no intention of ever letting go. As if sensing his thoughts, Laz turned and snuggled close, laying his head on Red's chest over his heart. An image of Pip, one of Red's fallen brothers-in-arms popped into his head and made him smile. Pip had dubbed him the king of hearts. Well, the only heart he wanted to be the king of belonged to the man in his arms, the king of *his* heart.

2
♥
LAZ
2
♠

Check out Lucky and Mason's story, *Join the Club*, the third book in the Four Kings Security series on Amazon and Kindle Unlimited.

# ABOUT
# THE AUTHOR

Charlie Cochet is the international bestselling author of the THIRDS series. Born in Cuba and raised in the US, Charlie enjoys the best of both worlds, from her daily Cuban latte to her passion for classic rock.

Currently residing in Central Florida, Charlie is at the beck and call of a highly opinionated sable German Shepherd and a rascally Doxiepoo bent on world domination. When she isn't writing, she can usually be found devouring a book, releasing her creativity through art, or binge watching a new TV series. She runs on coffee, thrives on music, and loves to hear from readers.

Website: www.charliecochet.com

Email: charlie@charliecochet.com

Sign up for Charlie's newsletter:

https://newsletter.charliecochet.com

www.ingramcontent.com/pod-product-compliance
Lightning Source LLC
Chambersburg PA
CBHW051127300726

48981CB00024B/579/J